FORKED TONGUE

LONDON 1997

The basement ceiling was covered in the shards of hundreds of smashed light bulbs. *No doubt some kind of conceptual artwork installation. The emphasis being on the concept rather than the art.* Mahvand hoisted up his stonewash jeans (that were forever slipping down), pulled his red hoodie over those dark, curly locks and pushed his way through the crowd towards the bar. At the far end by the stage, a lanky guy, with serious sideburns and a Victorian strongman moustache, was in animated conversation with a cat-eyed, bespectacled boho chick in Birkenstocks. Mahvand had seen her around: Bogdana Bogdonavich. Rumoured, according to scenesters and those with ivory tower aspirations, to be in the seventh year of a PhD entitled '*Ecriture Feminine* and Transgressive Representations of Womanhood in the Lyrics of Kate Bush.' *Things could be worse. A lot worse. I could have ended up in academia.*

He was just about to order a pint of his usual – Coca Cola, which, according to fellow comics aficionado and master of ceremonies Octavi, was THE gateway drug on account of all that sugar – when he overheard an American accent. *It isn't, is it?* At the spiral staircase end of the bar, a middle-aged man in a black polo neck and thick-framed, lensless specs was holding court. *It has to be!* It was no other than San-Franciscan queer comics artist turned graphic novelist Adam Hudson. *Why didn't Octavi let on that Adam was coming? Or did Adam intend to make a surprise guest appearance?* Mahvand was desperate to tell him what an inspiration he'd been when he was a gay teen growing up in the eighties. How he'd gone into mourning after one of his superheroes had died of AIDS. He checked himself. Adam was surrounded by his entourage – a sycophantic motley crew of mostly middle-aged men who hung on his every word and quaffed Dom Pérignon from plastic flutes. Mahvand ordered his pint and ear-wigged in on the conversation.

'Yah, Littlewood Studios have bought the film rights,' said Adam.

'What did I say?' said an emaciated man with a paisley cravat bunched around the scrag of his neck. '*The Castro Crusader* is pure genius. Cutting edge. Yet, as we all know, destined for commercial success. Tick, tick, tick!'

'If anyone deserves it, it's you,' cooed a Saudi shemagh-scarf-wearing, slim-young-thing, his arm interlocked through Adam's.

'Oh, it's just a small independent film company based in LA,' said Adam.

'Laa!' they cooed in unison. An eruption of laughter.

What, asked Mahvand to himself, circling the rim of his glass with his forefinger, would Octavi do? It was as if Octavi was right there by his side. If you're not prepared to network like a Z-list celebrity and self-promote like Narcissus on crack,

PHARMAKEIA

TIMOTHY GRAVES

around in his carrier bag and presented Adam with a copy of *Fallen Angels of Homo Heaven*.

'What's this?' asked Adam.

'My zine.'

'*Homo Heaven*, eh?' Adam said, laughing. 'Hey. Thanks, kid.' Adam turned his back and the posse immediately closed ranks, excluding Mahvand from talk that soon turned to *The Castro Crusader* and the negotiation of authorial royalties.

Mahvand slunk off to sit by himself at an empty table in the corner, fighting off the tears. *How dare they? I gave him a piece of myself. And what did I get? What do I ever get in return?* On any other occasion, the running commentary would have developed into a full-blown character assassination. Amongst other things, he would have berated himself for being socially inept, not one of the in-crowd, an artistic failure. But, that evening, as he sat at that table picking at the label on an empty beer bottle in that overcrowded little venue in the East End, a long-forgotten feeling of intoxication began to take hold. Surrounded by nobodies, wannabes and somebodies, his anger gradually gave way to a dark determination. He watched the familiar game of one-upmanship, as if in a trance, and right then and there made a pact with himself. *I'll do whatever it takes to raise my game. Whatever. It. Takes.* He repeated this to himself over and over, until he was eventually brought back to his senses by the vibration and rumbling of a tube train underneath. A rather panic-stricken Octavi pushed his way through the crowd to the stage. Mahvand stood and took his place twards the back of the venue.

Mahvand had first met Octavi a few years back at a queer comics convention in Waterloo. Over an overpriced fair-trade coffee and gluten-free flapjack, Mahvand had traded a self-published copy of his latest autobiographical zine, *Confessions of a Suburban Comix Geek,* in exchange for an episode of Octavi's *Kattalin Kemen,* which charted the ongoing trials and tribulations of a dope-smoking, middle-aged transsexual Basque terrorist.

Octavi adjusted the microphone on the stand. He was sporting a geek-chic look that was just beginning to take off in certain quarters of the gay scene: skinny jeans, low-cut V-neck T-shirt, and lensless, black-rimmed spectacles. The only exception was a pink feather boa that framed his Hitler-youth haircut. He tapped and blew into the microphone. A deafening screech followed.'Ladies and gentlemen! Whores and harlots! Poets and high priestesses of the craft! Welcome to Forked Tongue!'

Mahvand felt a genuine sense of pride for Octavi but couldn't help wishing he had just some of his confidence and charisma. There was a round of applause and several wolf whistles.

'London's one and only polysexual erotic literary soiree.' The overhead stage lighting picked up the slight tremor in Octavi's hands, the beads of sweat that had broken out across his forehead. 'To kick off our one-off comics extravaganza, I have the great pleasure of introducing the first act of the evening. He is a renowned cartoonist as well as an expert in the field of popular culture. Graeme Kant.'

And there he was, standing at the side of the stage, preened, and buff, allowing himself, thought Mahvand, a self-congratulatory little chuckle. Graeme's pencil-thin moustache that twiddled up Salvador Dali-style at each end annoyed Mahvand even more than usual. *That should be me up there. My work has far more relevance and universal appeal.* There was no abating the green-eyed monster when it took hold of Mahvand. He stood there in the dark and took some consolation in one of Octavi's favourite sayings: *there's no gym for the face.*

For the next twenty minutes, Graeme's PowerPoint presentation led the audience through the uncharted waters of his award-winning graphic novel, *Pig Head*. Mahvand stood squashed between a Marlene Dietrich lookalike in top hat and tails, who was poised with a cigarette holder in one hand, and a morbidly obese, middle-aged bloke, sporting a studded diamante dog collar and a leather harness. Mahvand wasn't sure how much more he could take, especially as a pungent aroma of body odour from the latter wafted in his direction.

Graeme's storylines were clearly semi-autobiographical (allusions to cottaging, saunas and pickups aplenty) and admittedly somewhat quirky. But his penchant for all things piggy? What was that all about? Every character, without exception, was drawn with a buff human body (apart from the waiflike villains), a pig's snout (to varying degrees of size) and little piggy ears and eyes. *Is Graeme seriously into what some gay men of a certain age are now calling 'Pig Sex'?*

Mahvand was now beginning to wish he was tucked up in bed listening to *Alien Sex Fiend* or *Inkubus Sukubus* while re-reading one of his prized Marvel Masterworks collections – *Son of Satan*. With the intention of leaving, he downed the rest of his Coca Cola and then sensed someone looking in his direction.

Words failed him. Metaphor and simile blushed and made a mad dash for the exit. A keen wordsmith by nature, Mahvand was momentarily left in literary limbo. A moment later, and the object of his affection was commanding all the accolades worthy of a modern-day male muse. He was the word become flesh. An other-worldly, exotic mix with an air of regal authority. A Saudi Arabian sex god with skin surprisingly as pale as the moon. That perfectly proportioned Roman nose, that closely cropped black hair flecked with grey (distinguished yet not quite daddy territory), and those eyelashes – Gran would have said they were wasted on a man; he was the whole package. And yet, more than all this, there was something in the way the stranger looked at him that gave rise to a hollow, burning sensation in the pit of Mahvand's belly: a yearning for something Mahvand could not name. He felt a rush of heat to his head and had to look away. When he could bear it no longer and glanced back, his sex god had disappeared. Mahvand stood on tiptoe and craned his neck, scanning the audience. A torrent of manic laughter erupted behind him. He turned to see the bloke in the dog collar and leather harness laughing hysterically like a deranged Buddha riding a pneumatic drill, his belly and man boobs jiggling ferociously. Mahvand gasped for air, his hands clammy with cold sweat. *Why, when I need my asthma pump the most, is it never at hand?*

By now, Octavi was introducing the next act: a man who went by the name of Belial – a performance poet who had gallantly stepped in at the last minute. (It was announced that the publicised guest speaker, Carol Ledbetter, whose underground comics explored the vagaries of various mental health disorders, had been rushed to A&E earlier that afternoon.) In place of applause, a quiet hush followed. Octavi looked around anxiously. There was a stirring in the crowd. Someone cleared their throat for the umpteenth time. A rockabilly chick covered in nautical tattoos, with a fringe cut to an inch below her hairline, made her way through the crowd and left. A young woman, dressed as a 1940s' burlesque dancer, replete with corset, suspenders, and drag-queen-standard make-up, tottered in her retro heels to the bar. *We're all born naked. The rest is drag.* Mahvand was wondering where he'd heard that, when the venue was suddenly plunged into darkness. Someone screamed. He felt a rush of cold air accompanied by a toxic smell that nearly made him gag.

Before Mahvand's eyes could adjust to the dark, Octavi shouted:

'*Encienda las luces!*'

The rumbling of another tube train drowned out Octavi's shouts, and further high-pitched commands issued from the stage. Then the music started up, softly at first, slowly building to a crescendo: *Ave Satani! Ave, Ave! Versus Christus!* Mahvand recognised the Gregorian chants. He had an extensive collection of horror DVDs at home – *The Omen* being one of his all-time favourites. In the darkness, and halfway through a rousing rendition in Latin of *We Drink Blood*, he couldn't help but think the worst. Had Carol's own history of manic depression played a hand in her impromptu A&E visit?

Suddenly, the stage was bathed in red light, overflowing with a billowing cloud of dry ice. A tall, athletically built man was standing centre stage, head bowed, dressed entirely in black: black suit and tie, black shoes that curled up at the toes Ali Baba-style and bowler hat. Slowly, he lifted his head. Mahvand couldn't believe his eyes. It was HIM – the handsome stranger. *What is he doing up there? And is it the lighting or is his skin actually translucent?* He threw his bowler hat Frisbee-like into the audience. Marlene Dietrich reached up to catch it but it hit her companion's harnessed man boobs fairly and squarely before falling at his rubber-clad feet. Belial undid his top shirt button and loosened his tie. A smile flickered across his face and he fixed his gaze on Mahvand. The music stopped abruptly. Belial bowed before the audience with a theatrical flourish. The French accent (which Octavi later assured him was distinctly Parisian) took Mahvand by complete surprise.

'There are many doors that lead to this world. The one I took blistered and burned. The path to that door twisted and turned. And all the while, I yearned, *Mesdames et Messieurs* ...' Belial pulled a red handkerchief from his trouser pocket and dabbed at each corner of his mouth. 'You have no idea how I yearned for your company.' He took a step forward. 'If I may be so bold, I feel, ladies and gentleman, a stirring.'

Mahvand detected a slight pelvic thrust.

'In my groin. Like Lazarus rising from the dead!'

A woman in front emitted a high-pitched laugh. Alarm bells went off inside Mahvand's head. *He's a psycho, a freak, a delusional maniac.* Then the prospect of public humiliation reared its ugly head. *Oh God. What if there's audience partici-pation and I'm summoned to the stage?*

'May I preface my little piece by saying that parody, ladies and gentlemen, is the highest form of flattery?' Belial coughed into a clenched fist, took a deep breath and began to recite.

'Finding myself (I won't say how)
In that dark wood,
Not quite halfway on life's journey,
I must confess, dear Dante
No leopard, she-wolf, nor lion saw I,
Nor virtuous pagan poet, nor philosopher of old,
Virgil, Socrates, Ovid,
Wandering in limbo
As you self-righteously foretold ...'

Mahvand recognised the poem as a reworking of the opening of Dante's *Inferno* but wondered why Belial, if that indeed was his name, had chosen to deliver it in a monotonous voice worthy of that junkie genius William Burroughs. *And what's with the deadpan expression?* Belial continued, conjuring Charon, hooded skeleton and ferryman of the dead, to lead Mahvand and the rest through the velvet black waters of Acheron, Phlegethon and Styx. Until now, Mahvand hadn't noticed the dark circles under Belial's eyes but found himself strangely charmed by the aesthetic imperfection. The heroin-chic look, which Octavi had assured him had made yet another comeback on the high-end fashion runway that season, lent Belial more than an air of a troubled, yet charismatic, Byronic hero.

Arriving at the gates of Hell, Belial announced in mock heroic tone:

*'Lasiate ogne speranza voi ch'intrate.'**

He removed his jacket, abandoned his monotone address, and quickened the pace. He denounced Dante as a charlatan and fraud, claiming that, wrought on that Iron Gate was an inscription of an entirely different nature: The Path of Excess Leads to the Palace of Wisdom.

Belial's voice suddenly switched to a deep baritone. It was as if an entirely different person, or indeed entity, were speaking through him. Mahvand felt as if the next verse was addressed to him alone:

'Demon dreamer, dear sweet boy,
From the path you stray.
Afraid of your own dark desires,
You keep the wolf at bay.'

Mahvand experienced a strange falling sensation in the core of his being but was reluctant to fully let go. A part of him still questioned the shift in content and style of the poem, the sudden change of voice. *Is Belial telepathically communicating this to me alone? What if everyone else is being led through some bastardised version of Dante's nine circles of*

---

* Abandon all hope you who enter here

Hell? He was aware of an intense pressure at the back of his head and a high-pitched ringing in his ears.

> *'Well hear this, wolf-king lover!*
> *Does your rosebud pucker?*
> *Do you twitch below and tremble?*
> *Standing on the precipice,*
> *My fallen*
> *angel.'*

What if I'm making it all up in my own head? No sooner had Mahvand begun to question his own sanity, than a childhood memory surfaced with such potency that it was as if Mahvand was experiencing it for the first time. It was so vivid that Mahvand completely forgot about the fashionistas, fetish freaks, and the beautifully beguiling man on stage. For he found himself, or rather a much younger version of himself, at a bazaar in central Tehran, mesmerised by the way a shaft of sunlight illuminated the gold and earth-red of a Persian carpet.

'And do you know why every carpet has an imperfect stitch deliberately woven into it?' asks his father, the familiar sound of the call to prayer blaring through a speaker from a nearby minaret.

Mahvand shakes his head. He is drawn instead by the peacocks and parrots and teardrops he sees in the silk carpet laid out by the moustachioed stall-holder.

'To remind us that mankind is imperfect. Remember this, son,' he says, ruffling Mahvand's hair. 'Only God' – Mahvand knows perfectly well what's coming next – 'is perfect.'

With his father's words of wisdom reverberating in his head, Mahvand rubbed his eyes and, still feeling somewhat disorientated, came up for air and back to the crowded, dimly lit basement in Bethnal Green. He gazed up at the man onstage standing knee-deep in dry ice, who looked like he'd made it to the summit of some cloud-capped mountain. 'Who are you?' Mahvand asked himself.

Like a bolt of lightning came Belial's telepathic reply: 'Demon to some. Angel to others.'

'Führe uns in Versuchung'*

The final words of Belial's epic poem were followed by a prolonged silence, which was eventually broken by the Marlene Dietrich lookalike who began singing off-key in a clipped Teutonic tone: *Ich bin von Kopf bis Fuss auf Liebe eingestellt!*** This was followed by the muffled sound of someone clapping behind him. Mahvand turned to see the man with the dog collar slapping his rubbered-up hands together. Others gradually joined in, and the clapping built to a rapturous applause interspersed with wolf whistles and shouts of 'Encore!', 'Belial!', and 'Pants Off!'

THUD!

A woman at the front, at the end of the row, went down. Mahvand couldn't take his eyes off her lower legs. They jutted out like the Wicked Witch of the East's after Dorothy's house falls from the sky and crushes her to death. Only she

---

* Lead us into temptation

** I am from head to foot, prepared for love

wasn't wearing stripy stockings and ruby red slippers. The Birkenstocks could mean only one thing: it had to be. It was – Bogdana.

Belial broke his pose and whisked the red handkerchief from his trouser pocket. He dabbed once more at the corners of his mouth, as if just having devoured some gourmet delight, then picked up his jacket, slung it over his shoulder, and stepped down from the stage. That was when the chant started up.

'BE-LIAL! BE-LIAL!'

Mahvand got the distinct impression that he was in attendance at some Nuremberg rally rather than a literary soiree in the heart of the East End. Looking like some high priest of the dark arts, Belial locked eyes with Mahvand (who stood there dumbstruck) before making his way towards the exit. Mahvand half expected him to return, take a bow, and thank his adoring audience. But there was no sign of the man who had awoken something that, since the zenith of his childhood, had lain dormant.

Mahvand fought his way through the crowd, hauled himself up the spiral staircase and ran out into the cobbled alleyway. It was raining heavily. He carried on running, past the door whore in a leopard-skin minidress and blonde Afro wig, past the railway arches and scrap metal yard, and back out onto the high street. Only he didn't see the drain near the kerb bubbling with water, nor the black cab heading at 'reakneck speed in his direction. But he felt every drop of cold water as it splashed below his waist.

' stood at the kerb in his sodden jeans, clutching his bag stuffed with untraded zines, and looked up.

The eyes that met his gaze were blood-red and filled with some kind of deranged craving, the set of gnashers instantly recognisable. Stretched across a full-length billboard, and above the slogan, *New Labour. New Danger*, was Britain's prime minister in waiting: Tony Blair.

NO PLACE
LIKE HOME

Mahvand tore the latest sketch of Belial from his sketch pad, scrunched it tightly into a ball and threw it across the room. Bullseye! It hit the framed poster of the moustachioed superhero Doctor Strange right in the centre of his golden Amulet of Agamotto. Faced with yet another empty page, Mahvand's vision blurred, and for a moment he was in danger of plumbing the depths of artistic despondency. He fought hard against it, sharpened his gaze and picked up the 2B graphite pencil. If only he could capture that sense of authorial majesty, a hint of devilish depravity. His hand swept in large strokes across the page and he began to reminisce about his trip to Rome with Gran and their visit to the Sistine Chapel. Belial may have held court last night, but now it was he, Mahvand Amirzadeh, who held the reins. He imagined he was Michelangelo's God from the Old Testament, reaching across the void, bringing Adam into existence

THUMP!

Mahvand's artistic musings were rudely interrupted by the whack of his gran's walking stick directly underneath his bedroom floor.

'MAH-VAND!' Gran's caterwauling, thickened from a forty-a-day B&H habit, rose above Marr's guitar riffs and Morrissey's fey falsetto on *This Charming Man.*

Mahvand reached for the knob on his hi-fi and turned the volume down.

'We've got comp'ny!'

He groaned, took two puffs from his inhaler, and went downstairs. The front room, or 'parlour', as Gran still referred to it, was thick with smoke. The ash from Gran's cigarette looked as if it was ready to drop, while Uncle Arthur was puffing away on his pipe like the East End's answer to Sherlock Holmes.

'There you are! Thought you'd been abducted by aliens,' said Gran, rocking back and forth in her rocking chair, a framed print of the *Sacred Heart of Jesus* hanging on the wall above her right shoulder. Despite her dour-faced expression, there was something of a French courtesan about her, as she'd over-applied the rouge and white foundation yet again and pencilled in a beauty spot above the right corner of her upper lip. And the significance of the pearl necklace was not lost on Mahvand. It only ever escaped the confines of her musical jewellery box – the one with the rotating ballerina – at weddings, christenings and funerals. *Is this the prelude to some big announcement?*

Mahvand was wearing black jeans and his T-shirt bore the name of one of his favourite bands, *The Fields of the Nephilim.* He was just about to take his place on the two-seater settee – the one with the dodgy spring and floral stretch covers – when he realised it had already been usurped by a woman in a lime-green chiffon blouse from number fifty-seven,

Petula Bishop. Mahvand clocked her plunging neckline. It revealed a cleavage ravaged by cheap foreign holidays and an addiction to tanning salons.

'Hello, Mahv, sweetheart,' said Petula, planting a kiss firmly on each of Mahvand's cheeks. 'Guess what? Yer gran read me tea leaves then did me Tarot. Apparently, there's some tall, dark, handsome man waiting in the wings.' She hiccupped and giggled. 'Who'd have thought, eh? Gracie's own flesh and blood.'

When it came to drinking tea, Gran insisted that she and Mahvand only ever use tea bags. Predicting the future for neighbours and friends was one thing. Family quite another matter. Mahvand glowered at Petula. She'd plonked herself directly under the black-and-white framed photograph of his mum hanging on the wood-chip wallpaper. The one his father had taken near their home in Tehran, only months before she died from crossfire in an armed street battle during the Islamic Revolution. Over the years, Mahvand's memory of what his mother looked like had begun to fade, but the photographic image of her lived on: it was of a young woman, still very much in love, leaning against a wisteria-covered wall, radiant in the late-afternoon sunshine.

Mahvand marched over to the bay window and reached inside the net curtain. He yanked both panels of double glazing apart, but the window would only open halfway as it caught on the overgrown laburnum tree outside. (Ever since his gran had told him as a young boy that the seedpods were deadly poisonous, the golden shower of yellow flowers had held a strange fascination for him.)

'How's it all going at the bookshop, son?' said Arthur, looking dapper in his navy blazer, pink cravat, and hand-kerchief poking out from the breast pocket.

'Not so bad,' said Mahvand, now perched on the edge of the settee next to Petula. 'Can't complain.'

Despite all his promises, Arthur had never so much as popped his head round the shop door. Mahvand put it down to Gran letting slip, all those years back, that Candy – the Geordie transsexual who manned the sex shop single-handedly down in the basement – was getting the 'snip down below'.

'Can't be easy for an ambitious boy like yourself though,' said Arthur. 'I mean, expect you'll be climbing that corporate ladder in next to no time? Manager, area manager, managing director, eh? Eh? Bright boy like yourself.'

Gran nodded in agreement. 'Oh, he's a bright boy all right. Takes after his gran in that department.'

He hated it when she referred to him in the third person whenever they had company.

'Got all his GCSEs, and that A level …' She paused. 'That A level in …' Mahvand registered the look of terror on her face. Then it was gone.

'Art, Gran. I got an A level in art.'

'And then there's all them years burning the midnight oil at university.'

Mahvand chose not to correct her. He'd never quite got over the fact that he'd gone to a polytechnic and not a university.

'He's a bright boy, my Mahvand,' said Gran.

'Handsome too,' added Petula, reaching over and giving his knee a good rub. 'Proper little Enrique Iglesias, ain't we? Bet you have all the young girls after you.'

There was an awkward silence. Gran had known he liked men, or at least men of the mature, swarthy variety, ever since she'd discovered the stash of *Hombres Latinos*, *International Leatherman*, and *Daddy* magazines under his mattress, alongside a video of Derek Jarman's *Sebastiane*. He'd been in his first year at North East London Polytechnic. But despite her fervent belief in the Good Lord, she'd simply told him that her Uncle Ernie from Bournemouth, God bless him, had always been a bit, you know, that way inclined. A bit ginger beer. A bit Clark Kent. And that he must never, on any occasion, ever forget to use 'preservatives', and left it at that.

'I'm OK as I am thanks, Arthur,' said Mahvand, with a distinct feeling that they were all ganging up on him.

'Come on, son. You can tell your Uncle Arthur. What are they paying you?'

'I get by. Don't I, Gran?'

'Well, now I come to think of it,' said Gran with a pinched look on her face, 'I could do with a bit more for yer upkeep. Money don't grow on trees, you know.'

The ticking of the cuckoo clock on the wall punctuated the silence. *Anytime now that blasted thing will shoot through the trapdoor.*

'Whatever they're paying you, I can match it,' said Arthur.

Mahvand stared at him nonplussed.

'I'm telling you, son. I can match it.'

Gran shifted in her seat. With one hand clasped to her chest, and in a voice usually reserved for answering the telephone, she said, 'Arthur has connections, you see. Business connections.'

'Let me handle it,' warned Arthur.

'I was just saying,' said Gran.

'Thought you might not be short of a bob or two,' said Petula, leaning towards Arthur. 'I said to myself, I did, when I first clapped eyes on you.' She was beginning to slur her words. 'I said that fella's not short of a bob or two.'

'Thing is …' said Arthur.

'The thing is,' said Gran, leaning forward and folding her arms, which had the effect of giving her double G bust an instant lift. 'What Arthur 'ere is trying to say is … Well, he's only gone and landed you a proper corn on the cob and everythin', 'aint you, Arthur?

Mahvand couldn't remember the last time he'd seen Gran this happy. She had this warm glow about her.

'Yer gonna be on …'

It was like she'd won the pools or something.

'TELEVISION!'

'Television?' said Mahvand, instantly rising to the bait.

'Television?' echoed Arthur.

'You been at the sherry again, Gran?' said Mahvand.

'Yer gran's got the wrong end of the stick, son. It's in ad-ver-tis-ing,' Arthur said, slowly articulating the word.

'That's what I said,' said Gran.

Arthur leant forward in the armchair, hands clasped together. 'It's a golden opportunity.' Now it was his turn to sound like he'd got a plum stuck in his throat. 'A position has been, how shall I say, made available. Yes, indeed. A fancy advertising firm over near Liverpool Street. My neck of the woods as it so happens.' He lapsed back into broad cockney. 'I dunno, son – you'll probably be making the tea, running errands and such like. Mind you, I started off as a barrow boy in Bishopsgate market. And now look at us.'

'Do you hear that, Mahvand? When anyone asks you what you do, you can say, I'm in—'

'ADVERTISING,' said Arthur, Gran and Petula in unison.

Mahvand felt as if he was being brainwashed.

'I'm in advertising,' said Gran in a silly, theatrical voice again, clasping a hand to her matronly bosom. She kept saying it over and over. Petula snorted with laughter. Mahvand simply stared at the opening and closing of Gran's mouth. He was convinced those dentures had a life of their own and imagined them still at it late at night, magnified by the tumbler of water, chitter-chattering next to her leather-bound King James copy of the Bible.

'Oh, don't it sound fancy? Advertising. Like another world. If anyone asks, I shall say, my Mahvand, I'll say, works in ADVERTISING.' The ash from her cigarette dropped down the front of her floral blouse. She brushed it off like a cow swatting a fly with its tail. 'Never look a gift horse in the mouth. You can do that drawing malarkey of yours and get paid for the privilege.'

'Now I didn't say it would be as easy as all that, least not to start with,' said Arthur.

Mahvand fixed his gaze on the mantelpiece. There, flanked on either side by two of Gran's beloved Royal Doulton figurines, was a framed sepia-coloured photograph of Gran and Great-grandfather Harbuckle onstage at Wilton's Music Hall. She was all of about fourteen – Shirley Temple curls, feather boa, and a corset that forced her hips back and pubescent breasts up. He, majestic in top hat and tails, and a moustache that twiddled up at both ends, took centre stage. Great-grandfather Harbuckle – the renowned psychic and Victorian magician. Or so the legend went. Mahvand wondered what Great-grandfather Harbuckle would have to say about his own daughter getting him to give up on his dream of ever becoming an artist. 'It's illustration, Gran. Not drawing. I've told you. I'm an illustrator. A cartoonist.' His voice was verging on the shrill.

Gran appealed to Petula, who looked like she was on the verge of passing out from too much sherry. 'There he goes again. What did I say? Always getting on his high horse.'

'What advertising company did you say it was?' asked Mahvand.

'I didn't,' said Arthur.

'Well, if it's that lot who did the Tory ad campaign—'

'Think I've crossed over to the dark side? What do you take me for, eh? It's footwear.' He reached for his tobacco and refilled his pipe. 'You'll be working for a globally recognised brand. A multibillion-dollar conglomerate.' He moved his lighter in a circular motion over the tobacco and puffed. 'It's Nike.'

'Over my dead body!' said Mahvand.

'Wash your mouth out!' said Gran, releasing a shower of spit in Mahvand's direction. 'Arthur's trying to help you out, is all.'

'I don't need helping out. And I certainly don't need to slave away for some Yankee advertising company in league with Nike.'

'Who's Nike?' asked Gran, exasperated.

'The devil, Gran. Corporate greed. Profit margins. Satan screwing the third world.'

Gran rolled her eyes to the ceiling. 'Whatever goes on in that head of yours, I'll never know.'

'Ever heard of child labour?' asked Mahvand.

'A right fine way to carry on when Arthur's gone out of his way—'

'It was just a suggestion, Mahvand,' said Arthur.

'We only want what's best for you,' said Gran, tears welling up in her eyes. 'We both do. It breaks my heart to think of you wasting away the best part of yer life in that bookshop.'

There was spittle on her lower lip. Mahvand fought an urge to get a tissue and wipe it off. He looked at Petula. She'd finally passed out on the sofa, her neck craned back, mouth wide open. She was making little rasping sounds in the back of her throat. The cuckoo clock marked time.

'I just want you to get a proper job,' said Gran, beginning to cry. 'One with prospects. A pension. Company car.'

The cuckoo burst out of its trapdoor announcing it was four o'clock. Petula's whole body jerked back to life. She looked around with startled eyes, as if she didn't know where or even who she was. It was an expression Mahvand had seen countless times on his own grandmother's face.

Mahvand stood up, fighting back the tears. 'I'm an artist! A cartoonist! That's all I've ever wanted to do.' He appealed to Gran. 'Can't you understand? That's all I've ever wanted to be.'

Gran pursed her lips and gazed up at the *Sacred Heart of Jesus*. '*When I was a child, I thought like a child, I reasoned like a child. When I became a man, I gave up childish ways. Corinthians 13.11.'*

This time, Gran had gone too far. Way too far. Mahvand stood up, walked into the hallway, grabbed his red hoodie, which was hanging on the stair banister, and slammed the front door shut as hard as he could. He was disappointed not to hear the sound of breaking glass on his way out.

He marched past rows of detached and semi-detached bungalows, hands dug deep into his jeans pockets, wishing he could teleport himself to any other place on earth. Freshly creosoted garden fences and neatly trimmed hedges hemmed each resident into a clearly defined patch they could each call their own. The Englishman and his castle. Mahvand imagined them defending it to the death with a thwack of a walking stick, shovel or pair of garden shears. Anything they could lay their liver-spotted hands on.

Garden gnomes, with red pointy hats and white beards, stood guard over front porches and carefully tended flowerbeds, belying the lives of quiet desperation he knew many of the residents led. At Rose Cottage he detected a twitching of net curtains and caught a glimpse of a ghost-like apparition – Miss Roberts, the spinster with a shock of white hair who'd turned into a near total recluse soon after her partially blind twin sister, Esme, had passed away during the night of the Great Storm of eighty-seven.

Mahvand turned into Honeysuckle Avenue with its larger detached houses, towering conifer trees and Jaguars or Mercedes parked in the gravelled driveways. He heard a pounding of footsteps behind him.

'Hold your horses, can't you?' Arthur called out, red in the face and breathing heavily.

Mahvand turned and waited for him to catch up.

Arthur put an arm around Mahvand's shoulder. 'Trying to give an old man a heart attack?'

They walked together along the eerily quiet, tree-lined avenue. 'Vote Conservative' posters had sprouted up in recent months behind bay windows and competed with 'Neighbourhood Watch' or 'Crime Stoppers' stickers for attention. Burglar alarms were fitted conspicuously under the roof guttering of some of the larger detached houses: part deterrent, part status symbol.

'You shouldn't have run off like that,' said Arthur.

Mahvand looked at Arthur's deeply furrowed brow. His comb-over had come unstuck and was blowing in the breeze. He reminded Mahvand of his much-loved but threadbare teddy bear, Flippy Floppy. 'I'm sorry, Arthur. It just felt like a bit of a stitch-up job back there.'

'Yer gran only wants what's best for you. You know that.'

Mahvand felt the thorn in his throat swell to a painful throbbing. 'Sorry about that job offer. It was Gran, wasn't it? She put you up to it.'

'She loves you, Mahvand. We all do. I know it's not been easy …' he paused, 'what with your mum and everything.'

They carried on walking towards the train station, past the little parade of shops and the plethora of estate agents and wine bars that had sprung up in this part of Essex in the last few years. Mahvand made this same journey five or six days a week. He knew every mound, crack and dip in the pavement, every grass verge and privet hedge, every pipe-smoking, fishing-rod-reeling, mushroom-squatting garden gnome; he'd even gone so far as to name some of them.

Arthur stopped outside a new coffee shop that had just opened up. 'I've been meaning to say something. About yer gran.'

Mahvand knew exactly what was coming. He was surprised Arthur hadn't brought it up before.

'She's not herself.' He paused. 'I wasn't going to say. But before, when you was upstairs, she was saying how ...' He took a sharp intake of breath. 'She was saying how she was looking forward to your mum coming home for Christmas.'

Mahvand felt crushed by Arthur's revelation. He knew Gran hadn't quite been herself recently but she'd never had a problem distinguishing between this world and the next. Nor one month from the other; it was barely spring.

Arthur smoothed over a tuft of hair that kept blowing up in the wind. 'I think it's high time we got a home help. Why don't I give social services a quick call? See what they can do, eh?'

Mahvand laughed. 'What's the point? She'd sooner move back to that East End tower block with the graffiti and the drug dealers and the smell of piss than have some stranger rooting round in her kitchen drawers.'

'She needs proper care,' said Arthur.

'We do all right.'

Arthur rested a hand on Mahvand's shoulder. 'I know you do your best. But what of the future?'

Mahvand knew what he was getting at. But not even Arthur could bring himself to say it. They walked under the railway bridge, weighed down by thoughts of the future and a family taboo. Mahvand couldn't help but glance up the steps that led to the car park and the graffiti-sprayed, near-derelict toilets that Gran had always warned him about. Where dirty old men do dirty things with other dirty old men, and young 'uns like himself, given half a chance. Mahvand looked at Arthur. He was kind, dependable, good for Gran. Mahvand was fond of him, but he found himself wishing, more than anything, that he was walking, not with Arthur, but with his own father. But what was the good of that? Since the death of Mahvand's mother and the rise to power of Ayatollah Khomeini, his father, by all accounts, had sought solace in shooting up smack.

That night, Mahvand stayed up into the early hours of the morning. Moonlight spilled into the bedroom, across the mountain range of crumpled clothes strewn across the floor, lighting up the extensive collection of comics stacked on shelves and the Wonder Woman print of his duvet cover. Gran had gone to bed some time ago. He'd heard the familiar sound of her laboured breath on the stairs, the muttering, and the creaking of her bedroom door as she shut it quietly to, no doubt thinking he was already in the land of Nod. The branch of an oak tree tapped his bedroom window. Mahvand looked out and spotted a red fox lurking by the garden shed. It locked eyes with him. They were eyes that seemed to know just what he'd been up to. And what would come to pass. There was something in its mouth. A rodent or small bird perhaps.

Sitting at his desk in his Superman boxer shorts, Mahvand entered that relaxed yet concentrated and luminous mental state of creative free-flow. He began doodling and abandoned any previous attempts to sketch a photographic likeness of Belial. He concentrated instead on what he did best – cartooning. Once he'd mastered the new cartoon version of Belial in all his fiend-like glory, he drew him in three different panels – a holy trinity of iconic moments: *Lust at First Sight; Poetic Parody; The Grand Exit.* His backgrounds were an experiment in style, leaning towards the expressionism of Munch's *The Scream* or the mind-bending surrealism of Escher's *House of Stairs.* Mahvand also experimented with bleeding the second panel into the next page, giving a sense of the moment haemorrhaging into timeless space.

He didn't notice how heavy his eyelids were as they flickered and began to close, nor his 2B graphite pencil and sketch pad as they released themselves from his grip. Not yet fully asleep, he imagined himself slipping through the gutter between the panels of a new graphic novel he would one day write – one which would debut Belial as 'Sex God of the Homoverse'. And from the limbo-like gutter of this erotic comics masterpiece, this blueprint for modern mythmaking, he descended the subterranean spiral staircase of sleep, before hurtling headlong into an all-too-familiar nightmare. One where he found himself standing yet again on the upper ledge of Canary Wharf Tower, knowing that any moment his foot would inevitably slip, his arms flail and he'd plummet over eight hundred feet to the concrete plaza below. Along with Big Ben, the Eiffel Tower and the Empire State Building, Canary Wharf Tower would rise from the depths of his subconscious and offer up its nightmarish precipice from which to fall, night after night.

He awoke with a jolt, his left leg suddenly jerking out and hitting the radiator. Two fifty-three. A random piece of information from his encyclopaedia on magic and the occult suddenly came back to him. *The witching hour, commonly believed by many pagans to be 3 a.m., is a time when witches, ghosts and demons exert their strongest power.* The red digits on his radio alarm clock blinked back in a series of dashes. Three minutes. He'd been asleep for three whole minutes. And at some point, as Mahvand had drifted off, his sketch pad had fallen in such a way that Belial was now hanging upside down, like the hanged man from the tarot card, trapped forever inside a cartoon panel, staring back up at him.

He gripped the adjustable seat of his chair with both hands to prevent himself from running into the hallway and bursting into Gran's bedroom. He scanned the room. The empty litre bottle of Coca Cola on the desk, his collection of superhero figures, even the air he breathed – everything seemed tinged with a sickly hue of yellow. Mahvand detected a supernatural sleight of hand at play; a sinister presence vibrated at the heart of everything.

'Presence'. No sooner had he acknowledged the word than he shuddered with the distinct feeling that someone, or something, was standing behind him. De-dum de-dum de-dum. A quickening of cardiac muscle behind breast bone. A throbbing in the flesh of his throat, the inner chamber of his ear. Sweat trickled down the nape of his neck. Summoning every last vestige of belief in a benevolent God, he closed his eyes and began to recite. *Our Father, who art in heaven …* He wanted, more than anything, to race to the finishing line.

To exorcise the evil presence. For 'Amen' to put a nail in the coffin of his fear. A fear quite unlike any other fear he'd ever experienced. A primal, other-worldly fear. A fear that filled him with supernatural dread. *Forgive us our trespasses, as we forgive those who trespass against us.* But the prayer refused to yield the next line. He repeated the previous line again. And again. *Temptation. That was it. Something about temptation. Jesus. What? Think!*

It was as if a chasm had opened up in his mind, and he caught, or thought he caught, a glimpse of a terrifying abyss. His descent from well-known city landmarks under slumber of sleep was no preparation for what he encountered now. A collapsing. Disintegration. A falling in on himself. He opened his eyes and heard his own voice splinter The Lord's Prayer into nonsensical fragments. *Deliver us from bread. Hallowed be thy trespasses. On earth as it is in evil.* The red digits on his alarm clock radio blinked back 2:59 like the eye of some malevolent trickster. It was at this heightened moment of blind panic that he felt, or thought he felt, the sensation of warm breath caress the nape of his neck. He could bear it no more and spun round.

Is it lurking in the wardrobe? Hiding under the bed? Oh God, was that a shadow that just flit across the ceiling? His hands were shaking like an old man's with advanced-stage Parkinson's disease. The radio alarm clock blinked back 3:00. His vision blurred. For a moment, he thought he might be dead. He couldn't quite feel where his body began or where it ended. And then, just as he felt himself about to black out, those words, that had thus far eluded him, bestowed upon him their benediction: *Lead us not into temptation.*

And deliver us from evil. In that moment, he felt himself fully inhabit his own body.

He'd never been so grateful to see the familiar sight of his extensive comic collection stacked on the shelves, each title ordered in strict chronology by date of issue. Nor Wonder Woman, warrior princess of the Amazons, staring up at him in her golden tiara and star-spangled knickers. There was only one possible and rational explanation for his flight into paranoid delusion. A fevered imagination had conjured substance out of shadow; his mind was playing tricks with him. Gran had warned against burning the candle at both ends.

Mahvand woke the next morning quite spent. Semen had dried in a patch and stuck to his boxer shorts. The only other time he'd had a wet dream of such magnitude was in the fog of mid-adolescence when a rather hirsute Tarzan, in nothing more than his leopard-skin loincloth, had swung across a huge ravine with a heroic, ululating yell. But this time his back felt strangely sore, just like it had last summer when he'd forgone the usual application of factor fifteen St Tropez suntan lotion and fallen asleep in the back garden on Gran's sun lounger in the midday sun.

He clambered out of bed, eyes heavy with sleep, and peered down the hallway. Gran's bedroom door was still firmly shut. He darted into the bathroom. When he turned to look at his back in the full-length mirror, he couldn't quite believe what was staring back at him. Had the early morning evil presence somehow shape-shifted into the form of a wolf man or Incubus and committed unspeakable acts while he slept? Or had he himself somehow summoned Belial through reproducing him on the blank page? Mahvand twisted one way, then the other, before reaching for the mirror on top of the glass cabinet. He removed his semen-stained boxer shorts and wiped the layer of dust off the hand mirror. With his back to the full-length mirror, he held it up for a complete reflection; his skin was covered in a criss-cross of scratch marks that ran all the way from his buttocks to the nape of his neck.

SOHO BOOKS

It was Friday afternoon and Mahvand had just started his shift. Nearly a week had gone by, and the scratch marks had all but disappeared. (He'd managed to convince himself it had been an allergic reaction to Gran's washing powder. Gran, not to be outdone by Petula Bishop, had switched to a new, biological brand.) Candy was manning the sex shop in the basement, while Mahvand sat perched on his stool behind the cash desk, a frothy mochaccino with extra cream and a Cadbury's Flake at the ready.

He looked up from his sketch pad at the customer who'd lingered long enough in the cookery section, towards the rear of the shop, for him to sketch her. While she pored over glossy pics of puddings, pasta and puff pastry, an uncanny likeness of her had taken shape on the blank page. She had a small down-turned mouth that seemed to speak of a life of putting up, shutting up and getting by. A crucifix dangled over her ample cleavage, and her tummy bulged over her slacks in a tight-fitting black top. Mahvand couldn't quite place her. Was she an out-of-townie in the West End whiling away the hours before escaping to a darkened auditorium and the fanfare of *Jesus Christ Superstar* or *Les Misérables*? Or was she secretly salivating over the culinary delights of Delia

Smith? No matter. He'd captured something of her mealy-mouthed expression and she was a welcome addition to the army of customer caricatures that populated his sketch pad.

Mahvand was also keeping one eye on Crystal – well known to the police and local shopkeepers in the area. She was a skeletal woman of indeterminate age, barefoot and swamped in a white, gold striped Adidas tracksuit. Enormous, hooped gold earrings dangled from her earlobes and the word 'H.A.T.E' was tattooed in faded black ink across both knuckles.

Crystal made a beeline for the pop music and celebrity section, which formed part of the front window display. Mahvand watched her every move through the mirror tilted at an angle above the entrance. She'd started to pick with her nails at the price sticker on a hardback chronicling the lives of Hollywood stars, nails that were dirty and bitten, with fingertips discoloured from nicotine. Mahvand had seen them up close. This random act was followed by another, as she placed the hardback first in the self-help section and then, after a suspicious backwards glance, on the top shelf with all the occult books. She then picked up *Diana: Her True Story*. There wasn't much Mahvand could do should she choose to shoplift and make a run for it. What with his asthma, he certainly wasn't going to chase her through 'Gay Central', dodging pedestrians, black cabs and mad cyclists. For what? To lay claim to a book which exposed the Machiavellian inner workings of the House of Windsor?

She sauntered over to the middle-aged woman in the cookery section. 'Spare any change, love?' asked Crystal in a Liverpudlian accent, her facial muscles twitching.

The doughy, dour-faced woman hid behind a large hard-back with a touched-up image of a raspberry pavlova on the front cover.

Crystal was undeterred. 'Need the bus fare home, see. Wouldn't ask otherwise. Cup o' tea wouldn't go amiss neither.'

Mahvand called out from behind the counter. 'Look. I think it's best you were on your way. '

'Oh, do you now?' said Crystal. She cocked her head, hooked her thumbs in both pockets of her trackie bottoms and sauntered over to Mahvand like a cowboy squaring up for a shoot-out. He wished he'd kept his mouth shut. There was no doubt in his mind that she'd graduated with flying honours from the school of hard knocks and was more than willing to prove it.

'What did you say?' she said, spitting each word out with a crazed look in her eye.

'I don't want any trouble,' said Mahvand. He'd heard a story about some crack monster in the States who'd ended up killing his own kid, convinced he was the son of Satan. Mahvand wasn't willing to incur the wrath of Crystal – not at the beginning of his late shift on a Friday afternoon with only Candy for backup. The last thing Soho needed was a crack-fuelled psychopath on the warpath.

But in his moment of hesitation, Crystal saw her chance. She grabbed his sketch pad. Mahvand tried in vain to snatch it back but ended up knocking over his half-drunk mochaccino into his lap. He jumped up from his stool like a demented jack-in-the-box, scalded by the hot water. The Cadbury's Flake, which he'd been looking forward to, was now on the floor in a puddle of cream. But worst of all – it looked like he'd wet himself.

'Now look what you've gone and done!' Mahvand shouted, grabbing fistfuls of air from behind the counter. 'Give it back!'

'Now, now. That's no way to treat a lady.' Crystal smiled, holding the sketch pad in the air just out of reach, goading him on. Mahvand couldn't help but notice her missing teeth.

The dour-faced woman, still lurking by the cookery section, peeked out from behind the raspberry pavlova. Mahvand thought he detected an element of *Schadenfreude* in the slight upturn of her down-turned mouth.

'Tell you what, Leonardo,' said Crystal. 'Give us twenty quid and I'll get me kit off and pose for yer. I'll be your *Mona Lisa*. What d'ya say, handsome? Beats turning tricks with some dirty middle-aged sleazebag down Berwick Street.'

Mahvand felt a tightness in his chest, took his inhaler out of his jean's pocket and puffed hard. 'Candy!' he yelled.

'That old tranny? Watch out! The circus is coming to town!' sneered Crystal.

By now Crystal had backed off and was in her element, holding court in the middle of the bookshop near the central display of photography and high-fashion hardbacks. She turned and addressed the next line to the woman in the cookery section. 'Didn't know Leonardo here was secretly sketching your ugly mug, did you, love? That's right, ladies and gentlemen. The fat cow in the corner with a face like a slapped arse. Who knows – could be worth a few grand in years to come. Your face. This shop. Who'll start the bidding?' She waved the sketch pad in the air. 'A tenner.

Twenty. Twenty-five to the gentleman at the back. Do I have any offers on twenty-five pounds?'

The shop bell rang, and in walked Ernest. A regular at Soho Books, he was the wrong side of forty, wore bifocal glasses and was sporting a new pudding-basin haircut. He clutched his trademark Tesco carrier bag full of breadcrumbs. Mary Poppins – that's what Mahvand had nicknamed him on account of his love affair with the flying vermin who pooped all over the West End. He stood dithering in the doorway. Mahvand prayed he'd remain there and block Crystal's path should she attempt a quick getaway.

'Is that me?' Crystal had flicked through the pad and come face to face with an unflattering version of herself propositioning someone for money. 'Is that what you think I look like? A fuckin' skank? A walking skellington? The Grim bloody Reaper? That your idea of a sick joke, Leonardo?'

It was now or never. Mahvand ignored all the advice the area manager had told him about not leaving the cash till unattended, and unbolted the side door to the cash desk. In a personal victory against the schoolboy bullies who still haunted him, he charged in the direction of the self-help section. With a newfound determination, he chased Crystal around the central display of high-fashion and photography hardbacks in a game of cat and mouse. On the third lap, Crystal bumped into an elderly gentleman clutching a hardback of Robert Mapplethorpe's homoerotic photography. With a look of horror on his face, the old man stumbled back and the book somersaulted into the air. It landed on the other side of the display, open at a black-and-white self-portrait of Mapplethorpe holding a machine gun in front of a giant pentacle. Crystal searched frantically for a quick exit but Ernest was still valiantly guarding the entrance. She turned and darted towards the wooden staircase and leapt down the stairs.

'Man the till!' shouted Mahvand.

'Right you are,' said Ernest, who gave Mahvand a military salute and marched over to the cash desk, pleased to be of any assistance.

Mahvand was in hot pursuit. He wasn't quite sure what he'd do if he caught up with Crystal. Pin her up against a wall? Wrestle her to the ground? He didn't fancy his chances. But being an artist was his gift to the world. His reason for getting up each morning. And that particular sketch pad was a painstakingly and faithfully recorded account of the flotsam and jetsam of Soho life: the pimps and prostitutes who'd loiter on the corner of Berwick Street, the homeless down and outs who'd come in asking for cigarettes or fifty pence, the recent influx of Brazilian gay boyz who'd hang outside Cafe Costa sipping cappuccino like they owned the joint. Who knew? Perhaps one day some of the sketches might even form part of an art exhibition on the local area. There was no way the likes of a Liverpudlian crack whore was making off with all that.

Down in the basement, a bearded, middle-aged bear type in leather chaps, clutching a hard-core S&M porn video to his chest, let out a high-pitched gasp as Crystal pushed past him and into the rear of the shop. Overhead on the TV screen, above the assortment of jockstraps and bottles of poppers, two US military cadets with swinging hard-ons were wrestling in a muddy field in nothing but their military caps and army boots. Crystal had positioned herself strategically behind an assortment of dildos, handcuffs and a life-size blow-up doll of Brad Pitt.

Candy was behind the till, painting her nails in a new gold lacquer: *How Many Carats?* She gave Crystal the once-over and blew nonchalantly on her nails. All six foot two of her then stood up and tottered out from behind the till in six-inch stilettos. Her Crimplene sea-green dress was more suited for evening wear, or a mermaid's convention, than a basement sex shop in Soho. She placed both spatula-shaped man-hands on her hips and pouted.

'A friend of yours, Mahvand?'

Mahvand was on the verge of tears. 'She's got my sketch pad.'

'And what d'yer expect Mutha te do, leik? Wrestle the lass te the fuckin' ground?'

'You can't go drawing people without their say-so,' said Crystal. 'It's a criminal offence,' she added smugly.

'Thief!' cried Mahvand. 'That's nearly two years work in there.'

'Well you should have thought of that before you pimped us all out in the name of art,' said Crystal.

'Now look 'ere …' said Candy.

'Crystal,' said Crystal.

'Charmed, Ahm sure. Ahm Candy. Candy Darling. Yee may have heard me name bandied around town?'

'Muscling in on my territory?' said Crystal.

'Madam Jojo's … The Two Brewer's in Cla'am? Cabaret artiste, sex shop impresario, entertainer extraordinaire.' She stepped forward and extended a hand. 'Pleased te meet yer acquaintance.'

Crystal remained at the rear of the shop, cowering behind the Brad Pitt doll.

Candy's voice suddenly dropped an octave. 'Alreet. Let's dispense wi' formalities, shall we? Just hand ower the book, man? Then maybe we can all get some bloody peace an' quiet round heor.'

The bearded guy in chaps walked away in a huff, stomping his way up the stairs to street level in his Dr Martens, a bright yellow handkerchief trailing out of his left jean pocket.

'See – you're scaring me regulars away. He wez this much away frem purchasing *Armageddon 2: The Second Cumming*,' said Candy.

'I scared him away?' said Crystal. 'Have you looked in the mirror recently?'

'Why ye brazen little hussy,' said Candy hoisting up her dress.

'Keep taking the hormones, love,' cackled Crystal.

Candy got no further than the vintage leather and water-sports porn collection before she tottered and stumbled. Her turquoise patent stiletto shoes (not used to anything more strenuous than a catwalk strut) buckled from under her. She reached out in desperation to the shop floor dummy, which was kitted out in full-body rubber regalia and 1940s' government-issue gas mask. But to no avail. Down she went. Her chestnut-brown wig had become displaced in the fray, and the fringe was now level with her over-plucked eyebrows. She looked up at Mahvand and reached out a perfectly manicured, lacquered hand. 'Christ, me foot. Aa've twisted me fuckin' foot, man!'

Crystal was now standing on the other side of Candy and laughing, the gaps between her rotten teeth hideous and fleshy like a carved pumpkin mouth on Halloween. 'Now that's a sight for sore eyes.' She turned to Mahvand, rolling up her sleeves. 'Come on, hot stuff. Show us what you're made of.'

Mahvand was just about to commit tranny roadkill and step over the hulking great body of Candy, when he caught a glimpse of her face, contorted with pain and humiliation. He couldn't just leave her lying there, so he offered her his hand. Crystal took advantage and charged towards the staircase, taking the steps two at a time all the way up to the ground floor. Mahvand watched her skinny frame in the oversized Adidas tracksuit disappear from view at the top of the stairs. No doubt she'd make off, not only with his treasured sketch pad, but with as many overpriced hardbacks as she could carry, before legging it past the strip joints and lap-dancing emporiums and into Old Compton Street. At the very least, he'd end up with a formal warning from the area manager, if not losing his job.

Candy hobbled back to her stool behind the cash desk, leaning on Mahvand for support.

'I'm so sorry, Candy,' said Mahvand.

'Divvent yee worry yourself. Ah will be alreet the morra, ye bugger.'

Mahvand paced up and down. Where would his cherished caricatures and portraits finally end up? Sold, no doubt, for a couple of quid so she could put it towards buying a rock

of crack. *Why is it always one step forward and two steps back?*
Part of him, although he'd hate to admit it, was already
regretting having chosen Candy over his art.

'She's violated the inner sanctum of my imagination,'
cried Mahvand. 'I'll never sketch again.'

Candy reached for a bottle of poppers and sniffed deeply
from each nostril. 'Strictly medicinal, mind.'

'I'll never sketch again!'

'So divvent be getting any ideas.'

Mahvand felt the waves of humiliation. First Adam
Hudson. Then Gran quoting Corinthians in front of the
likes of Arthur and Petula. And now a Liverpudlian crack
whore in possession of his artwork. But this latest setback
and public humiliation just served to add fuel to the fire.
So there, in amongst the dildos, handcuffs and blow-up sex
dolls, he summoned a dark determination, just as he had all
those weeks ago at Forked Tongue.

'Be a doll, shut up shop and fetch us a bag of frozen peas,
why divvent yee. Money's i' Mutha's purse.'

'I think I can stretch to a bag of peas, mother.'

She threw him the bunch of keys and he trudged up
the stairs.

'Does this happen to belong to you?' said a familiar voice
in a deep baritone at the top of the stairs.

The first thing Mahvand noticed were the autumnal
shades of leather on his brogues, then the Prada briefcase
wedged between his feet. He took in the navy pinstriped
trouser leg, diamond-studded cufflinks, Arabic features
and aviator sunglasses. Shafts of sunlight streamed down
the staircase, bathing Belial's porcelain white skin in an

etheric body of golden light. He was holding up Mahvand's sketch pad like Moses on Mount Sinai holding out the Ten Commandments on the tablets of stone. Mahvand climbed a few steps and, in a gesture of supplication, reached up. Belial handed him his sketch pad. In that moment a wave of relief swept through Mahvand. It was not just his sketch pad that Belial was handing back; it was a part of himself.

'Thank you.' It wasn't until Mahvand examined the sketch pad more carefully that he noticed a single spot of what looked like blood on the front cover. What lengths had Belial gone to, to secure his prized possession?

'Pretty impressive,' said Belial.

'Sorry?'

'Your sketches. How can I put this?' He bent down and his eyes narrowed perceptively. 'They speak to me of a yearning for greater things.'

It was as if Belial could see into his very soul. Then the voice of reason kicked in. How could he? Belial, along with everyone else, would never know how he lay in bed at night imagining his name on the rolling credits for his award-winning zine-turned-graphic-novel-turned-indie-film: *Fallen Angels of Homo Heaven.* Nor would he ever know his greatest shame and most cherished of fantasies – the one where he proudly takes his place on the couch on *This Morning* with Richard and Judy, while shamelessly plugging both graphic novel and movie, to the backdrop of the Liverpudlian Albert Dock.

Mahvand could hear Ernest's voice harking back to the Blitz and rallying the customers. 'Keep calm and carry on shopping!'

'Where did Crystal go?' Mahvand asked, fully emerging from the basement.

'The charming young woman in possession of your artwork but not a full set of her own teeth?' asked Belial, raising one eyebrow. He turned to the shop door which was wide open. 'Let's just say she may have seen the error of her ways. I don't think she'll be bothering you again.'

Mahvand thanked Ernest for holding the fort and told him he could choose a book free of charge for his efforts. It was like Ernest had just been awarded the Military Cross for gallantry in military operations, and, after closing the shop door, he snuck off to browse in the self-help, or what Mahvand had nicknamed the 'Self-Hell' section.

'I don't think we've been formally introduced,' said Belial, holding out his hand and grinning in a manner disturbingly reminiscent of Tony Blair. '*Enchanté*.'

Mahvand caught a glimpse of the exposed inner mechanism on Belial's watch. No doubt astronomically expensive, and clearly vintage, he felt he was bridging more than one world as Belial firmly shook his hand.

'I'm Mahvand.'

'Mah-vand.' He seemed to savour each syllable as if they were an exotic delicacy. 'Farsi. "Light of the moon", if I'm not mistaken?'

'How did you—?'

'Let's just say, monsieur, one has done one's research.'

'I saw you at Forked Tongue,' said Mahvand.

'Did you now?' Belial said, laughing knowingly.

The memory of that night suddenly came rushing back: the instant attraction from afar, the venue being plunged into sudden darkness, Belial's bizarre yet mesmerising performance. Had Belial sought him out or was it just a coincidence that he was browsing for books in his shop? He was too shy to ask.

Belial gestured to the far corner of the shop. 'By the way, I couldn't help but notice your occult section needs revamping. There's a dearth of literature on Aleister Crowley, sex magick, and the secret art in general. It would be an honour to suggest some welcome additions.'

'Well if it's books on the occult you're after, Watkins bookshop—'

'Actually, it's you.'

'Sorry?'

Belial locked eyes with Mahvand. 'I'm after.'

The fluttering sensation in Mahvand's stomach intensified. He was flummoxed for a verbal response, but the stirring in his groin was unequivocal.

Belial held his gaze then said breezily, 'I'd like to invite you to dinner. That is, of course, if you're free?'

Mahvand found himself staring into Belial's eyes. He was Mowgli hypnotised by the great serpent Kaa and, at that moment, would have given anything to have dived into those two dark depths.

'Shall we say a fortnight on Saturday? There's the small matter of a business arrangement I'd like to discuss.'

Mahvand's romantic aspirations were suddenly dashed to pieces. Again he found himself wrong-footed, unsure of Belial's intentions. 'What line of work are you in?' he managed.

'I'm a dealer.'

Mahvand was struck by a vision of a gun-wielding, Havana-cigar-smoking Columbian cocaine baron with a gold tooth, and shipments of cocaine arriving in a speedboat on the Cornish coast. Despite his initial moral indignation, Mahvand's curiosity was piqued.

Belial laughed. 'An art dealer.' He handed Mahvand his business card: *M. Lebeau-Chevalier, Conceptual Art.* On the back was an image of an eye inside a glowing pyramid. It reminded Mahvand of the all-seeing eye in Doctor Strange's Amulet of Agamotto. 'Phone me.'

Mahvand was suddenly distracted by a manly voice in a heavy Geordie accent yelling from the basement.

'Hev yee got those ruddy peas yet, man?'

When Mahvand turned back, the shop door was wide open; Belial had gone.

YOUNG BRITISH ARTISTS

Thoughts of Belial consumed Mahvand's every waking hour. On his way to work on the 7:34 from Shenfield to Liverpool Street each morning, jammed against his fellow passengers, who looked like they were on their way to the gallows, Mahvand would strain to keep his eyes open. Face pressed up against the glass or else someone's armpit or shoulder, his flickering eyelids would eventually close and shut out the world. Moments later he'd be clinging on to Belial's back, whizzing past the intergalactic giants of the Milky Way, or else finding himself locked in passionate embrace in front of a Frida Kahlo, or Picasso, at some exclusive, champagne-clinking art gallery opening in Manhattan or Berlin. Each earthbound fantasy was unashamedly aspirational and built on the sandcastles of romantic cliché – an unusual twist for a boy who prided himself on his countercultural credentials and political correctness. But as the train pulled out of Romford, Ilford, or Gidea Park, he'd remain oblivious to the blur outside of terraced housing, office blocks, and hoardings advertising everything from Tamagotchi to New Labour. With one-pointed fixation, he'd replay ad infinitum the exact moment his saviour had handed him back his stolen sketch pad: those grey eyes, flecked with the fire of amber, like a matador's goading the bull to its final death throes. Spirited away, Mahvand would search for a way in, longing to penetrate that transparent veneer of cornea, and pour his entire being into Belial's. He was reminded of Octavi's assertion that lovemaking was the desire to inhabit the same space as the beloved. Well, he desired to inhabit Belial's space in the most intimate of ways, to become one with Belial's cardiac tissue, or be propelled, as a red blood cell or platelet, at great velocity through vein or artery in one exhilarating, death-defying, visceral adventure. The ultimate act of transcendental transmogrification. A cannibalistic union. Inverted Holy Communion. From 'I'm yours', to 'I'm you.' And, as the commuter-crammed train hurtled towards the chrome, steel and glass of the city, Belial's words, 'I sense you have a yearning for greater things', would gather momentum, until Belial appeared in all his majesty, replete with horns, cloven hooves and the whites of his eyes inked with the murky black waters of Acheron and Styx.* Mahvand would rouse from his wayward fantasies at Liverpool Street station somewhat dazed and quite spent.

He'd arranged to meet Octavi at a bar in Hoxton Square the following Saturday. A pop-up gallery was host to the opening night of *Vulgarity* at the far end of the square. So they stood outside to witness the media circus, Suede's *Beautiful Ones* still playing on the jukebox – Octavi in purple leggings and a tartan poncho, sucking the life out

---

* Ancient Greek mythology: rivers in the infernal regions of the underworld

of a ready-made rollie, Mahvand in his red hoodie, nursing a pint of Coca Cola. They were surrounded by the usual arty-farty types: girls in kooky prints, pixie ankle boots and ironic plastic jewellery; straight boys in vintage Levi jeans from Japan or San Francisco, wearing T-shirts bearing the names of increasingly obscure record labels. Then, of course, there were the usual smattering of media whores and wannabes masquerading as somebodies, all jostling for position in their chosen field – be it photography, graphic design, fashion, DJ'ing, jewellery design, film or conceptual art. Mahvand had lost count of the number of conversations he'd endured with devastatingly beautiful yet fame-hungry 'ME, ME, ME' types who hadn't shown the slightest bit of interest in him or his comics work. That night he was glad Octavi was there to ward off any potential vampiric beauties out on the prowl for a human looking glass.

Amidst a flurry of flash photography, a rake of a guy in skinny jeans, replete with Jarvis Cocker spectacles, stepped out of a yellow Porsche with an entourage of equally waiflike girls. Mahvand could just make out the words emblazoned across the front of his T-shirt: *Art washes away from the soul the dust of everyday life*. It was just the kind of messianic inspiration he needed. He'd been bursting to unleash his secret all evening.

'Remember the performance poet at Forked Tongue?' said Mahvand. 'Stepped in at the last minute?'

'The freak who played "Ave Satani" while I desperately tried to get the bloody house lights to work?' said Octavi.

Mahvand nodded. 'Belial.'

'You mean Jean-Baptiste,' said Octavi.

'Sorry?'

'I thought you knew,' said Octavi. 'Belial is his stage persona.'

'Oh.'

Octavi threw his cigarette stub on the floor, stamped it out and put on an exaggerated French accent. 'Zat, monsieur, is his real name. I sought I told you.'

Mahvand wondered why Belial hadn't said anything at the bookshop. Jean-Baptiste. Mahvand couldn't quite put his finger on it, but there was something strangely familiar about the name. Was it a character in a movie? Something he'd read? Then it dawned on him. Of course. Jean-Baptiste. It was French for John the Baptist. Along with an image, from his *Children's Illustrated Bible*, of Christ walking on water, and Satan hurtling head-first down from heaven, the bearded, severed head of John the Baptist had more than made its mark on his impressionable young mind.

'He's invited me to his house,' said Mahvand. 'For dinner.'

Octavi stared at him through his lensless spectacles.

'In Hampstead.'

'Is that wise?' asked Octavi.

Mahvand searched Octavi's face for an explanation as to his friend's lack of wholehearted endorsement.

'I think we both know the guy's got a screw or two loose,' said Octavi.

Mahvand's voice rose an octave. 'He rescued my sketch pad from that rancid crack whore.'

'What, so now he's your knight in shining armour?' Octavi placed a hand on Mahvand's shoulder. 'Look, I wasn't going to tell you this—'

'Why can't you just be happy for me?' said Mahvand. 'You're always on at me about not going on enough dates. For not ...' he paused, 'putting myself out there enough.'

'A friend of mine – he said there was something distinctly "dark" about Jean-Baptiste.'

Mahvand stepped back. 'But you're constantly telling me that no life is truly lived until you've at least flirted with the dark side.'

'*Cariño*, there's dark,' said Octavi, leaning in, 'and there is consorting with demons.'

There was an awkward silence. Mahvand stared at the bubbles in his Coca Cola fizzing to the surface. Pulp's *Common People* started up on the jukebox inside.

What if Octavi is right? A demon might be stretching it a bit far. But who's to say he isn't a complete nutjob. He was brought abruptly back to reality by the sound of breaking glass and an alarm. He turned in the direction of the pop-up gallery. The front window bore a gaping hole, and the shattered glass that remained intact now resembled a giant spider's web. A retro 1950s' rockabilly chick covered in tattoos, sporting a red rose in her hair, strutted out of the entrance of the building with a histrionic look of horror on her face. The paps and members of the press had positioned themselves at various vantage points in the street to capture the unfolding drama and sense of panic. Mahvand spotted a figure in a black hoodie sprinting down a side street. A man in a black suit and ear piece was in hot pursuit.

'Do you think it was the public outrage over the masturbatory scene at the cenotaph what done it?' asked Mahvand.

'Or was the shot of the artist pissing on the statue of Winston Churchill the real deal deal-breaker?'

Half the clientele outside the bar were now standing in the middle of the road, regrouping in an act of voyeuristic solidarity.

'Wouldn't surprise me if it was deliberately staged so as to maximise publicity,' said Octavi. 'I can just see the morning papers. "Vandalism at *Vulgarity*", or perhaps just a front-page photo of the smashed window. "Is this Young British Art at its Best?"'

Mahvand fixed his gaze on a young man in a tartan bow tie and purple velvet suit slumped outside the gallery, an octopus of blood dripping down his shaven head. His thoughts turned to Jean-Baptiste. *If he is a practitioner of the dark arts, what's his speciality? Voodoo? The Evil Eye? Full-moon man-orgies in Epping Forest?*

'Did your friend really say Jean-Baptiste was demonic?' Mahvand asked, trying to control the slight quiver to his voice.

'A shard of ice in his soul. Those were his exact words,' said Octavi.

Mahvand was reminded of the shards of all those smashed light bulbs on the ceiling at Forked Tongue. His arms were suddenly covered in goosebumps.

'Look, I wasn't going to tell you, but seeing as you really have no idea what you're playing with.' There was something mask-like in Octavi's theatrical expression. 'The last guy he went out with … by all accounts, it ended disastrously.'

The sound of a siren drowned out the last part of Octavi's confession, and Mahvand was momentarily distracted by the woman with the flower in her hair striking theatrical poses in front of the smashed window for one of the photographers as if she was Carmen Miranda in *Copacabana*.

Octavi put an arm around Mahvand's shoulder. 'Some sort of magic ritual, apparently. Out in the Peak District. Or was it the Lake District? One of the two. '

'He's a magician?' asked Mahvand.

Octavi took a rollie out of his 1920s' vintage cigarette case. The flame from his art deco lighter licked the sprouting hairs of tobacco. 'Don't say, *cariño*, I didn't warn you.'

Mahvand snuck his hands into the side pockets of his red hoodie. A childhood memory of himself performing his own magic ritual hijacked the moment. It carried the image of a young boy suspended in mid-flight, leaping from his bedroom wardrobe under cover of darkness. But it was the incantation the boy used to utter – *Witches! Demons! Come to me!* – just prior to landing in a prepubescent, preorgasmic state of ecstasy that, even now, all these years later, left Mahvand feeling deeply ashamed and more than a little uneasy. Yet it was this same transgressive frisson that attracted him to Jean-Baptiste like metal to a magnet.

Octavi had a dreamy, faraway look in his eye. 'Rumour has it Jean-Baptiste's last lover ended up in a lunatic asylum.' Mahvand followed his gaze. It led straight to the boy in the Blondie T-shirt. 'Paranoid schizophrenia. Or so they say.'

'Who's to say he didn't have it before he met Belial? I mean, Jean-Baptiste.'

'Ashraf. I remember now. That was his name,' said Octavi.

'Ashraf?' Mahvand stared at Octavi open-mouthed. 'That's Persian.'

'Who knew?' said Octavi. 'Maybe he has a thing for hot, young Persian boys?'

Mahvand stared at the spider's web of shattered glass in the pop-up gallery at the end of the square. He couldn't shake the feeling that Jean-Baptiste was more than just your common-or-garden sexual predator. *Monsieur Lebeau-Chevalier. Oh, God. What if he'd received an invitation to the private viewing? Is he somewhere inside the building right now?* Mahvand glanced up to the third floor. His pint of Coca Cola nearly slipped from his grip. Someone at the window was staring back.

A siren and flashing blue light momentarily diverted his attention as an ambulance careered into the square. When Mahvand looked back up at the window, the figure had gone.

'Shall we go back inside?' asked Mahvand as a paramedic began to attend to the man with the bloodied shaven head.

The warmth of the bar and Placebo's *Nancy Boy*, blaring out from the jukebox, soon began to take the edge of Mahvand's paranoia. They were on firmer ground as they began to chat about Brit art, Nu Labour, and Octavi's revamped narrative poem, written from the viewpoint of a talking arsehole.

Lying in bed later that night, Mahvand put Octavi's words of warning down to nothing more than idle gossip and perhaps a touch of the green-eyed monster. Failed artists, he mused, would stop at nothing (Hitler being a case in point). And yet, teetering on the edge of his awareness, was a deeper acknowledgement; from his first glimpse of Jean-Baptiste at Forked Tongue, there had been a shift in the tectonic plates at the core of his being.

Mahvand slept in fits and starts. When he woke, he felt even more exhausted than when he'd gone to bed. But then he had spent a good part of the night dodging an intermittent ejaculation of lava from the bowels of the earth – all the while clutching a compass that could not tell north from south, nor west from east.

GOLDEN DAWN

Above the door, two stone gargoyles, with pterodactyl wings and snarling mouths, stood guard over the threshold to Jean-Baptiste's property. Mahvand thought it somewhat inauspicious that he should be visiting Golden Dawn when it was still dusk. Something a bit topsy-turvy about it all. Like the sun and the moon being in the sky at the same time. He reached for the brass knocker. To his surprise, the door was ajar.

'Belial!'

Mahvand immediately chastised himself for not having used his real name, tentatively pushed the front door and stepped inside. After walking along a winding hallway, at the end of which was a fibreglass arm mounted to the wall clutching a smashed light bulb, he turned into the main reception room. Flames flickered behind a cuboid of glass that jutted out from a granite wall. White marble steps that led to an upstairs gallery gave the illusion of being magically suspended in mid-air. It wasn't until Mahvand looked underneath one of the steps that he realised the entire staircase was in fact supported by some kind of clear Perspex. Huge, jellyfish-like light fittings loomed large over-head, their amorphic shapes reflected in the white marble floor tiles. Under the jellyfish, an arrangement of white sofas looked as if they belonged in some futuristic VIP airport lounge. Mahvand looked down and noticed he was standing on a black-and-white animal skin. *An accident waiting to happen.* He stood there awkwardly clutching the bottle of Australian Chardonnay, his *Alien Sex Fiend* T-shirt and Dr Martens boots an anachronism in a showroom of sharp edges, gleaming surfaces and cutting-edge design. A life-size portrait of Chairman Mao on the far wall stared back at him. With his green-and-yellow skin, he bore more than a little resemblance to a human reptile. *What was it David Icke had said about reptilian overlords taking over the world?* It wasn't until Mahvand clocked a painting of a tin of Campbell's condensed tomato soup above the fireplace, and a blue-haired Marilyn Monroe, that he realised he had to be in the presence of a private collection of Andy Warhol's 1960s' pop art.

'Mah-vand.'

Mahvand's whole body jerked. He spun round and staggered back on the animal skin. The French accent was unmistakable. But having deliberately left his glasses at home, the figure at the top of the stairs remained blurry. When Jean-Baptiste came into focus, it was as if he'd stepped straight out of a Noel Coward play. Gone was the tailor-fitted black suit and Ali Baba shoes. And in its place, classic 1930s' vintage clothing: tweed trousers and waistcoat, burgundy jacket, and a yellow handkerchief perched in the breast pocket. Under his shirt he was wearing a matching burgundy and yellow paisley cravat. Jean-Baptiste seemed to glide towards him.

Mahvand held out the bottle of wine, unable to contain the slight tremor in his fingers. 'Sorry it's not chilled.' He hadn't a clue which wine to get and had sought advice from the acne-scarred Oddbins sales assistant from Shenfield who'd assured him that New World wines were the way to go.

'Chardonnay. How thoughtful,' said Jean-Baptiste, leaning in and kissing him gently on the lips. Mahvand breathed in Jean-Baptiste's perfume – a heady concoction of musk and orange peel, with perhaps a hint of sandalwood. When Jean-Baptiste pulled away, Mahvand felt as if he was levitating a few inches from the floor.

'Please. Take a seat.' Jean-Baptiste gestured to the seven-seater white sofa. With the other hand he flicked a switch on a remote control device. A soprano aria blared through his state-of-the-art sound system. *'Con onor muore.'* Jean-Baptiste placed the Chardonnay on the floor and reached for the bottle of Bollinger in the ice bucket near the wall of fire. He poured two crystal-cut flutes of champagne and handed one to Mahvand.

'Sorry?' said Mahvand.

'To die with honour. *Madam Butterfly.*'

'Oh.' Mahvand sat on the edge of the sofa, fighting the urge to bite his already badly bitten fingernails.

'May I say,' said Jean-Baptiste, who sat opposite him on the L-shaped sofa, 'thou art, *mon cher*, rich in beauty.'

Mahvand felt himself blush and didn't know where to look. No one had ever quoted Shakespeare quite like that to him before. He fixed his gaze on Chairman Mao.

'Shall I tell you who you remind me of?' asked Jean-Baptiste. '*Un jeune prince Persian se précipant.*'

Mahvand stole a glance. He'd learnt enough French at school to realise Jean-Baptiste was comparing him to a young Persian prince. Shadows cast from the fire flickered like impish sprites across Jean-Baptiste's face. *And you* – he thought but dare not voice – *are my guardian angel.*

Jean-Baptiste stood up and offered Mahvand his hand. 'Dinner is almost ready.' When they reached the dining room, Jean-Baptiste said, 'I like each room to express a certain *je ne sais quoi.*'

Mahvand felt as if he'd entered an Aladdin's cave for comic book aficionados. Every spare inch of wall laid claim to silver-framed posters and first editions of comics from the 1940s. Then he realised. All the comic book characters were magicians of some sort: Doctor Occult, Ibis the Invincible, Zatara, Mandrake the Magician – even Sargon the Sorcerer.

'I've been an avid collector,' said Jean-Baptiste, squeezing his hand, 'ever since I was a boy.'

Mahvand turned and looked into his eyes. It was as if they were at Soho Books and Jean-Baptiste had just handed him back his stolen sketch pad from the top of the staircase. When he looked back, on the far wall, above the glass-top table that seemingly floated in mid-air, he spotted a Roy Lichtenstein. *How did I miss it?* It was his favourite ever Lichtenstein – *Drowning Girl.* He'd only ever seen the comic book panel.

'Is it—?'

'An original?' Jean-Baptiste nodded.

Mahvand walked up to the canvas with the reverence one might expect from an American or Japanese tourist encountering *Mona Lisa* or *The Last Supper* for the first time. It was as if the girl had literally cried herself the swirling sea she was drowning in. He re-read the words inside her thought bubble '*I don't care! I'd rather sink than call Brad for help!*' Those words had somehow always struck a chord.

'There is something of Picasso's weeping women in the piece, don't you think?' Jean-Baptiste said, walking up to Mahvand and resting a hand on the small of his back. 'Forgive me. You must be famished.' He lit the candelabra and pulled out a high-backed, black plastic chair with jagged spikes for legs.

The meal was something of an ordeal for Mahvand. Although Jean-Baptiste assured him the foie gras was part of France's cultural and gastronomical heritage, he couldn't help thinking of the geese that were force-fed corn in his name to fatten their livers. And the Coca Cola from a classic 1950s' glass bottle did little to quell the knowledge that the half-chewed meat that got stuck halfway down his gullet once belonged to a pond-dwelling, ribbiting amphibian.

After dinner, Jean-Baptiste offered Mahvand his arm and escorted his guest along a long, winding passageway. In his other hand, Mahvand carried a bottle of Coca Cola and imagined they were two dandies from the Victorian era strolling down the streets of London or Paris. *If only Candy could see me now.* The passageway hosted a gallery of black-and-white photographs, all of Jean-Baptiste, and many taken on various mountaineering exhibitions. A composite picture was beginning to emerge of his host as the all-round Renaissance man: art dealer, performance poet and mountaineer.

They stopped before one particular photograph of a bearded Jean-Baptiste camped outside a small tent at the foot of a glacier. 'K2, or *Chogori* as the locals call it. Part of the Karakoram range in the Himalayas. Do you know what it's like over twenty thousand feet?'

Mahvand hiccupped. 'Cold?'

'Without air the brain cells die. The brain shuts down. Then the rest of the body follows. We lost a member of the expedition team a few days after this photograph was taken.'

Mahvand felt something brush against his legs. A pair of emerald-green eyes looked up at him.

Jean-Baptiste laughed. 'That's Shiva. He doesn't miss a trick.'

Eventually they came to a wooden padlocked door. Jean-Baptiste removed a bunch of keys from his trouser pocket. As if by way of explanation, he said, 'Of course, the space where one exhibits one's art is just as important, perhaps more so, than the works of art themselves.'

On the opposite wall, a steel bookshelf, coiled like the fossilised shell of an extinct mollusc, held a number of hardbacks at odd angles. Mahvand scanned the titles in a desperate bid to glean more information about his host: *Sexuality, Magic and Perversion; Beelzebub's Tales to His Grandson; The Satanic Bible; Owning Art; The Aeon of the God Horus; Lilith and Archangel Samael; De Lamiis et Pythonicis Mulieribus; Ancient Callings of the Dark Lord Seth; The Himalayas; Do what Thou Wilt; The Devil in Love*. He, himself, in his late teens, had developed a bit of an obsession with Aleister Crowley and was more than a little intrigued by the films of Kenneth Anger. But this? *Why didn't I heed Octavi's words of warning?*

'You know what they say about curiosity,' said Jean-Baptiste, rattling the key in the lock.

Mahvand removed his asthma pump from his pocket and took a few puffs in quick succession. 'Can't we see it another time?'

'*Carpe diem*!' said Jean-Baptiste.

That's what Octavi's always telling me. Maybe they're both right. Maybe I just need to let go and live a little. 'I can't be back too late. Gran will be wondering what's happened.'

Jean-Baptiste kissed him gently on the lips. 'As you wish.'

Mahvand found himself stooping low, gripping the rail. His eyes hurt with the glare of a single light bulb swinging from a white flex on the ceiling. He spluttered and picked at the remnants of a spider's cobweb that clung to his face. At the bottom of the stairs he was greeted by a host of grotesque effigies that, with the right incantation, looked as if they might come to life at any moment. He searched the exposed red brickwork in vain for a window. An air vent. A secret door.

'I come down here from time to time,' said Jean-Baptiste. 'And ponder life's little …' He ran his finger along the top of an oval-shaped mirror on the wall and examined the dust. 'Conundrums.'

A damp, putrid smell hung heavy in the air. Mahvand was struck by the religious or rather sacrilegious nature of many of the exhibits. A plasticised sculpture of an aged priest in a scarlet cassock was laid out on the floor, a contorted look of terror on his face. He clutched a cratered piece of rock above his stomach. Mahvand crouched down. The exhibit was called *Holy Father Crushed by Meteorite*.

'Celestial interference. The irony of it all,' said Jean-Baptiste, almost to himself.

One of the most disturbing pieces of art was a sculpture of a young child in nothing more than a pair of the latest trainers with two penises moulded onto its forehead like horns.

'A risky financial investment, I admit. But I simply had to have it. I think the English expression is "It's so bad, it's good",' said Jean-Baptiste, absent-mindedly caressing one of the sprouting penises.

More a case of the emperor's new clothes, thought Mahvand, who'd already seen quite enough.

On the far wall were a collection of framed photographs. Mahvand was immediately drawn to the one entitled *Narcissus Now*. It showed a beautiful young man with curly blonde hair staring into a muddy pool of water under a billboard advertising a range of male cosmetic surgical procedures. Underneath was a quote from Ovid's *Metamorphosis*: '*Both boys and girls looked to him to make love, and yet that handsome figure of proud Narcissus had little feeling for either boys or girls.*'

'Narcissus is a character in one of my comics,' said Mahvand.

'Is that so?' said Jean-Baptiste half-heartedly. 'Life is full of little coincidences. But surely …' he paused and gestured to a rubber mould of a person hanging upside down with what looked like duck feathers stuck to his back, 'your underground zines have more in common with this artist.'

So. Jean-Baptiste had read *Fallen Angels*. Why hadn't he mentioned it earlier? Was he merely building up to that moment when he would casually slip into the conversation the exact nature of his connections in London's literary scene or the film industry? Mahvand approached the rubber cast and read the inscription: *Fallen Angel.*

Jean-Baptiste smiled knowingly. 'More than a passing resemblance to your own artwork, wouldn't you say?'

Mahvand felt a sudden pang of compassion for his own comic book creations. 'It looks nothing like it,' he protested. 'My fallen angels are beautifully drawn. And this ... well, to be perfectly honest, it's ...' He racked his brain for a suitably damning adjective. 'It's diabolical.' As soon as the words were out, he was struck by a terrifying thought. What if the rubber cast belonged to Ashraf? What if Octavi had got it all wrong and Ashraf wasn't languishing in the ward of some psychiatric hospital? What if his corpse – he reached out to the wall for support – was decomposing somewhere in the grounds of Golden Dawn?

Jean-Baptiste, unperturbed, put an arm around his shoulder and offered him a piece of fatherly advice. 'Not the appearance. It's the concept that is king in conceptual art. Here, granted, the aesthetic is intentionally hideous. But what of the concept?'

It suddenly dawned on Mahvand that he was in a basement with a virtual stranger, surrounded by a host of Hammer House of Horror exhibits. *What if Jean-Baptiste suddenly produces a dagger? Or beats me to a pulp with his bare fists?* He couldn't help but think this was the perfect location. In the basement. Under lock and key. Was this where he lured all his victims before bludgeoning them to death? Was Jean-Baptiste just the latest in a long line of gay serial killers? A wave of nausea, accompanied by a vision of his own rubber cast hanging in some exclusive conceptual art gallery of the future, welled up inside him. *No one knows where I am.* His vision blurred. He wanted to vomit. 'Why are you showing me all this?'

'This is the future, Mahvand. Your future. That is, if you want it to be.' He reached out and caressed Mahvand's cheek. 'Painting. Portraiture. It's dead. Dead as a dodo. Or at least cryogenically suspended, shall we say? Today, more than ever, it's through conceptual art that we can choose to become the gods we only sought to worship in the past.'

Shiva was sitting at the head of the *Holy Father Crushed by Meteorite* exhibit, his eagle eyes staring in Mahvand's direction. It all made sense. Mahvand shuddered as he realised the awful truth. Shiva was Jean-Baptiste's familiar.

What was that? Oh God, there it is again. Like some kind of wild animal howling. Whatever it was, it seemed to be coming from Jean-Baptiste. But how could it? His lips – they weren't moving. Mahvand was struck by a terrifying thought that made him doubt his own sanity. That strange, inhuman sound – it had to be coming from somewhere deep within Jean-Baptiste's own body. He pulled away and stepped back. And there, in place of Jean-Baptiste's heart, inside the dark, empty space of his ribcage, two fluorescent yellow eyes stared back. Behind the bars of human bone, a hologram of a wolf in green-yellow, yellow-green light began to snarl in slow motion and bare its teeth.

'Is something the matter?' asked Jean-Baptiste, with a knowing smile.

Transfixed, Mahvand watched as the holographic wolf opened its jaws so wide that its teeth and tongue filled the ribcage, and then, as if its sole intent were to tear some human flesh, it leapt from Jean-Baptiste's heart towards his own. As Mahvand lost his grip on the glass bottle, the apparition dissipated, at mid-point on its trajectory, into thin air. Mahvand stood there agog, staring at the shards of glass and the spilt dark liquid that frothed on the concrete floor like some rabid dog. He'd seen things before. Things that other people just didn't see: strange lights, shadows that flit across the ceiling at night, mere glimpses of a world beyond this one. But nothing like this.

His fingers began to form into fists. He looked up and locked eyes with Jean-Baptiste. A surge of energy animated his whole body. Suddenly he was pushing with all his might, pushing hard against Jean-Baptiste's chest. A bejewelled fist slammed into his right shoulder, but it was Jean-Baptiste who slipped, tripped and staggered backwards. Shiva hissed and sprang out of the way. Jean-Baptiste crashed into the fibreglass sculpture of the child with penises sprouting from its head. Mahvand saw his chance and grabbed the rail at the bottom of the staircase. He gave one backwards glance at Jean-Baptiste sprawled on the floor as if he was a victim of a hit-and-run, and then launched himself up the stairs as if his life depended upon it.

THE PROPOSITION

Candy, an ardent supporter and lifelong member of the Labour Party, had arrived early that morning, sleep-deprived yet raring to go. She'd decked the basement sex shop out in a sea of red balloons and reams of Union Jack bunting fit to rival any royal wedding street party this side of the Watford gap. She'd cleared the counter of cock rings, tit clamps, ball stretchers, and chastity belts, and replaced them with an assortment of twiglets, salted peanuts and things on sticks. But the *pièce de résistance* to her election victory spread was the symbol of the New Labour campaign – a red rose, in a single flower vase she'd nicked the other week from Pizza Express on Dean Street.

Mahvand stood next to Connie Lingus, Candy's drag queen flatmate, who was wearing a rather sinister-looking Cherie Blair face mask. Connie had her arm draped around Mahvand. Both stood, necks craned back, staring up at the TV screen. But instead of the usual continuous loop of alpha-male grunting and groaning, close-ups of puckered arseholes and monster cocks, they witnessed history in the making: a messianic Tony Blair, smiling like a Cheshire cat, addressing the party faithful at the Royal Albert Hall.

'A new dawn has broken, has it not?' said Blair. 'Today, on the eve of this new millennium, the British people have ushered in a new era of politics.'

An already-drunk Candy, dressed as Ginger Spice, z-snapped her fingers, as if she was some sassy, hip-hop chick from the ghetto, and sauntered over to Mahvand in her sequined Union Jack minidress, ginger wig and ridiculously high platform shoes. She handed Mahvand a polystyrene cup of Coca Cola sporting a fancy cocktail umbrella, as if they were living it up on some Club 18–30 holiday in Benidorm or Gran Canaria, rather than making their own entertainment in a basement sex shop in Soho that never saw the light of day. 'So, Casanova,' she said, flicking her new head of hair with the back of her hand. 'Why have yee been moping around leik a wet weekend for the last month? An may Ah remind yee, dowtah, this is a party. Not a frigging wake.'

'Think I'll make meself scarce,' said Connie in a thick Brummie accent, who then sashayed over to the counter and helped herself to a handful of twiglets and a Spumante top-up.

'Have I?' asked Mahvand.

'Dowtah, let's put it this way. If we swapped positions an' Ah wez upstairs flogging books, looking aal glamorous wi' me Cher wig an pert titties – courtesy of a hot, young plastic surgeon on Harley Street – d'yer really think the takings would have taken such a dive ower the last couple of weeks?'

A presidential-looking Tony Blair, in a police escorted motorcade, cruised along the Mall towards Buckingham Palace to the roar of jubilant crowds waving Union Jacks.

Mahvand hadn't told a soul about that night at Golden Dawn. What was the point? No one would have believed him. Apart from Gran. But she'd have told him to end it then and there. Still, he couldn't help but wonder if those hideous, so-called works of art might have something to do with Jean-Baptiste's business proposal. And if they did, surely he owed it to himself to pursue it. But more than all that, although he was loath to admit it, Mahvand still mooned after him. So he ignored all the warning bells, refused, yet again, to fully accept he had inherited Great-grandfather Harbuckle's visionary powers, and turned a blind eye to the holographic wolf and Jean-Baptiste's obsession with the occult.

Still, there was no getting away from Candy when she was on your case. But he decided right from the start to keep the lid firmly shut on that silently snarling wolf. Candy listened, intrigued, captivated, and before long it was clear to Mahvand that she too had come under Jean-Baptiste's spell. (This was hardly surprising, as she was forever harping on about Quentin Crisp's 'Great Dark Man' that had thus far eluded her in her own life.)

'Well, make amends,' said Candy. 'Swallow yer pride. Crawl back te Hampstead wi' yer tail between yer legs.'

'I phone. He never picks up. I've sent all the sketches I did of him registered post. Nothing.' Mahvand paused. 'I just want to apologise. For running out like that.'

Cut to Tony outside No. 10 Downing Street and the world's press hankering after that perfect front-page picture. Cherie is clinging to his arm while grinning inanely like the Joker in *Batman*. The Blairite sprogs are smiling awkwardly, in clothes, Candy later told Mahvand, she was sure had been worn to revive the flagging fortunes of C&A.

'Yee divvent want te come across as a Desperate Dan. No one leiks a total keeno. Keep him on the back boiler. But divvent, whatever yee dee, become a bunny boiler. Wi' yer sultry, canny good looks, and youth on yer side, yee should be sowing yer wild oats while yee can, man.' She paused. 'I'd have yee mesel' if Ah wasn't twice yer age and hadn't gone ahead wi' the vaginoplasty.'

Despite Candy's flippancy and camp default mode, Candy rarely judged. Mahvand decided to confess. He had to tell someone. 'In the weirdest way imaginable, I sort of did meet Jean-Baptiste. Last weekend, Octavi hooked me up with this guy, Kevin.'

'Yee dark horse. Ah knew yee had it in yee.'

'I sort of fancied him.'

'Sort of?' said Candy incredulously. 'There's no halfway house when it comes to matters o' the cock, pet. Or the heart for that matter.'

'Decent looking, well-meaning, works in computing,' said Mahvand.

'There goes me hard-on,' said Candy.

'I thought it might help me get over Jean-Baptiste.'

D:Ream's *Things Can Only Get Better* was now blaring out of the telly to a montage of carefully selected images from New Labour's campaign trail.

'It just made everything that much worse,' said Mahvand.

Connie had begun to waltz down the aisles with a speedo-clad, blow-up sex doll of a well-endowed Brad Pitt, sporting an oversized *Britain Deserves Better* T-shirt.

'Dowtah, what are we going te dee wi' yee?' said Candy.

'We ended up kissing and—'

'Divvent tell me. He had halitosis?'

'Try again,' said Mahvand.

'Slobbered aal ower ye leik a lovesick Labrador?'

Mahvand shook his head, dreading yet strangely relishing the moment when his Kafkaesque confession would finally be unleashed on an unsuspecting Candy.

'He wez a tonsil tickler?'

Mahvand looked into her eyes, emerald-green like Shiva's, courtesy of the coloured contacts, the lashes thick with mascara. 'He turned into—'

'Aye?'

'You're not going to believe me.'

Cut to Peter Mandelson striding purposefully out of No. 10 Downing Street with a thin-lipped, fixed grimace and black briefcase in tow.

'Just spit it out, man,' said Candy.

'Jean-Baptiste.'

It took a moment for Candy to fully register what Mahvand had said. 'Let me get this straight. You're telling me that well-meaning, sweet-but-boring Mr Computer Geek turned into the Great Dark Man?'

'I swear to God.'

'People divvent just turn into other people, Mahvand. Look, if you're gunna turn this into another late-night episode o' *The Twilight Zone* or one of yer weird comic byeuks, Mutha's gonna need a serious nicotine fix.' She pulled a squashed pack of Benson and Hedges from her silicone-injected cleavage, lit one, and took a deep drag.

'We've aal done it, pet,' she said, blowing the smoke out of the corner of her mouth. 'I've lost count of the number of times some borderline attractive closet from Milton Keynes or Surbiton has slobbered aal ower me while Ah close me eyes an imagine Ahm deein it with George Clooney or Richard Gere.' She looked over to where Connie was still waltzing in the aisles with Brad Pitt. 'Still, it could be worse,' she said with pursed lips. 'Guess who that one's imaginary man is?'

Mahvand shrugged his shoulders.

'Barry Manilow.'

*

Over the coming weeks, Jean-Baptiste's stranglehold over Mahvand began to loosen. Jean-Baptiste clearly was never going to contact him again. After being physically assaulted in his own home, what possible reason could he have? So Mahvand decided to put it all behind him. He began to sketch in public again – quirky-looking customers, hot gay boys sunbathing in Soho Square, the Radical Faeries in their Doc Martens, negligees and rainbow feathers picnicking in Phoenix Gardens. He stayed up late into the night printing and stapling dozens of copies of *Fallen Angels of Homo Heaven* and was overjoyed when Gosh Comics and Gay's The Word agreed to stock it. He managed to clock up some overtime at the bookshop and even got round to mowing the lawn and trimming those unruly rose bushes in the back garden. And on one unusually warm evening in late May, he found himself in the West End. Phoebe Goldstein, late eighties countercultural comics icon from San Francisco, was at Forbidden Planet giving a seminar about her work.

Being back at Forbidden Planet was like reliving his childhood. Action figures from the fifties to the present day peered down from the locked cabinet that stretched half the length of the shop floor: Superman in his tight red pants; the Incredible Hulk, a green fireball of fury and funny hair; and Wonder Woman with her star-spangled knickers, tiara and indestructible bracelets.

'Hey! Mahvand, dude. Wanna trade?'

It was Alex. He was about Mahvand's age, wore John Lennon glasses and spoke with a lisp. His self-published autobiographical zines featured the romantic trials and tribulations of a bipolar, bisexual anarchist who wore round wire-framed glasses and battled with a speech impediment.

Mahvand was not overly keen on Alex's whole faux-naive style of cartooning, with its stick men and hastily drawn speech bubbles. But he knew Alex had a bit of a soft spot for him and couldn't bear the idea of being the one who bailed on a trade-off. He reached into his Foyles carrier bag. In exchange for *Bi Trouble* he pulled out a copy of *Fallen Angels of Homo Heaven* and handed it to Alex. Then TJ, the store manager, comics aficionado and heavyweight boxing champion, who hailed from the suburbs of Tijuana, began to usher everyone to their seats.

Phoebe Goldstein seemed to glide effortlessly in her pink Birkenstocks from the rear of the shop to where the microphone, screen and projector were set up. Her tie-dye dress, gathered in at the waist with a gold sash, drew attention to her curvaceous hips. She raked her fingers through a mane of silver hair and adjusted her shawl – black with golden tassels, embroidered with roses and wild flowers.

'I don't think we'll be needing this,' she said in a cheery Californian accent, putting the microphone to one side. She smiled at Mahvand. He looked into her sunken sky-blue eyes and fought the urge to stand up and announce to everyone how Phoebe's comic book *Tits 'n Clits* had changed his life. He lowered his gaze. Phoebe's hands were just like Gran's – ghostly white and paper-thin with liver spots that had multiplied as if they were frog spawn.

'Let's cut to the chase, shall we?' said Phoebe. 'First off, I've never felt comfortable working in a male-dominated comics world. Guns, fast cars, gratuitous violence and super-heroes scheming to take over the world. Not for a young girl who grew up with flower power, the summer of love, and LSD. As a woman used to the fog that rolls in from the Pacific Ocean, let me tell you, I'm interested in telling different types of stories.'

Mahvand listened, enthralled, as his comics guru told stories of female camaraderie, feminist ideals, and the personal empowerment that comes from belonging to a vanguard countercultural movement. She was Glinda, the good witch from *The Wizard of Oz*, dispelling the dark forces of DC comics, patriarchal power structures and Bible-Belt politicians.

Phoebe kicked off her Birkenstocks and clicked on the laptop. The bangles on her bony wrists jingle-jangled as the light caught the topaz and aquamarine of her rings. On the overhead screen, Pandora in *Pandora's Box* was a real woman, drawn and inked to show some weight around the thighs, hips and rear. *Pandora's Box* struck a chord with Mahvand as, just like *Fallen Angels of Homo Heaven*, it was mythical, magical and transgressively erotic. But unlike the original Greek myth, Phoebe's *Pandora's Box* was more an orgiastic, Dionysian celebration of lesbian love than cautionary tale. Phoebe showed several slides of Pandora performing cunnilingus in a range of sexual positions and settings, on a whole host of Greek goddesses: Athena, Persephone and Aphrodite. While *Red Hood,* her second graphic novel, chronicled a young woman's journey through a dark wood and her sexual encounters with a host of well-known fairy-tale characters. Even Mahvand felt a sense of unease by the panel showing Dick Whittington's anal penetration of a joyous Red Riding Hood, while Peter Pan and Tinker Bell got it on, each panel drawn in swirling, expressionistic lines and inked with an explosion of psychedelic colour.

Phoebe closed her presentation with a discussion of censorship laws, and then opened up the floor to a Q&A session. After sitting through a lengthy and somewhat meandering discussion about artists identifying as 'queer' without actually being queer, and a serious contender for Weight Watchers who would not shut-the-fuck-up about Phoebe's black wheelchair-bound lesbian character not looking 'empowered' enough, Mahvand finally plucked up the courage to ask his question. 'What advice would you give a comics artist wanting to break into the industry?'

'Don't sell out. Be authentic. Keep your integrity. It's not all about fame and money.' Phoebe laughed. 'Certainly not in this game, anyway. Be proud to be part of a countercultural, underground movement.' She paused. 'Yes, the gentleman at the back.'

'*Bonsoir.*'

The French salutation immediately gave birth to a fluttering sensation in the pit of Mahvand's belly, a sudden pounding inside his chest.

'Your question?' asked Phoebe.

'I applaud you, madame, in your no-holds-barred Dionysian celebration of erotic forces.'

I must play it cool. Don't give in. But, like an addict on the verge of a major relapse, Mahvand just couldn't help himself. A moment later he'd turned round. And there, leaning against a poster of the 1940s' Green Lantern from the cover of *All-American Comics*, was Jean-Baptiste. Gone was the country gentleman look, and in its place was something much more casual: thigh-hugging jeans, trainers and a tight-fitting T-shirt that bore an image usually found on the back of a one dollar bill – the all-seeing eye.

Phoebe laughed. '*Merci*, monsieur.' She shifted on her chair and adjusted her shawl. 'But do you have a question?'

'I was wondering, madame ...'

Mahvand thought there was something of Belial in the way he addressed Phoebe.

'Do you think comics, as an art form, can ever be considered a suitable vehicle for depicting ...' he paused, 'esoteric knowledge revealed via the gateway of blood-engorged genitalia?'

A murmur went through the audience.

'I am referring, madame, to what the English so quaintly used to refer to as "a bit of how's your father".'

'Indeed. I prefer the term Synergistic Energy eXchange. For me, it captures the quintessential essence of sexual union, monsieur,' said Phoebe. 'But continue.'

'If I may speak candidly, it seems to me that sequential

visual art can never quite capture that defining moment …' he paused again, 'of alchemical transmutation.' He addressed the next line to Mahvand. 'When *désir sexuelle* is superseded by a power much greater than pure animal instinct, or indeed, some misguided belief in the cultural construct of romantic love. I am talking, madame, of the power of the will.'

There was an awkward silence. *What on earth is Jean-Baptiste talking about? Is he on drugs?*

Phoebe's eyes narrowed perceptibly. 'Believe it or not, I am familiar, monsieur, with the central tenets of sex magick.'

'Then you are aware, madame,' said Jean-Baptiste, 'that the explosive moment of orgasm can be harnessed for, let us say, purposes other than reproduction. Or indeed, sexual pleasure.'

Phoebe cleared her throat. 'As I'm sure you're aware, the sexuality I portray through my art is of a playful, exploratory nature. I use comics to conjure joyous images of coitus and cunnilingus.' She lowered her tone. 'I believe tantra has so much to teach us in harnessing our sexual energies.'

'Tantra, you say?'

Something in the way Jean-Baptiste seemed to sneer reminded Mahvand of the snarling wolf he'd seen trapped behind rib and breastbone.

'I'll leave the white light religion stuff to you, madame.' Jean-Baptiste coughed into a clenched fist. 'One further question, if I may?'

An overweight Welshman sitting at the end of the front row in a short-sleeved shirt with sweat stains in the armpit area called out. 'Look boyo, I don't know who you think you are—'

'Your question?' said Phoebe, her brow now furrowed, hands clasped tightly on her lap.

'*Oui*, madame. It's about comics.'

She chuckled. 'Well, folks do say I'm a comics artist.' A ripple of laughter went through the audience.

Mahvand imagined Jean-Baptiste was not the kind of man that took kindly to being laughed at.

'A fanatical devotion to comics,' said Jean-Baptiste. 'Have you ever wondered what Freud, for example, might have to say about it?' He paused. 'Infantile regression, if I'm not mistaken.'

Mahvand stared at him in disbelief. Hypocrite! *If he has such a deep aversion to comics, why on earth does he have the likes of Ibis the Invincible, Zatara and Mandrake the Magician in pride of place in his dining room?*

The Welshman stood, jabbing his finger in Jean-Baptiste's direction. 'Who let this bloody lunatic in?'

A woman beside Mahvand with closely cropped hair stood up and cocked her little pinky. 'I wonder what Freud would have to say about the likes of you. Drive a big car, do you?'

TJ marched over and positioned himself next to Jean-Baptiste, his arms crossed as if he was some heavy-duty bouncer at a nightclub in one of Mexico City's less salubrious districts. Mahvand was left reeling from Jean-Baptiste's betrayal, trapped at the front in his child-sized chair. *Whatever did I see in him? He's arrogant. Unhinged. And now, apparently, my very own personal stalker. Phoebe, Octavi, even Alex; these are my people.* He fixed his gaze on Phoebe's slide of Red Hood down on her knees, in amongst the runner beans and herbs of Granny's walled garden, performing fellatio on the Big Bad Wolf.

'And which art form gets the thumbs up from you? In your humble opinion,' asked Phoebe.

'Conceptual, madame. Tracy Emin being a fine example of a homespun, feminist conceptual artist.'

'Honey, female comics artists were doing that "art as therapy" thang back in the sixties, long before the likes of Ms Emin,' said Phoebe.

Mahvand's bum was practically numb. The wolf's face stared back in a fixed, preorgasmic grimace, as if he'd done himself an injury.

'*Une observation petit*,' said Jean-Baptiste.

'If you don't mind me saying, not a very informed one,' replied Phoebe.

Mahvand heard TJ shout something in Spanish. Phoebe suddenly held up her hand as if she was a bodhisattva signalling the Buddhist mudra of fearlessness and protection. 'No. Let him stay,' she said. Her eyes danced with the fire of a free spirit. 'He may well learn something.' Another ripple of laughter.

Mahvand sat there seething over Jean-Baptiste having hijacked some half-baked Freudian theory to support his own prejudice about comics fans and comics artists. The rage simmered inside him as he remembered everyone who'd made similar judgements: the kids at school, a tutor at his Art Foundation course in Chelmsford, even Gran. And as for gay men with a certain image and lifestyle to prop up (the plastics) they were the worst. He could hear them all now rising up against him in a rousing chorus of disapproval. Grow up. Comics are for kids. Live in the real world. Comics aren't real art. They're not real writing.

Geek-Freak!

After Ms Goldstein had skilfully steered the debate through the potentially perilous waters of post-feminist discourse and queer theory, Mahvand could bear it no longer. He shifted position in his chair and turned round. But in place of Jean-Baptiste, he was greeted by an enlarged image on the back wall of Green Lantern's magic-ringed fist.

*

Just before midnight, Mahvand left Forbidden Planet and walked towards Tottenham Court Road tube station. He gazed up at the white summer moon and the stars that glittered like metal. Carried away with his own flights of fancy into the realm of nymphomaniac vampires, devastat-ingly attractive older men whose eyebrows met in the middle, and insatiable sex demons, he didn't notice the black stretch limousine slow down and crawl alongside the kerb. Then, glancing in the shop window of Woolworths, in amongst the pick 'n' mix and a bald-headed shop dummy of indeterminate sex, he saw the limousine keeping pace with him. He stopped. The limousine stopped.

A tinted window towards the rear of the limo sunk into the bulk of black metal to reveal a man with slicked-back black hair, and skin as pale as the moon, hiding behind a pair of aviator sunglasses. He was holding a joint between thumb and forefinger and blew a smoke ring of marijuana in Mahvand's direction. It wobbled before dissipating into the night air.

'Get in,' said Jean-Baptiste.

Mahvand marched on, gripping his carrier bag full of untraded copies of *Fallen Angels*. The streets were packed with people emptying out from the pubs. On the other side of the road, a gaggle of girls in miniskirts, stilettos and Jennifer Aniston hair had linked arms and were singing an inebriated version of *Wannabe* by the Spice Girls.

'We need to talk,' said Jean-Baptiste.

Mahvand stopped. 'We have nothing to talk about.'

'*Au contraire*. You owe me an explanation. That night when you ran off like a frightened rabbit.'

'I have a train to catch.'

'Miss it,' said Jean-Baptiste.

'Go to hell!'

Jean-Baptiste smiled lasciviously. 'If only you knew.'

Mahvand carried on walking. The limousine kept pace alongside him.

'I never got the chance to fully explain my business proposition.'

'You totally embarrassed yourself in there. And me,' said Mahvand.

'*Accord*. Now we're even. Get in.'

'I never thought you thought I was ...' Mahvand paused, 'a complete retard.'

'Have it your way,' said Jean-Baptiste. 'Go back to Granny. Keep working at that run-down, second-rate bookshop. Sketching nobodies at 'Gay Central' while dreaming of being a somebody. Filling speech bubbles with riveting auto-biographical insights. Penning spellbinding captions. Keep telling yourself that it doesn't matter if no one reads them. If you make a loss. If you don't get reviewed.' Jean-Baptiste took a sharp drag of his joint and exhaled the pungent weed into the night air.

Mahvand noticed his own breathing was becoming rather erratic. The word 'somebody' reverberated in his head.

'Perhaps you're not cut out for what I had in mind. Maybe you just don't have that … that artistic vision.'

Mahvand stopped again. He wished he hadn't. For he saw himself reflected in the mirrors of Jean-Baptiste's sunglasses: shoulders stooped, those dark, curly locks Gran was always itching to get her scissors into, the carrier bag still stuffed with copies of *Fallen Angels*.

'Who was it once said we're all in the gutter? But only some of us are looking at the stars?' said Jean-Baptiste.

No one told Mahvand Amirzadeh he was in the gutter. Nor that he lacked artistic vision. Least not some arrogant, up-themselves, filthy-rich arsehole from Hampstead with a creepy collection of conceptual art exhibits in his basement. The fact that he'd quoted Oscar Wilde made Mahvand even angrier. He took one last look at himself reflected in Jean-Baptiste's sunglasses then marched round to the other side of the limousine, yanked the door open, and climbed in.

When his eyes had adjusted to the marijuana fog, it was as if he'd entered the starship Enterprise. TV screens were lit with black-and-white static. Red lights from several monitors and the surround sound system stared back like tiny demonic eyes. The minibar, draped in folds of red satin, stretched along one entire side. Champagne flutes, cocktail glasses and multicoloured bottles of liquor sparkled under fluorescent tubing. He'd never been inside a limousine before and was determined not to be impressed. *This is what rat-arsed girls from the cultural wastelands of Essex, all fake tan and hair extensions, hire on their hen night*, he reminded himself. *I am not, repeat, not, impressed.*

The credits of *Bareback Bastards from Borstal* scrolled down on a large plasma-screen TV. Mahvand sat on the adjacent seat that resembled a silver inflatable portion of a bouncy castle and started to cough.

'Please. Make yourself at home,' said Jean-Baptiste, who flicked a switch. Mahvand's seat automatically reclined. 'And in case you're wondering, I travel this way by virtue of necessity. After a series of drink-driving offences, some jumped-up, geriatric judge, in his infinite wisdom, decreed that I should never get behind a steering wheel again.'

Mahvand forced himself into an upright position and stared out of the tinted window. He was just in time to see the mouth of the Palace Theatre spewing a rather inbred-looking bunch of out-of-townies out of *Les Misérables* and onto the streets. He turned to Jean-Baptiste. 'Your business proposal?'

'Look, I apologise.' Jean-Baptiste paused. 'Sounding off like that in the comic shop. It was childish of me.'

'The proposal,' said Mahvand.

'I was angry at you. For running off into the night like that.' Jean-Baptiste sat up and spread his legs wide so his crotch became the apex of a giant 'V' shape. 'Anyhow. As the English say. It's all water under the bridge.'

Mahvand did his best to quash an image of his own head and shoulders firmly lodged between Jean-Baptiste's legs. But instead the image metamorphosed into something darker, something far more disturbing: himself emerging from Jean-

Baptiste's loins as an adult-sized, fully formed newborn.

Jean-Baptiste leant forward. 'I take it you are familiar with the work of Ms Emin and Monsieur Hirst?'

'The love tent. The dead shark. Isn't everyone?'

'*Exactement*! It's making Saatchi an absolute fortune.' He clasped his hands as if about to close an important business deal. 'I want you to rival their stake in the market. Push boundaries. Explore depravity and the darkest recesses of the human mind. All through the medium of conceptual art, of course.'

'I'm not sure I follow,' said Mahvand.

'I'm willing to sponsor you. Set you up with a studio. Do the PR for your debut exhibition. Turn you into the celebrity conceptual artist London has been crying out for.'

'Me, a conceptual artist?'

'Mahvand Amirzadeh. The new messiah of conceptual art.'

'You're crazy,' said Mahvand. 'I haven't the faintest idea about conceptual art.'

'What's there to know? If Emin can exhibit a tent with dedications sewn inside to her teddy bear and aborted foetus, Andres Serrano can photograph a plastic crucifix in a glass of his own urine, and Hirst can make millions with the carcass of a dead cow, you, *mon cher*, can create something equally sensational with your concept of a fallen angel.'

An image of the human rubber mould hanging upside down in Jean-Baptiste's basement fought for Mahvand's attention. 'I'm a comics artist. That's what I do. That's who I am.'

'You're so much more than that,' said Jean-Baptiste.

'Underneath that shy exterior, you're a seething hotbed of subversion. I can tell.'

'You're insane.'

'I have every faith that you will create something sensational.'

'You've got the wrong guy,' said Mahvand.

'Start with the idea. The idea is king. The concept is god.'

'But the last piece of 3D artwork I did was a papier mâché model of a volcano. At primary school.' Mahvand was feeling light-headed. Floaters were dancing in his field of vision. *Is it the passive smoking from all that dope?* 'Why me?'

'You mean, why me?' said Jean-Baptiste.

'Sorry?'

'It was you who chose me.'

'I don't understand,' said Mahvand, who took his inhaler from his pocket, shook it vigorously and puffed.

Jean-Baptiste smiled. 'You choose not to.'

Mahvand placed his fingers on the car door handle. Jean-Baptiste reached across and placed his hand on top of Mahvand's. It was the first time Mahvand had noticed the ring. The threads of gold against the cobalt-blue seemed to contain their own secret magic.

'You're either with me,' he whispered in Mahvand's ear. 'Or against me.'

Moonlight shone through the open window as they sped past the imposing facade of an eerily quiet Lyceum Theatre. On either side of the Greek pillars, gigantic posters bearing an image of the crown of thorns advertised the new production of *Jesus Christ Superstar.*

'Left-wing sentimental drivel masquerading as an historical account of the *Révolution françàise.* And a rock opera culminating in the suicide of a Galilean carpenter's son,' sneered Jean-Baptiste. 'If God, as Nietzsche rightly proclaimed—' He abruptly fell silent as if aware of having said far too much already.

Mahvand tried to remember why he'd got into the limousine in the first place. While he was mentally retracing his steps from *Forbidden Planet*, Jean-Baptiste had come and sat next to him. Mahvand noticed crumbs of white powder caught amongst his nostril hair. He could smell the alcohol on his breath.

'What's this?' said Jean-Baptiste, gently prodding Mahvand's stomach.

While Mahvand was searching for a stain or hole in his red hoodie, Jean-Baptiste tickled him under the chin, forcing him to look up, and zeroed in for the kill. His lips were dry, the stubble rough against Mahvand's flushed cheek. But this time Mahvand found himself kissing back. It was as if he was locking lips with one of his own creations: a comic book fallen angel from *Homo Heaven* made flesh. His fingers inched their way up thigh-hugging denim, brushed against cotton and the all-seeing eye, caressed lips, cheekbone and earlobe. He fumbled with 501 buttons, tugged at a rather stubborn Prada belt, then found himself down on his knees lodged firmly between those thighs. Jean-Baptiste lifted his arms and the T-shirt was off; Mahvand was in. But it wasn't long before he fell victim to a strange kind of whispering. Multiple voices, airy charms, made claim to his inner ear. 'Make the jump, Mahvand!' they whispered. 'Make the jump!' Mahvand gazed longingly, lustfully at the beatific vision before him.

Jean-Baptiste gently pulled back. 'Remember. If no one remembers who you are, it's as if you never existed.'

Mahvand experienced a moment of blind panic and confusion before something inside him rose up in defiance. *It's not true. There's more to life than making a name for yourself. Much more.* But the nature of what that 'something' was never came to fruition. Jean-Baptiste's words had washed away that emerging wisdom, just as the afternoon tide, all those years ago, would wash away his seashell-decorated fortresses on the mudflats of Southend. And in its absence, Jean-Baptiste's voice began to merge with the strange whisperings, until they were one voice: his voice. *Yes. It's true. Art does offer an alternative way to achieve some semblance of immortality.*

'Of course,' said Jean-Baptiste, examining his perfectly manicured fingernails, 'if you're not up for the challenge, I'll understand. Not all of us are looking at the stars, *n'est-ce pas?*' He leant forward. 'Nikolai! Stop the car.' The limousine came to a screeching halt outside Holborn tube station. 'I think we're just about done here.'

'Sorry?' asked Mahvand.

Jean-Baptiste glanced at his watch. 'You don't want to miss that last train home.'

'But I thought—'

'Granny ...' he paused, 'will be waiting.'

Through the tinted glass, Mahvand could just make out the hordes of late-night revellers, theatregoers and harried-looking workaholics spilling into Holborn tube station. A woman with a pink fluffy halo attached to her head lay slumped outside the station in a pool of her own vomit. It was an image superseded by that of Gran, slumped in her armchair in front of the telly.

'Remind me. Why is it the English never rose up against their royals in revolution?' Jean-Baptiste stretched his arms up above his head. Mahvand marvelled at the slow-motion sequence of movement, the bird-like bend at the elbow and wrist, the final outstretch of each finger: One. After. The. Other. As if Jean-Baptiste was destined for flight. As if he saw all human endeavour, and the accompanying historical cataclysms, from some great vantage point. Those fingers – surely the envy of world-class classical pianists – seemed to bend backwards before assuming the sign of heavy metal fans and devil worshippers worldwide – that of the 'Horned One'. The ethereal whisperings in Mahvand's ear became indistinguishable from Jean-Baptiste's epic poem and political posturing: *Standing at the precipice, my fallen angel. Make the jump. Never rose up against their royals in revolution?* An arrow was aimed straight at Mahvand's heart, its tip dipped in the fire of dark secrets, anointed in the black shining of Jean-Baptiste's mind. *Precipice. Jump. Revolution?* How part of him yearned to be taken under his wing; how he longed to relinquish his own earthbound existence, and, in some metaphysical leap of faith, join HIM.

'Ahh,' sighed Jean-Baptiste, almost, thought Mahvand, in recognition of his newfound, age-old longing.

'I'm with you,' Mahvand heard a voice say, just as the whispering gathered momentum. It was only then that he realised – that voice was his. Only then that he fully understood; the whispering itself was a form of worship. At this recognition, the voices rose in defiant jubilation, and Mahvand got the distinct impression that he was encased, not by the bulk of black metal now parked on double yellow lines outside Holborn tube station, but by the inner sanctum of some glistening, coal-blackened cocoon. And it was this cocoon that provided the brief gestation period for an idea so abhorrent, an insight so contrary to Mahvand's true nature, that he reached out yet again for that door handle. For he knew. And what he knew chilled him to the core. The voices in his head were whispering salutations to the Great Whisperer Himself. The Lord of Lies: His Infernal Majesty.

There was a moment's hesitation. A dawning of white light on the horizon of Mahvand's being. A sudden battle cry for his soul. But it was too late. An electrical current from his left forefinger was shooting up the inner aspect of his arm, obliterating any residual selfhood, and filling him, from the toe to the crown, full of dark, fathomless desire. He glanced up at his hand. The tip of Jean-Baptiste's forefinger was touching his.

This simple gesture triggered a memory from late adolescence. And for a brief moment, he saw his NHS-bespectacled seventeen-year-old self inside the Sistine Chapel, staring up at Michelangelo's *The Creation of Adam*.

'I'm with you,' said Mahvand.

Jean-Baptiste was smiling, his eyes brimming with tears. '*Mon enfant.*'

'I'm making that jump.'

KAOS

Mahvand couldn't quite figure out why Jean-Baptiste had had a sudden change of heart and had asked Nikolai to head out into Essex. He didn't quite buy the line about an unforeseen early morning meeting with Nicholas Serati at the Tate, but something warned him off any further questioning. As they'd hurtled along the M25 to Shenfield accompanied by a medley of Britpop songs, Jean-Baptiste had racked up line after line of cocaine. 'Of course, what you always collect,' Mahvand remembered him saying, 'is yourself.' That, and 'Money creates taste.' Mahvand had politely refused the offer of cocaine, smiled, nodded in all the right places, and stared at the motorway signs through tinted glass. Part of him wished he'd never set foot inside that limousine. The other part wanted nothing more than for the limo to do an abrupt U-turn and head back to London so they could carry on where they had left off.

It would be nearly three weeks before Mahvand saw Jean-Baptiste again. In that time he'd maxed out his library card and devoured every book there was at his local library on conceptual art. On his days off from Soho Books, he'd fully immerse himself in the city's contemporary and conceptual art world. In search of inspiration, he'd go at gallery-pace through central London's exhibition spaces, stopping every now and then to view a piece of conceptual art from different vantage points, waiting for its inner secret to reveal itself to him. He'd ticked all the galleries Jean-Baptiste had recommended off his list: the Whitechapel Gallery, Saatchi Gallery, White Cube, the Tate and the Serpentine. Then, of course, there was the odd degree show and the pop-up galleries that had sprung up in and around Shoreditch and the Isle of Dogs. But what he discovered became the fodder for nightmares rather than inspiration: plasticised body parts hanging from the ceiling, white walls spattered with blood, photographs of magnified bullet wounds, and, of course, the politically correct crucified trio, entitled *God*.

The telephone rang late on Friday night. Gran and Mahvand were halfway through a second helping of rhubarb and custard and one of Gran's all-time favourite movies: *Brief Encounter*. Gran paused it at the point where Celia Johnson's character says, 'I've fallen in love. I didn't think such violent things could happen to ordinary people.' It was Jean-Baptiste. He'd made an executive decision. They were to meet in a nightclub called Kaos. 'It's not far – Kings Cross,' he'd said. 'In a converted warehouse. Oh, and before I forget, there's someone I think you should meet.' Jean-Baptiste conveniently forgot to mention that Mahvand should come suitably attired; Kaos was a full-on fetish night.

*

Mahvand was greeted at the entrance of the club by the bald-headed club promoter, who wore a full-body black rubber apron. *Is it too late to turn back?* Her arms were sheathed in black rubber gloves up to the elbow, her forehead and upper chest pitted with acne scarring. The tattoo of a pitchfork was inked onto her right shoulder. Hecate: guardian of entrances and crossroads. Mahvand knew his Greek mythology.

Hecate took a mean drag of her cigarette. 'Ditch the denim,' she growled.

To the sound of wolf whistles, and the penetrating gaze of a skinhead with an inverted cross tattooed onto his skull, Mahvand wriggled out of his jeans, and, shielding his Superman-clad shrunken manhood behind two hands, entered the club. After depositing his jeans and red hoodie in the cloakroom, he made his way to the main dance area. A sudden rush of dry ice stung his eyes. He was momentarily blinded by strobe lighting. The bass hit him hard in the chest. When the smoke began to clear, he was face to face with a tranny sporting a wide-brimmed black hat and veil, balancing on stilts. Mahvand couldn't make up his mind if she more resembled Morticia from the Addams Family or some kind of Gothic bee keeper.

He pushed his way towards the DJ booth and a spiral staircase in the corner. In the upstairs gallery he was confronted by a whole host of fetishists clad in flesh-hugging rubber, leather and latex. To his left, an elderly man, with more than a whiff of Darth Vader about him, was writhing out of time to the music in an oversized gas mask with a concertinaed funnel for a snout.

Mahvand watched the carnival of chaos down on the dance floor with a mixture of wonderment and unease. *Where's Jean-Baptiste?* At one end of the bar, a middle-aged man with a beer belly, dressed in nothing more than killer heels, jockstrap and a niqab, was voguing out of time to a hard-core remix of Candi Staton's *You Got the Love*.

As Mahvand was beginning to plan his exit strategy, the music suddenly stopped. An explosion of strobe lighting lit up an empty raised platform. A figure slowly began to emerge from the smoke, presumably through a trapdoor. A spotlight illuminated his features. He looked like the model in the latest Dolce & Gabbana advertising campaign, except this one was covered in facial piercings and bore a tattoo of a pentagram on his chest. His arse cheeks fell in two delicious scoops over the supporting elastic of his black jockstrap. He slowly craned his neck back, looking up to the giant glitter ball in a gesture of divine supplication. Mahvand was shocked to discover his own innate cannibalistic tendencies, as he fought an impulse to rush down to the main dance floor and take a bite out of that prominent Adam's apple. Then the D&G clone slowly stretched out his arms and turned round. Attached to his shoulders were a gigantic pair of wings. Mahvand strained his eyes. Was the the strobe lighting playing tricks with his vision? *Are they really covered in black feathers?*

Something soft tickled Mahvand's cheek. He looked up. A giant piece of netting was hanging loose from the ceiling. It was snowing black feathers. There were hundreds of them. He cupped his hands and scooped some off the floor. He examined them under the frenzy of strobe lighting, fending off an intrusive image of Hecate and her cronies plucking thousands of crows. The old man in the mask danced a merry jig as if he was Rumplestiltskin and had just confounded the miller's daughter for the umpteenth time.

The feathers nestled in between the straps of leather on his neighbour's harness. They carpeted the floor. Mahvand looked up in wonder as if he was a child witnessing his first fall of snow.

He followed the trajectory of a single feather and observed how it seemed to fall slower than all the others. Suddenly, it wasn't the feather that was falling. It was himself. He was a child again, jumping from the top of his wardrobe, the light from the full moon spilling into his bedroom: a monthly bedtime ritual inspired, in part, by a muscle-bound image of Lucifer in the Old Testament section of his *Children's Bible* falling headlong from the ethereal sky.

Suddenly he found himself struggling against a vice-like grip. A voice whispered in his ear: 'Put on the wings and arouse the coiled splendour within.' The arms released their grip. Mahvand turned around. Jean-Baptiste was standing breathing heavily, dressed in nothing more than boots and black Turkish wrestling trousers. 'I am the snake that giveth knowledge and delight. Lust! Enjoy all things of sense and rapture. Fear not that any God shall deny thee for this.'

Mahvand decided it was probably best to ignore Jean-Baptiste's 'Garden of Evil' rant but couldn't help but eye his six-pack enviously. Each muscle and sinew, as white as snow, was perfected to within an inch of its life.

Jean-Baptiste reached for Mahvand's hand. 'There's someone I'd like you to meet. Remember?'

They squeezed past a hirsute, muscle-bound guy in an NYPD uniform who was chomping away on a cigar, and went down the spiral staircase back to the main dance floor. A group of men in animal-face rubber gimp masks were hanging out by the entrance to the darkroom. *It's not every day that you get to see a horse, a fox, and a dog in human form passing the time of day over a pint.*

Just before entering the darkroom, Mahvand got his first glimpse of Jean-Baptiste's strange tattoo. It was nothing like the tribal tattoos that were all the rage in certain quarters of the gay scene, and was etched onto his lower back, across his sacral vertebrae:

As they traversed the labyrinthine twists and turns of the darkroom, Mahvand realised where he'd seen it before. On a prescription for his Ventolin inhaler. *But why would anyone in their right mind get that done just above the parting of their arse cheeks?*

When they reached the other side, Mahvand instantly recognised him from the front pages of certain tabloid newspapers and the *Ten O'clock News*. It was none other than London's renowned celebrity conceptual artist, and well-known socialite, Daimon Mount-Stuart. There he was, *the* Daimon Mount-Stuart, sweating profusely outside the main entrance to the toilets in rubber shorts and a singlet with the words *Fuck, Suck, Spank, Wank* splashed across the front. Mahvand made a conscious effort not to stare at the stump on his right shoulder.

'And this,' said Jean-Baptiste, 'is Daimon.'

Mahvand felt as if, just by virtue of being in Daimon's presence, his own stock had risen. He clocked the pierced nipples and Vivienne Westwood braces.

'How do you do?' said Daimon, firmly shaking Mahvand's hand.

'Daimon had a very "out there" video installation exhibition,' said Jean-Baptiste, 'at an industrial warehouse. Where was it?'

'Yah. Near Canary Wharf,' said Daimon in a public school accent that evoked memories of *Brideshead Revisited* and Merchant Ivory films. 'Lots of white noise interspersed with scenes from a local abattoir.' He raked his fingers through his shoulder-length, dirty-blonde hair. 'I guess you could say "death" is one of my territories.'

'Doesn't all art, in some way, explore time's winged chariot,' said Jean-Baptiste.

Mahvand instantly got the Andrew Marvell reference, having studied the metaphysical poets at sixth-form college. He suddenly felt included in a way that was rare for him to feel with other men, particularly gay men.

Daimon turned to Jean-Baptiste. 'Shall we partake in the sacrament?'

Jean-Baptiste nodded. He slipped the toilet attendant, who was guarding an array of perfumes and deodorants, a crisp five-pound note, and they squeezed into the toilet cubicle at the far end. Jean-Baptiste turned the latch on the back of the door and locked it shut.

Mahvand didn't know where to look. He was sandwiched firmly between Daimon and Jean-Baptiste. If this was the beginning of some porn-inspired, three-way action, he wanted out. The floor was strewn with typical toilet-cubicle-clubbing detritus: empty sachets or wraps of drugs, discarded water bottles and a mush of trodden-in toilet paper. The toilet was missing a seat, and one wall was full of the usual graffiti: the telephone numbers for sex, the hastily drawn sketches of superhuman penises spurting mountains of cum. But Mahvand remained flummoxed by one particular message scrawled in red pen: '*There is no God but You.*'

Sweat was dripping off Jean-Baptiste in rivulets down the muscular contours of his upper back. He produced a glass pipe from a pouch inside his leather trousers and a clear plastic sachet from the inside of his boot. Kissing the bulbous end of the pipe, he said, 'I like to think of this pipe as a glass portal to another world.' He looked up to the exposed light bulb and carefully tipped something from the sachet into the pipe. Daimon handed him a butane jet lighter and he applied the blue flame an inch or so below the bulb.

'Welcome to the world of crystal,' said Daimon, laughing, 'where everything suddenly becomes—'

Mahvand spotted a tattoo on the inside of Daimon's forearm. He felt a pang of jealousy in the pit of his stomach. The design was identical to Jean-Baptiste's. *Have they been lovers?*

'Crystal clear,' they said in unison.

Do they mean crystal meth? Methamphetamine? Mahvand had seen the 'Before and After' mugshots of crystal users in a magazine article about the crystal epidemic in the States: the zombified stare, the facial scabs and sores, the infamous 'Meth Mouth'. But it didn't make sense; both JB and Daimon were facially flawless.

'Picked this up in the US,' said Jean-Baptiste, as if reading his mind. 'I like to think that encoded in the very DNA of every drug is some kind of spell or enchantment.' He held the pipe up to the light and examined it. '*Diaboli Virtus in Lumbar Est.*'

It was as if he was invoking some unholy entity.

'The virtue of the devil, is—' said Jean-Baptiste, fixing Mahvand with his penetrating gaze.

He's just playing at being Belial. Don't let it get to you.

'In His loins.' He proceeded to roll the pipe between forefinger and thumb, still looking up to the light. 'It's all the rage on the club scene in New York. Won't be too long before it takes off over here, I shouldn't wonder.' He paused. 'I should take you there someday. The music is out of this world.' His eyes had a haunted, manic look. 'An infernal, discordant clanging. As if everyone has taken an iron rod or metal pipe and beaten the very gates of Hell itself.'

Mahvand watched, mesmerised by the thick yellow smoke that encircled the shaft of the pipe and the blue flame that burned the crystals. So much like the mystic energy bolts, shaped and hurled by Narcissus in *Fallen Angels*.

Jean-Baptiste inhaled slowly. He seemed to hold it in his lungs before exhaling two streams of thick yellow smoke through both nostrils, so it seemed to Mahvand that Jean-Baptiste himself was on fire. Like Phoenix from the X-Men.

Daimon offered the pipe to Mahvand, who coughed and waved his hand furiously to disperse the smoke. 'I don't take drugs.'

'Just say …' Jean-Baptiste paused, 'YES. And remember – if it feels good, it can't be bad, *n'est pas?*'

Mahvand eyed the latch on the back of the cubicle door with a sense of impending doom. He hadn't as much as had a toke on a spliff. Ever. There was no way he was going to lose his drug virginity to crystal as if he was some trailer-trash teenager from Nevada. *I can reach across, unlock the door. And keep walking.* He felt Jean-Baptiste's hands caress his body, felt fingers slipping inside his briefs. *But I'll be walking away from the one and only opportunity of ever being—*

Daimon was holding the pipe to his lips.

A somebody.

'Inhale slowly. And remember. Hold it deep down in your lungs,' said Daimon, kissing him on the forehead.

He could feel Jean-Baptiste's lips caress his left ear. 'Thee I invoke, O Bornless One.'

Some. Suddenly Mahvand was spluttering and coughing up a cloud of thick, yellow smoke. *Body.* There was a strange taste in his mouth. Toxic. Metallic. He touched his lips. They were sore. It took a few moments for him to realise he must have burnt them on the shaft.

'Good man,' said Daimon, who seemed to give Jean-Baptiste a conspiratorial smile, and added, 'or should that be, Good Man?'

As Daimon performed a crystal-meth blowback on Jean-Baptiste, a high-voltage electric current shot from the base of Mahvand's spine to the back of his skull. Every last vestige of anxiety and self-consciousness was obliterated by a brilliant white light. Waves of indescribable pleasure coursed through his entire body. It was as if a veil had been lifted and he now saw and felt things as they truly were.

'It's curious,' said Jean-Baptiste, handing the pipe to Daimon. 'I've always thought of cocaine, crystal and speed as being – how can I put this?' The tip of his tongue licked his upper lip. 'A bit like a family.'

'Yah. The unholy trinity,' said Daimon, laughing.

Under any other circumstances, Mahvand would have been horrified at the sacrilegious nature of what Daimon and Jean-Baptiste were saying. But with the sudden release of massive amounts of dopamine in his brain, he couldn't help but see the funny side.

Grinding his teeth, Jean-Baptiste placed one arm around Mahvand and the other around Daimon. 'You know what that makes us, don't you?' said Jean-Baptiste. He paused for dramatic effect while Daimon seized the moment and performed a blowback on Mahvand. 'The Three Musketeers. *Tous pour un, un pour tous!*'

Mahvand felt a stirring in his loins and a familiar yet overwhelming sensation of falling. Falling through Jean-Baptiste. Through himself. Through Daimon. Just as surely as if he were a falling feather or a child again leaping Lucifer-like from the top of his bedroom wardrobe.

When they had retraced their steps through the labyrinthine passages of the darkroom and reached the main dance floor, Mahvand stood in all his newfound glory, pierced by an onslaught of laser beams, as if he was a modern-day St Sebastian.

'Back in the room!' shouted Daimon, punching his one fist in the air just as a Hardbag House remix of Porn Kings' *Up To No Good* kicked in.

'This calls for a celebration,' said Jean-Baptiste. 'I'm off to the bar.'

'Where do you get your inspiration from for your pieces of conceptual art?' asked Mahvand, eager to seize the opportunity, now Jean-Baptiste was out of earshot.

'Must we talk art?' said Daimon wearily, wiping his brow. 'I can think of plenty of other things we could discuss.' He hooked his braces off his shoulders with his thumb and struggled out of his T-shirt. Mahvand wasn't sure whether it was the done thing to offer assistance.

'I'm serious,' said Mahvand.

Daimon put his arm around Mahvand's shoulder. 'You're dangerous, you are. You'll get me into all sorts of trouble.' He reached across Mahvand and lit his cigarette. 'Let's just say there are things one can do to harness one's creative energies.'

'What things?'

Daimon smiled knowingly. 'Now that would be telling.'

Jean-Baptiste was already walking towards them cradling a bucket of champagne on ice. In his other hand, three upside-down flutes dangled from between his fingers.

'Look. You'll just have to ask the master,' said Daimon.

'Follow me,' said Jean-Baptiste with something of the Pied Piper about him. 'There's something I want to show you. It's a complete trip.'

Jean-Baptiste led them back to the bar then veered off to a room dedicated to psychedelic trance and decked out with fairground mirrors. In one curved mirror, a short and stumpy version of Mahvand stared back, like some horny sex dwarf in search of Snow White's cottage. In another mirror, his Superman underpants had rippled and stretched to fill the entire length of the glass. When Mahvand turned around, he found himself irresistibly drawn by the sultry Latino looks of the DJ behind the booth. That was, until he clocked his T-shirt; inside a nuclear mushroom cloud, he could just make out the word *Choronzon*. But what really perturbed Mahvand was the elderly gentleman in drag sitting to the side behind a makeshift table. He was wearing a grey wig identical to Gran's and a floral overall just like Petula's. A middle-aged muscle Mary who looked as if he'd be more at home on a builder's site, kitted out with a builder's hard hat and orange overalls, sat rolling his eyeballs, gurning away. Mahvand left Daimon and Jean-Baptiste to take a closer look. What he saw shook him to the core. The drag queen had arranged a set of cards face down in a pattern only too familiar to Mahvand. Staring intently at Mahvand with rheumy, turquoise eyes, he turned the card. Even though it was upside down, Mahvand recognised the image: two dogs, flanked on either side by two towers, howling in unison under the watery moon. His mouth was bone dry.

'Everything OK, sweetheart?' said the Tarot-reading drag queen, revealing a mouth in need of some serious dental treatment.

Mahvand wondered if Jean-Baptiste's prediction of crystal meth taking off in London might be a bit behind the times. He detected an underlying sinister tone to the drag queen's voice.

'Why don'tcha draw up a seat? Pretty boy like you. Don't you wanna see what the cards have in store for ya?'

Mahvand felt as if he was at some weird fairground. He half expected the Elephant Man or some buxom bearded lady to come waltzing through. A hand touched his shoulder. He turned around. It was Jean-Baptiste.

'Ça va?'

'I have to get out of here.'

'You're kidding, right?'

'My head. It doesn't feel right.'

'It's the crystal,' said Jean-Baptiste.

'My chest.' Mahvand's breathing was becoming erratic. 'It feels tight.'

'*Respirez,* monsieur.' Jean-Baptiste began to massage Mahvand's neck and shoulders. '*Respirez.*' His fingers set to work on his scalp. He used both thumbs to slide them across Mahvand's forehead and ease the tension at his temples.

Mahvand turned around. 'I've got to get out of here. That drag queen. The mushroom cloud. The moon.' Jean-Baptiste smiled. For a split second, Mahvand thought his mouth was full of gaping gum and blackened stumps for teeth. 'Your teeth!'

Jean-Baptiste grabbed his elbow. 'I've just bought a bottle of *Bollinger Blanc de Noirs.* Have you any idea how much that costs?' The blackened stumps flickered back to the perfect array of pearly whites.

'Enjoy every penny's worth. I'm getting the night bus.' Mahvand marched off in search of the cloakroom and nearest exit, the psychedelic trance vibe giving way to tribal house beats.

Jean-Baptiste caught up with him outside the club. 'I'm sorry. I pushed. Too far. Too soon. It's just …' The moon hung motionless, trapped inside the steel girders of a nearby electricity pylon. Nikolai stood astride, leaning against the limousine in a fitted black suit, Bogarting a spliff. The pungent smell of marijuana hung heavy in the early morning air. He opened the door for Jean-Baptiste, who gestured for Mahvand to get in first. Suddenly the night bus and that long wait at Liverpool Street station didn't seem so appealing.

'To Hampstead. Then drop the limo off at the depot,' said Jean-Baptiste.

'Yes, sir,' said Nikolai

'Take me home,' said Mahvand, sitting opposite Jean-Baptiste.

Jean-Baptiste leant over to the drinks cabinet and poured himself a shot of vodka. 'It's 2 a.m. and you're telling me you'd rather be asleep in the suburbs?'

'It's Gran – She'll be worried. I didn't tell her I wasn't coming back.'

'Sleep when you're dead.' Jean-Baptiste produced a pocket-sized mobile phone. 'Phone her. Tell her you're coming back with me. Go on. What are you waiting for?'

Jean-Baptiste pressed the phone firmly into Mahvand's chest. Mahvand hesitated before pulling the aerial out and punch-dialling the landline number. *What if Gran's already asleep?* He imagined her slowly rising from her rocking chair in the sitting room and shuffling to the hallway in her burgundy slippers.

'It's dead. The line. It's dead.' Mahvand passed the phone back to Jean-Baptiste.

'Relax. I'm sure British Telecom will send an engineer out in due course.'

'Something's happened. I just know it.' Mahvand wiped the sweat from his brow. His heart slammed repeatedly into his chest like a clenched fist. 'You tricked me into taking that crystal.'

'I did nothing of the kind.'

Mahvand's voice rose an octave. 'I told you I didn't want it.'

'Oh, come now,' said Jean-Baptiste. 'How easily you forget. It was you, *mon cher*, who sucked on the glass pipe like…' he paused, 'a newborn suckling on its mother's teet.' He lit a cigarette and took a drag. 'Free will, Mahvand. Don't start feeling guilty now.'

'But I've never taken drugs.'

Jean-Baptiste smiled. 'I guess one could call crystal meth an acquired taste.'

'Not until tonight.'

'Don't you ever get tired of carrying around all that guilt? All that anxiety and shame? Think about it, Mahv. I can call you Mahv, can I? Something that feels that good. How can it be bad?'

'You don't understand,' said Mahvand. 'I have to see Gran. Something's happened. I know it has. I'm all she's got.'

'*A votre sante!*' Jean-Baptiste lifted his glass, knocked back the rest of the vodka in one, and slammed the glass down.

'I'm her only grandson.'

Jean-Baptiste edged closer to Mahvand and began toying with his curls. 'OK. You win. Here's what we'll do. We'll go back to Granny's house. And if we find she's been eaten by the Big Bad Wolf, I'll strangle the beast with my bare hands.' He smiled lasciviously. 'Something tells me you'd rather like that, wouldn't you?'

Jean-Baptiste gave the order. Nikolai stepped hard on the gas pedal, and the car wheels screeched as it headed towards the M25.

PHOENIX FROM
THE FLAMES

A bellow of ash and smoke rose from the horizon into the night sky as the limousine turned left at the church. Mahvand barely registered it, as he filled his lungs yet again with toxic yellow fumes and began to savour that strange metallic taste to the discordant overtones of what Jean-Baptiste referred to as post-industrial dark ambient music. He peered through the tinted glass window, clutching a bottle of Coca Cola, and watched the semi-detached bungalows with their hanging baskets, potted plants and privet hedging pass him by in a stupor of yellow street lighting. What would they all think if they could see him now? What would everyone he'd ever known think if he ever became a household name? He swayed to a crescendo of church bells and a distant siren, imagining celebrities from the telly and the glitterati of the art world flocking to his debut exhibition. *Whatever. It. Takes.* At first he thought the siren was part of the music. Then a flashing blue light flooded the back of the limousine. Terrified that they were just about to be pulled over by a police car, Mahvand ducked down. It wasn't until Nikolai slowed down to let the vehicle pass that Mahvand realised that it was, in fact, an ambulance.

Turning into Laburnum Tree Avenue, Mahvand was mesmerised by the flames – red, amber, yellow, purple – dancing high above the roofs of the houses, licking up into the air with the wind. The limousine cruised along as if behind the wheel was some sleazy, late-night kerb-crawler looking for business. Neighbours lined both sides of the street. Two men were unpacking camera equipment from the back of a van. Mahvand watched the drama unfold in silence behind the heavily tinted backseat window. Miss Roberts, the elderly spinster from Rose Cottage, clutching onto her Zimmer frame with one hand, was mouthing something to a police officer and pointing to something further along the street. Mr Hargreaves, a widower of twenty years, came running out of his bungalow in stripy-blue pyjamas and a silk dressing gown. Mahvand caught it all: the expression of disbelief and horror, his arms flailing in the air, the way his dressing gown trailed behind him as he ran up the driveway. Mahvand felt nothing; it was as if he was watching a silent disaster movie in slow motion. He wiped his brow and asked Jean-Baptiste to unwind the window. Jean-Baptiste flicked a switch and the tinted glass disappeared to reveal a world in Technicolour and full sound. Mahvand heard shouting further along down the street, someone sobbing, and was blinded by the flashing blue light of the ambulance. Then an almighty CRASH. The limousine was filled with the acrid stench of smoke. He finally came to his senses and realised; it was his house that was on fire.

'Stop the car! Let me out!' he yelled.

'Do you think that's wise?' asked Jean-Baptiste, pouring himself yet another vodka. 'It sounds like pandemonium out there.' He smiled knowingly. 'In fact, I'd go as far as to say that it reminds one of the storming of the Bastille during the French Revolution.'

The limousine stopped outside Rose Cottage. Mahvand wrestled with the door handle, yanking it back and forth, sick with fright. His only thoughts were of Gran. *Is she still in there? Is it too late?* Suddenly the door opened and he found himself standing in the middle of the tarmac. Even at the distance of a couple of hundred metres or so, his face burned with the searing heat of the fire. Flames danced rebelliously on the roof as if they were drug-fuelled go-go dancers with attitude giving it some on a podium. They poured through the front door of Laburnum Tree Cottage and out of the windows on the ground floor. A fire engine and two ambulances were parked further down outside the inferno, their flashing blue lights a throwback to the strobe lighting at Kaos. Firemen stood at various vantage points, their yellow helmets beacons of hope as they doused the fire with giant arcs of water from their hoses. But as the flames continued to lick high up into the air, Mahvand knew it was already too late.

'Mah-vand!'

Mahvand spun around. And there, standing by her front garden gate, with a fag in one hand and a sherry glass in the other, was Petula. She was dressed in a silk kimono dressing gown and pink, fluffy, high-heeled slippers, eerily lit by the flashing blue light of a stationary police car.

'Oh, Mahvand. I'm so sorry,' said Petula.

'Where's Gran?!' shouted Mahvand, shielding his face from the searing heat of the fire.

'She's in here, sweetheart. We all are.'

Mahvand detected an evil glint in her eye. He shouted above the roar of the fire. 'She's not dead?'

'You'd best come in.' Petula put an arm around him and huddled him in through the front porch. The painting in the hallway – of the naked woman splayed out on a rock under a full moon – should have reassured with its kitsch familiarity. Instead, it hung under the Artexed ceiling like a bad omen.

Walking on through to Petula's lounge, Mahvand stopped in his tracks when he saw two sombre-looking policemen. They were standing on Petula's sheepskin rug under the glass-beaded chandelier. Arthur was sat at the dining table, trying again and again to get a flame from a lighter to light his pipe, his head all bandaged up as if he was a soldier wounded in action. And there, sitting in an armchair near the gas fire, wrapped up in a pink terry-towelling dressing gown, was Gran. Mahvand felt his legs go from under him and reached for the back of the sofa.

'She's not—'

'She'll be right as rain,' said Arthur. 'Dozed off not long before you showed up.'

Mahvand felt as if his world had just jumped tracks and, thankfully, an even more terrifying version of reality had just been averted.

'She's had oxygen and has been checked out by the ambulance crew. Apart from a few cuts and minor smoke inhalation, she's fine,' said Arthur, beginning to cough.

This is all my fault. If I hadn't gone to the club. Mahvand became suddenly aware of how hard he was clenching his jaw, how thick and tight the muscles in his shoulders felt. He sat down on Petula's red crushed velvet sofa, his foot tapping to an imaginary beat, and gave the taller policeman a sideways glance. *Can he tell? Tell what I've been up to?*

The silence was broken by the tune to *London Bridge is Falling Down*: Petula's doorbell. She stubbed her cigarette out and went to answer it.

'And you would be?' asked the policeman with the furrowed brow and centre-pattern balding, fixing his gaze on Mahvand.

'Gracie's grandson,' said Arthur.

'Well, at least you're accounted for, son,' said the other copper, whose handlebar moustache made it difficult to imagine any lip behind it.

'And where were you tonight?' said the first.

Mahvand looked away, ashamed that he hadn't even told Gran of his whereabouts, and that, even in the midst of all the chaos, he found himself longing for another hit of crystal.

'He was with me.'

Mahvand looked round. And there, standing in the doorway with rolled-up shirt sleeves, wiping his brow, as if he himself had just lent a hand in putting out the fire, was Jean-Baptiste. For a brief moment, his skin seemed almost translucent again, the facial muscles and network of veins clearly visible beneath the surface.

'And you are?' asked the moustachioed policeman.

'Jean-Baptiste Lebeau-Chevalier.' He handed the policeman his business card. 'You could say I'm a friend of the family.'

Arthur cleared his throat and glowered at Mahvand. Petula looked like she was going to say something then giggled coquettishly.

'That,' said the policeman, 'won't be necessary Mr— '

'Please.' Jean-Baptiste shook the policeman's hand. 'Call me Jean-Baptiste.'

Petula gestured for him to sit down next to Mahvand on the sofa. She poured two cups of Earl Grey from a porcelain pink teapot fashioned in the shape of a pouting fish, which, for a moment, Mahvand became convinced was opening and closing its mouth. Flicking her hair with the back of her hand, she said, ''Elp yourselves to milk and sugar, boys.'

The policeman with centre-pattern balding turned to Mahvand. 'I think we're about done here. Mr Bowen has given us a full account. Of course, there will be a full investigation to ascertain the exact cause of the fire.'

The moustachioed policeman continued, 'That's beyond our remit. But I'm sure the chief investigating fire officer will be in contact with you in due course with the outcome of the investigation.'

Mahvand looked out through Petula's bay windows and net curtains. The fire still raged. He pictured his comic collection that had taken him years to build up – every single edition of *Doctor Strange, The X-Men, Son of Satan* – all of it going up in smoke. The books from his childhood: *The Magic Faraway Tree*, the illustrated works of *Grimm's Fairy Tales*, his own sketches and early autobiographical underground zines – now just reduced to ash.

Petula showed the policemen out then came back to the lounge. 'Such lovely coppers,' she said. 'The younger one complimented me on my nude portrait in the hallway. My Brian used to hate that picture, he did. Just goes to show.'

'You have impeccable taste, madame,' said Jean-Baptiste, sipping his tea with his little finger cocked out. 'You should allow me the honour of accompanying you to Sotheby's sometime.'

The sudden realisation that the fire would have also destroyed the only mementos of his mother, struck Mahvand with all the force of a punch to the gut.

'Oh, I'm not sure about all that,' said Petula, giggling.

He felt his heart slamming against his breastbone and was struck by another terrifying thought. It wasn't just his home that was burning. It was the whole world.

'I'm more of a car-boot sale sort of girl,' said Petula.

'How the pair of you can be talking about art at a time like this is beyond me,' said Arthur, refilling his pipe. And turning to Mahvand, he added, 'God knows I'm not pretending to be your father. Not for one minute. But what you did. Leaving yer gran on her own like that. Sick with fright, she was. That's why I came round.'

Mahvand stared out of Petula's bay window at the burnt stump of the laburnum tree in what used to be the front garden. It looked like something from a post-apocalyptic landscape. 'How did it start?' he managed.

'The fire? Who knows?' said Arthur.

'Didn't I always say that one day those Benson and Hedges would be the death of her,' said Petula.

'All I remember was waking up in the spare room,' said Arthur. 'Something was burning. I opened the bedroom door. The hallway was thick with smoke.' He paused. 'If

I hadn't been there, I dread to think what might have happened to yer gran.'

'Arthur saved the day. Proper little hero he was,' said Petula. 'Carried yer gran out of a burning building in his bare arms, he did.'

A piece of masonry suddenly came crashing down outside, sending flying embers high into the air. Gran woke with a start and looked disorientated. 'Where am I?'

'We thought it best to let you rest,' said Arthur.

'What are you lot doing in my house at this time of night?'

Arthur gave Mahvand one of those looks. 'It's the shock. She's still in shock.'

Mahvand knew it was something else. He also knew she'd sooner die than see out the rest of her days in an old folk's home that stank of pee and boiled cabbage.

'This is my house,' said Petula loudly, articulating each word carefully as if she was talking to a partially deaf person. 'THERE WAS A FIRE, Gracie.'

Gran stood, shuffled to the bay window and lifted the net curtain. Wisps of white hair gave her a ghost-like appearance. *Her collection of acrylic wigs must have gone the same way as my comics collection.* Gran's right hand started to shake. 'It's not a dream?' she asked, her voice quivering.

'No, Gran,' said Mahvand, making a determined effort not to grind his teeth. 'It may feel like a nightmare. But unfortunately this is real.'

'Would you like a drop of sherry?' asked Petula, walking over to the drinks cabinet. 'Might help calm your nerves, dear.'

'Me Royal Doulton figurines. Mahvand's comics. Did yer manage to save any of 'em?'

Arthur shook his head. 'It was all I could do to get both of us out in one piece.' He paused. 'You're lucky to be alive, Gracie. We both are.'

Petula went to her sideboard cabinet, eyes welling up, and fetched a box of tissues. She dabbed at her eyes and gave her nose a good trumpeting.

'I wanna go home,' said Gran.

Petula walked over and put an arm around her. 'We'll find you another home, Gracie. You'll see. Everything'll be all right.'

Gran shrugged her arm off. 'What are you talking about? I already have me own gates of Rome. Why on earth would I want another one for?'

Arthur took her arm and guided her back to the armchair.

Gran looked Jean-Baptiste up and down. 'And who might you be?' She paused. 'One of yer fancy men, Petula?'

Jean-Baptiste walked over to Gran, knelt down and kissed her hand. '*Enchanté*, madame.'

'He's a friend of our Mahvand's,' said Petula.

Gran folded her arms. 'Is he now? Well, there'll be none of that funny business. Not under my roof.'

'I can assure you my intentions are entirely honourable, madame,' said Jean-Baptiste.

Gran suddenly looked around as if she'd lost her bearings. ''Ere, what have you done with me cuckoo clock?'

'I just came to offer my sincere condolences,' said Jean-Baptiste.

'Why? Who's died?' said Gran.

Jean-Baptiste pressed his business card into the palm of her hand.

'What on earth do I want with this?'

'It is my belief, madame, that one day your grandson will become a great artist.'

'My Mahvand? We'll see what the tea leaves have to say about all that, shall we? Hand it over.'

'Madame?' said Jean-Baptiste.

'The teacup, dear.' She reached out her hand. The veins that bobbled to the surface were even more bulbous than Mahvand remembered. As if they were strange green bulbs pushing at the surface of the skin. He imagined them bursting through the epidermis, her hands suddenly home to a whole host of weird and wonderful flowers.

'I think it's time we made a move,' said Jean-Baptiste, checking his watch.

Arthur glowered at Mahvand. 'You're not going anywhere, son. There are things need sorting. The insurance claim. Where you and yer gran are going to stay.'

'Turn the cup three times to the left,' said Gran.

'This is insane,' said Arthur. 'Gracie, you're destitute, homeless, and you want to play gypsy Rosie-fucking-Lee?'

A glimmer of recognition and then sadness flickered across Gran's face. Then it was gone. 'What are you talking about? Making things up at your age. Should be ashamed of yourself.' She turned to Jean-Baptiste. 'Close your eyes, dear. Turn the cup three times to the left then place the cup upside down on the saucer.'

Jean-Baptiste hesitated.

'Do it if it'll make her happy,' said Mahvand, who thought Gran's ability to predict the future was a bit hit and miss.

Jean-Baptiste lowered his gaze.

'Please,' said Mahvand, who suddenly became aware of a painful throbbing in his left eyeball.

Jean-Baptiste glanced at his watch as if he was about to leave then took a deep breath and closed his eyes. He turned the cup three times, placed it upside down on the saucer then gave it to Petula who handed it to Gran.

'I'm going to check on things outside,' said Arthur. 'At least one of us has a grip on reality.' He hobbled to the door with an expression of pain on his face. The slamming of the front door signalled his departure.

Gran hunched over the teacup to study the tea leaves. Strands of white hair had fallen forward and were covering her face. Mahvand found it slightly unbecoming. *What on earth will Jean-Baptiste think?* He was ashamed to find himself reminded of the three grey crones from ancient Greek mythology who shared a single detachable eye. Just as he became convinced he was going to burst a blood vessel in his own left eyeball, Gran straightened her back and placed the teacup on her lap. She looked up, her rheumy blue eyes fixed on Jean-Baptiste. She said nothing. She didn't need to. Her pursed lips said it all.

'What is it?' asked Petula. 'Can you see an older woman in the picture? Attractive. Born home-maker. Romantically inclined?'

The teacup on Gracie's lap had begun to rattle.

'Come on, Gracie,' said Petula eagerly. 'Put us out of our misery.'

Gran turned to Mahvand. Through gritted teeth, she said: '*Enter ye at the strait gate.*' She gripped both arms of the armchair, pushed herself forward, and delivered her next line to Jean-Baptiste. '*For wide is the gate, and broad is the way, that leadeth to destruction. Matthew 7:13.*'

Jean-Baptiste burped. Loudly.

Mahvand thought it somewhat out of character. But right then he was more concerned about Gran. She must still be in shock. He walked over, knelt down, and held her hand, his own hand twitching from the crystal. 'It's OK, Gran. We'll find somewhere else to live. I won't leave you.'

Gran placed the cup and saucer on the side table then used the armrests to propel herself into standing position. She slowly raised both hands to the ceiling as if she was a pastor in a Southern Baptist church. 'Behold! I send you out a sheep amidst the wolves.'

Jean-Baptiste burped again – a burp of almost inhuman proportions.

Jesus! Is that what crystal meth does to you? Will it be my turn next? Mahvand reached for Gran's outstretched arm and tried to guide her back to the armchair. She was having none of it and, with an amazing show of strength, pushed him off.

'It's not too late,' said Gran, waggling her index finger at Jean-Baptiste, who was gripping his stomach with both hands.

'Stop it, Gran. You're scaring everyone.'

'It's not too late to turn to the Good Lord.'

Jean-Baptiste was now in the full throes of a full-on belching fit.

Mahvand appealed to Petula. 'Can't you do something?'

'I hear peppermint tea is very good for indigestion, dear.'

'Not him. Gran!'

'That one needs more than peppermint Rosie Lee,' declared Gran. 'What that belching Beelzebub needs is an exorcist from the Vatican!'

Mahvand suddenly yearned for the anonymity and deafening beats of Kaos. He turned to Jean-Baptiste. Was it his imagination or were parts of his body beginning to jerk as if he was having some sort of epileptic seizure?

'I trust the investigation into the fire rules out anything ...' said Jean-Baptiste, still clutching his stomach, 'untoward.'

'Arthur was right. This is insane,' said Mahvand.

'Get out my fuckin' cat and mouse!' screamed Gran, sending a half-drunk glass of sherry hurtling in Jean-Baptiste's direction. He ducked just in the nick of time, avoiding onward collision with the missile, but was nevertheless doused with a nutty-smelling brown liquid as the glass smashed against the double glazing.

'It's not your house!' said Petula, slurring her words.

Jean-Baptiste stood and kissed Mahvand on the cheek, but not before releasing one almighty burp. 'You need to be with your family at a time like this.'

Mahvand caught Jean-Baptiste by the elbow. 'She's having a funny turn. That's all. She doesn't mean it.' He paused. 'Don't leave me here.'

For a moment Jean-Baptiste seemed to waver.

'Please. I've got no one else.'

Mahvand thought he saw a flicker of a smile then Jean-Baptiste was brushing past him and walking into the hallway. He was just about to call out, when, for the second time, he heard the front door slam shut. Moments later, there was a screech of brakes and the sound of a vehicle speeding off down Laburnum Tree Avenue.

Later that morning, Gran took the spare room and Arthur kipped down on the blow-up mattress in the lounge. Mahvand tossed and turned on a red sea of crushed velvet, the oblivion of sleep kept at bay by the methamphetamine still coursing his veins and Arthur's incessant snoring. Every now and again he'd draw the tasselled dining room curtains and duck under the nets. And each time he was confronted with the same bored-looking policeman guarding the same smouldering remains, fallen masonry and rubble that had once been his home. The only thing that changed was the position of the sun in the sky.

Arthur was interviewed by the chief investigating fire officer later that afternoon and drove back to Poplar in his Ford Escort soon after. Petula and Gran spent the next few days rummaging round local charity shops and drinking endless cups of tea while Mahvand crashed from post crystal-meth exhaustion. There was something invalidish about him as he convalesced on Petula's sofa or picked at thread in the carpet. He'd never felt so alone, so cut off from everything, in his entire life.

In the early hours of the third night he was rudely awoken by a tapping sound that seemed to be coming from the window. At first he thought it might be a fox or stray cat rummaging around for food near the rubbish bins. Then it stopped. Mahvand covered his head with the duvet and tried to recapture the moment just before he had risen from a trapdoor onto the podium at Kaos dressed as Doctor Strange.

Now it sounded as if someone was throwing small stones at the window. Mahvand went to investigate. When he pulled back the curtains, he gasped out loud. Only a veil of net curtain and a pane of glass separated him from Jean-Baptiste.

He knew that if Gran woke up and saw him, he risked reigniting her Christian wrath and waking the neighbours. So, after struggling into jeans and trainers, he opened the front door as quietly as he could and let himself out. Jean-Baptiste was on the other side of the road leaning against the limousine, crowned by the full moon, a cigarette smouldering between his fingers. He was dressed in leather trousers and a black leather jacket. Mahvand crossed the street, the gutted remains of Laburnum Tree Cottage laid bare under a starlit sky. The policeman guarding the property had been replaced with a 'Do Not Enter' sign.

'Didn't think I'd see you again,' said Mahvand.

'Oh, you know me.'

No, I don't. I don't know you. You're like sand that slips through my fingers. There was a heaviness in his heart that his head barely acknowledged.

'I've been thinking,' said Jean-Baptiste. 'Why don't you move in with me?'

Mahvand searched his eyes for something vaguely resembling the truth. *Is this a trick?* He looked up to Petula's latticed, darkened bedroom window where his grandmother was no doubt still fast asleep. *Or does he really care what happens to me?* 'What about Gran?'

Jean-Baptiste tilted his head back and blew the smoke out through his nostrils. 'Oh, Mahvand. Shall I tell you who you remind me of?

'Who?'

'A guilt-stricken Catholic nun.'

'Thanks.'

'When are you going to realise? You have your own life to lead.' Jean-Baptiste glanced up to where Gran was sleeping. 'And so does she.'

Mahvand stared at the ruins of his home. He would have preferred if the house had been razed to the ground, rather than to be confronted with the charred remains of the sofa with the dodgy spring or the new fridge freezer she'd bought on hire purchase, now covered with ash and blackened with stalactites of melted plastic.

'Anyway, she can always bunk up with the former East End barrow boy,' said Jean-Baptiste, his face lit by the yellow glare of a street lamp.

'You mean Arthur,' said Mahvand.

'Or that painted whore who fails to appreciate the ironic kitsch of her own car-boot-sale collection.'

Mahvand suddenly wished Jean-Baptiste would just go far, far away and leave him be. He felt reluctantly drawn to the charred remains of his home like a family member at a morgue or a hospital who has to say goodbye to their nearest and dearest. He walked around the front of the limousine and ran his fingers along the police cordon.

'What are you doing?' shouted Jean-Baptiste.

'What does it look like?'

'But it's not structurally safe.'

'I think we crossed safe a long way back.'

Mahvand lifted the cordon and crept under. He picked up a brick, scraped his fingertips along its rough surface and looked up at the white summer moon. If he could, he would have propelled himself towards the horizon like Sirius, the man god of romantic love in *Fallen Angels* and be engulfed in the lunar deity forever.

Jean-Baptiste ducked under the police cordon. Mahvand walked towards where the kitchen would have been. The sink and the metal girders that provided the structural foundations of the house were still intact. But in place of the Formica flooring, a rubble of bricks and fallen debris lay on the floor in random formation, like it was some godforsaken piece of modern art up for the Turner Prize. Mahvand looked up. His bedroom was now just a big expanse of open sky.

Jean-Baptiste was behind him again, laying a hand on his shoulder. 'Out of the ashes of the nest and the old bird, rises the new phoenix.'

From their very first meeting, Mahvand had had serious reservations about Jean-Baptiste. But he quashed them and withheld judgement, in part, it was true, because he'd fallen badly for his chameleon-like charm and those chiselled Middle-Eastern features. The fact that he also stood a chance of actually making it as an artist, albeit a conceptual one, made it even easier to hang on in there. But standing in the very spot where Gran used to rock back and forth in her rocking chair, it felt as if a piece of him had died inside; he could deny the truth no longer. The real Jean-Baptiste had stepped forward. He was nothing but a two-bit showman. An incurable narcissist. Incapable of loving anyone but himself. Mahvand wanted to land him a punch then and there, but his trembling fingers refused to form themselves into a fist. So he held out his arms. 'What are these, you arsehole? My wings?' He started to run, dodging bits of charred timber, bricks and fallen masonry, squawking and flapping his arms. 'Watch me rise from the flames!' he yelled ironically.

'A phoenix doesn't squawk. It sings!' shouted Jean-Baptiste.

Mahvand kept running in all directions and squawking in defiance like a demented parrot. Jean-Baptiste ran after him. Mahvand scooped up a pile of ash and debris in both hands and threw it in Jean-Baptiste's direction. Jean-Baptiste wrong-footed him. Mahvand fell over a fallen girder and put out his hands to break the fall. Jean-Baptiste came up from behind, lifted Mahvand to a standing position, and restrained him.

'Enough!' yelled Jean-Baptiste. 'You'll hurt yourself.'

Mahvand wrestled against Jean-Baptiste's arms that held him in a vice-like grip. 'Who are you?' Jean-Baptiste was squeezing him so tightly he could hardly get the words out. 'Is your heart even human?'

'Listen to yourself. You're as mad as your grandmother.'

Mahvand managed to break free from Jean-Baptiste's grip. He was laughing hysterically. 'You must be one of the most arrogant, narcissistic men I have ever had the misfortune of meeting.'

'I know it may feel like the end, Mahvand. But really it's just the beginning.'

'Don't you get it? I want my home back. My life. I want things the way they used to be.'

'Can't you see?' said Jean-Baptiste. 'This is your rebirth.'

Mahvand bent down and picked something up. The fire had devoured half of a copy of *Fallen Angels*. As he opened the charred remains of his zine, part of it fell away in his hands. He was left with a panel showing a decapitated Hedonisus riding a rainbow unicorn. He dropped to the carpet of ash on both knees, his mouth wide open. The screams, when they came, were silent. Tears streamed down his cheeks. He cried for a mother he could hardly remember. For a father who, by all accounts, had turned to a life of petty crime to support a spiralling addiction to heroin. And he cried for his grandmother, who, in her late eighties, was homeless for the first time in her life and slowly losing her mind.

Jean-Baptiste knelt down beside him and cradled Mahvand in his arms. He held him like that, singing softly in French, until Mahvand's sobbing subsided. Mahvand knew he shouldn't give in, the last thing in the world he should do is succumb to Jean-Baptiste's charms, but he'd come to the end of the road; he was exhausted. And at that moment, he felt protected and cared for in the same way that, as a young child, he'd felt towards his own father. 'Fuck me,' Mahvand whispered through his tears.

Jean-Baptiste started singing again. Mahvand's French wasn't good enough to decipher the meaning of the words but it sounded like a lullaby. He wrapped himself around Jean-Baptiste. '*J'ai envie de toi. Baises moi.*'

Jean-Baptiste looked around. 'What of the neighbours?'

'Fuck the neighbours.'

Jean-Baptiste laughed. 'I'd rather fuck you.'

Mahvand reached up and kissed him.

'Not here,' said Jean-Baptiste. 'But I know just the spot.' He stood up, offered Mahvand his hand and led him behind what remained of the rear living room wall.

Taking off his leather jacket and spreading it on the ground, Jean-Baptiste said, 'Lie down and turn over.'

Mahvand did as he was told and lay on his front. Jean-Baptiste hoisted him back onto his lap, undid his belt, the buttons on his jeans, and slowly pulled down his underpants.

Mahvand, who was beginning to have second thoughts, said, 'I've never done this before.'

'I know.'

'No one's ever—'

'I'll break you in. Gently. I promise.'

Mahvand watched as Jean-Baptiste removed a pack of something from his trouser pocket and tore it with his teeth. He felt a wet and rather cold sensation around his back passage. Then a finger gently began to probe. He clenched his buttocks and grimaced. This was the last place he'd expected to lose his virginity. The words, whispered in a thick French accent, sealed his fate:

'You were born to take the seed of another man, boy.'

Mahvand took a sharp intake of breath and yelled; Jean-Baptiste was in. At first, he desperately wanted Jean-Baptiste to take it out. But in a few moments, the pain and discomfort had all but subsided and Mahvand discovered his buttocks had a life of their own, clenching and relaxing in rhythm with Jean-Baptiste's thrusting.

As Jean-Baptiste kept fucking, an image began to form just above the blackened stump that used to be the laburnum tree. At first, the image was blurred, the outline hazy. But with each pelvic thrust, it came nearer, became clearer, until Mahvand experienced an overwhelming sense of déjà vu.

Only then did the image give birth to itself and become fully three-dimensional.

'It's not real!' shouted Mahvand, who saw a vision of five rotating blue and green spheres covered in a swirling white mist. They reminded him of gigantic versions of those treasured Swirly marbles he used to keep in a shoebox under his bed. But it wasn't until four of the rotating spheres began to orbit the largest one that he realised he was witnessing some bizarre planetary configuration: an unholy replication of Mother Earth herself. And on each of her four planetary offspring, identical in colour formation if not in actual size, misshapen growths had sprung up across both northern and southern hemispheres like gigantic tumours.

'Yes it is!' he heard Jean-Baptiste cry above him.

'No! It's not!'

'Yes! It! Is!'

It was then that Mahvand realised; they were cities. *Is this a vision of the future?* He crooked his neck and looked behind. *A vision of the past?* Jean-Baptiste's elbows were jutting out as if they were baby pterodactyl wings, his hands were up above his head, palms facing outwards, fingers contorted in such a way that they resembled antlers. *Is this my doing?* Mahvand watched on incredulously. Jean-Baptiste tilted his head right back and gazed up to where Mahvand's extensive comics collection would have been, the whites of his eyes like two moons. *Or his?* The middle two fingers bowed down in prayer to the centre of each palm. Mahvand sensed a fork in the road before his whole body spasmed; the antlers had become horns. Then it came. First, the contorted expression on Jean-Baptiste's face, reminiscent of the Big

Bad Wolf's orgasmic grimace from Phoebe's PowerPoint presentation. Then, that long-awaited squirting sensation that really touched the spot. As Mahvand opened his eyes, the final, enduring image was of the largest planet Earth spontaneously combusting.

When Mahvand got to his feet, his arse was throbbing and he was covered in ash. A wet trickle ran down the inside of his thigh. Under the shrouded sky, bathed in the silver light of the moon, he could see it was bright red.

APOCALYPTIC
VISIONARY

Mahvand had often thought life was a bit like a game of snakes and ladders. In recent weeks, he felt he'd had more than his fair share of all things serpentine, so when Jean-Baptiste asked yet again whether he would like to move in with him, Mahvand acquiesced, left Petula's gaff in the chauffeur-driven limo, and moved into Golden Dawn. A month later, JB flew to New York to put in an appearance at Christies and to promote an up-and-coming contemporary artist who hailed from Nebraska. Before he left, he handed Mahvand the keys to his own art studio. 'Think of it as an investment,' he'd said, cracking open a bottle of champagne. 'I'm investing in Mahvand Amirzadeh.' Mahvand couldn't quite believe his good fortune. If losing his home was akin to sliding, head first, down a giant python, receiving the keys to his very own art studio somehow reminded him of William Blake's *Jacob's Ladder*. Then it struck him; Jean-Baptiste was the angel standing on one of the lower rungs holding out a helping hand.

The studio was on the top floor of a block on Curtain Road in Shoreditch, or 'Ditch' as Mahvand's fellow bohemian Ditchonians referred to the place. It was late evening and

Mahvand was waiting, with a nagging sense of self-doubt, for Daimon Mount-Stuart to arrive. The pieces to his debut piece of conceptual art, *Mankind as a Cancer on the Face of the Earth*, lay half-finished on his workbench. Half an hour later than expected, while Mahvand was berating himself for not having gone down to see Gran and Petula that week, he heard a familiar voice shouting down in the street. He downed his paintbrush, slipped the front door key into a sock and lobbed it out of the window. (Whoever owned the freehold in the block still hadn't got round to installing a buzzer system.)

'So how's the new messiah of the conceptual art scene?' said Daimon, ducking his head and walking into the studio. Mahvand wondered if Daimon actually subscribed to the viewpoint on his T-shirt: *All Americans Are Wankers.* Or was it just political posturing?

'Hardly,' said Mahvand, whose own T-shirt was splattered with blue and green paint. 'I feel more like a first-year student at St Martin's.'

'And what's with the area? Ghastly! No cashpoint, nor shops of any description for miles around. Then I have to contend with something falling from the sky like Chicken-frigging-Licken. Only it's not a bloody acorn. It's a manky old sock.'

'Welcome to the neighbourhood,' said Mahvand grinning awkwardly. He'd forgotten how Sloaney Daimon's accent actually was.

'I can hardly see how they're describing this area in *Time Out* as up and coming. Oh, I'm sure it's all frightfully bohemian. But I'm not sure how they can possibly say east is the new west.' Daimon flicked his dirty-blonde hair away from his forehead.

They walked over to Mahvand's work station. 'Work-in-progress,' said Mahvand, standing nervously, with his arms folded. '*Mankind as a Cancer on the Face of the Earth.*' The five, half-completed, green and blue papier mâché spheres on his workbench were arranged in order of size. Pieces of scrunched-up brown sticky tape were attached at random above and below the equator to represent cancerous growths. It suddenly struck Mahvand that he might have gone too far.

Daimon took a step back but said nothing. His expression gave nothing away. From the studio below, Bob Marley's lyrics to *Sun is Shining* filled the silence. A faint whiff of Mary J. wafted through the open window. Mahvand felt a hot flush of embarrassment and stood there feeling like the emperor who'd just discovered he was stark bollock naked.

'Well,' said Daimon at long last. 'They definitely show promise.'

From Daimon Mount-Stuart, these were great words indeed. Mahvand let out an inner sigh of relief.

'You've certainly managed to pull off that whole faux-naive style. I mean – fuck the tyranny of technique. If it looks like a six-year-old could do it – you're onto a winner, right?'

Mahvand wasn't quite sure whether to take it as a compliment or an insult so he brushed it aside and handed Daimon a paintbrush. After a careful application of green paint to the islands of Southeast Asia on the second largest sphere, Daimon put down his brush and seemed deep in thought. He then began to smirk until eventually he was bent double and laughing hysterically. 'I'm sorry, old sport. You have to admit it. It's all a bit four horsemen of the apocalypse. I mean, where on earth did you come up with this shit?'

Mahvand told him how his artistic vision for the piece had appeared just before Jean-Baptiste had shot his load. Retelling that part of the tale brought the strange sex magick experience out of the shadows and into the cold light of day. Mahvand was suddenly struck by how ridiculous it all sounded.

But Daimon wasn't laughing anymore. 'Did JB tell you to do that before you guys had sex?'

'Tell me what?'

'To harness your will. Focus on a piece of artwork you wanted to manifest prior to *la petite mort*?'

'What are you talking about?'

'He didn't instruct you in any tantric visualisation exercises beforehand?'

Mahvand couldn't help but wonder whether that's exactly what Jean-Baptiste had done with Daimon. *Am I just one in a long line of lovers?* His tone of voice was guarded. 'No. Why would he?'

Daimon sidestepped Mahvand's question, stepped back, and seemed to be admiring the work in a more considered way. '*Mankind as a Cancer on the Face of the Earth*. Yah. It speaks to me now with its own kind of visceral truth. I, like, totally dig the concept. But …' he hesitated. 'For me, there's still something missing here.'

Mahvand took a deep breath then confided in him about the spontaneous combustion of one of the model Earths.

'That's it! That's what you do when you exhibit the piece. Well, not you. Not if you don't want to, that is.' He took out a pack of cigarettes from his back pocket, hooked one out with his thumb and forefinger. Mahvand lit it for him. 'I mean, I could do it for you.'

'Do what?'

Daimon was gesticulating wildly with the cigarette. 'Set fire to one of the globes. To the whole God-damn lot of them if you like.'

Mahvand stared at him open-mouthed. He had Daimon down as many things but a pyromaniac wasn't one of them. 'You can't be serious.'

Daimon took a deep drag on his cigarette. 'Set the world alight, why don't you? With my good name behind it, you can sell the ashes for some ridiculously obscene amount and watch as your artistic reputation goes stratospheric! Mahvand Amirzadeh – Artist! Arsonist! Apocalyptic visionary! The Daily Wail will hate you.'

Mahvand wanted to tell him to rein it in. That there were limits. He stopped in his tracks. Who was he to tell Daimon Mount-Stuart what to do? So, instead, he simply said, 'Won't there be fire regulations to consider?'

'It's genius!' said Daimon. 'A hybrid conceptual-performance art event. We could even do it to Mozart's *Requiem Mass*.'

'Look. I don't want any trouble.'

'But you really should get an assistant to do all the dirty work. One hears the graduates from Goldsmiths these days are actually quite good.'

There were friends and foes along the path to artistic success. On Daimon, Mahvand decided, the jury was still out.

'By the way. I meant to ask. What did you make of JB's book?' asked Daimon, who proceeded to take a wrap of cocaine out of his wallet and rack up a line with surprising dexterity on the glass top of one of Jean-Baptiste's conceptual art cast-offs: a pig suspended in a vitrine filled with formaldehyde solution.

Mahvand put his paintbrush down on the workbench. 'What book?'

Daimon stood up, grunted at the back of his throat and grimaced. He hesitated before saying, 'Oh, come on. Don't tell me he hasn't told you about it?'

Mahvand felt himself blush. This was something that he as Jean-Baptiste's— Well, what was he? His lover? Boyfriend? Protégé? Their relationship had never been officially declared. Anyway, whatever he was, he had the right to know if he'd been published.

Daimon handed him the tightly rolled twenty-pound note. 'Look. You have to promise me you won't tell him … that I told you.'

'Of course,' said Mahvand, walking towards the vitrine.

'I mean it, old sport.'

'I promise,' said Mahvand, who couldn't help but wonder what else Jean-Baptiste was keeping from him.

'You know what he's like. Temperamental. Flies off the handle.'

Daimon walked over to the open Edwardian sash window and stood with his back to Mahvand.

Mahvand used one nostril then the other to snort Daimon's huge line.

'It's called *The Book of Belial*,' said Daimon.

'Belial?' said Mahvand. 'I don't get it. Why use his stage name?'

Daimon laughed. 'Is that what it is?'

Why can't Jean-Baptiste trust me enough to open up? Mahvand suddenly wished that he was there in the studio so he could have it out with him.

'Has he mentioned the will to power?' asked Daimon

'Not exactly,' said Mahvand, joining Daimon for a cigarette at the window.

Daimon put an arm around Mahvand. 'I shouldn't be telling you all this.'

They looked out across the sprawling council estates and the neighbouring office blocks in Liverpool Street. A group of Bengali boys were kicking a tin can in the street below.

'Has he told you anything of the Brotherhood of the Skull and Crossbones?' asked Daimon.

Mahvand recalled seeing the symbol on the packet of rat poison Gran kept under the sink. He'd also seen it, as a child, somewhere in the countryside near an electricity pylon. But Jean-Baptiste hadn't said anything about the symbol.

'Look. Maybe you're better off asking Jean-Baptiste,' said Daimon.

Mahvand was taken aback by the strangest of feelings. If he could have articulated it, he would have said it was as if Daimon was the brother he'd never had. 'I'm asking you.'

'If you've been initiated, the rituals – they involve ancient Egyptian forms of worship, Buddhist mantras, visualisations. A smorgasbord, really, of New Age beliefs and ancient religious practice. It's all about harnessing subconscious energies and invoking entities that supposedly exist on other planes of reality.' Daimon inhaled deeply. 'I have to admit

– it helped my career enormously. I was a nobody before I joined. And now. Well …'

Mahvand gazed up at the moon. It looked like a human skull. He knew the answer even before he'd asked the question. 'Jean-Baptiste was the founder, wasn't he?'

'I guess you could say he pointed the way,' said Daimon.

'Do you have a copy of the book?'

'Maybe.'

'Can I see it?' asked Mahvand.

Daimon laughed. 'You're what's called a "Sleeper". You haven't been initiated. Esoteric knowledge and all that.'

'I need to know what I'm getting myself into.'

Daimon squeezed his shoulder. 'Ah, Mr Amirzadeh, take it from me, if you play with fire—'

Mahvand turned, walked over to the armchair that Chaz, his white Rasta neighbour had given him as a moving-in present, and sat down. He stared at the 'found objects' he'd collected from local skips, which included an industrial metal cog and the dismembered limbs of several shop mannequins. His heart was racing from the recently ingested, super-strength cocaine. Suddenly it all seemed like a pile of old shit. It wasn't clever. It wasn't groundbreaking or avant-garde. He'd turned his back on his first love – comics – and for what?

Daimon walked over and crouched next to him. Once again, he put his arm around Mahvand. This time there was a tenderness to the touch which caught Mahvand off guard and prompted yet another confession. 'Part of me thought Jean-Baptiste might be …'

'Yes?'

'A demon.' Mahvand laughed nervously. 'I mean, how stupid was that?'

'And you still moved in with him?'

'I must be attracted to the dark side,' said Mahvand, light-heartedly. His heart would have told a different story. It felt like a bird that would never escape the wrought iron bars of its cage.

Daimon's hand reached down and pulled Mahvand's T-shirt out of his jeans. 'Maybe, a bit like Milton, JB's of the devil's party without knowing it.'

Mahvand felt cold fingertips work their way up to his nipples.

'Or am I talking about someone else?'

Do something. Divert his attention. Change the topic of conversation. But don't piss him off. You need him on your side.

'Put all your mortal fear and human prejudice aside. Just for a moment. Imagine he were to suddenly materialise. Here. Right now.'

'Who?'

Daimon gave a conspiratorial smile. 'I think we both know who I'm talking about.'

'Jean-Baptiste?'

Daimon laughed then fell silent. 'He, who refused to bow down to Adam. That which has the power to shape-shift at will.' He paused. 'His Infernal Majesty comes in many guises. And, as I'm sure you know, is known by many names.'

A cavernous silence opened up and filled the room. Daimon stood and walked back to the window. With his back to Mahvand, he rested both hands on the window ledge. 'The Master Puppeteer, Prince of Darkness, Beelzebub,

Mammon, Father of Lies, Satan, Abaddon, Beast, Leviathan.'
He turned to face Mahvand, bathed in the light of the moon.
'Or – my all-time personal favourite – Old Serpent. Imagine
if He were to reveal himself in all his diabolical, fiend-like
glory. Know what I think?'

'No,' said Mahvand in a whimper.

'I think, *mon cher,* it would be love.' He paused. 'Love at
first sight.'

There was a moment's hesitation. After everything Jean-
Baptiste had done for him. After everything he himself had
promised. But the rising sexual tension, and the transgressive
pull of making art without much heart, proved too much.
Mahvand stood up and walked back towards Daimon.
He reached for his hand, before nuzzling his head against
Daimon's chest. Anaesthetised by the last line of cocaine, he
shut his eyes and shut out the world. As a child, he would
dig away with his bright yellow spade in Gran's vegetable
patch, convinced he could dig his way through to Australia.
Just then, he was filled with a similarly childish fantasy. But
this time he imagined what it would be like to dig his way
into Daimon. To force his way inside the ribcage and take
shelter in that bloody chamber from his own contrary state
of being that pulled him first one way then the other.

Mahvand suddenly froze. He opened his eyes.

Daimon pulled back. 'Hadn't you better answer it?'

His new Nokia 6110, one of many gifts from Jean-Baptiste,
was vibrating in amongst the pile of plastic, dismembered
limbs. The dead pig looked out from behind the glass panels
of the vitrine. Its little piggy eyes seemed to know. Know
exactly who was on the other end.

Mahvand picked up the phone. He pushed the aerial out and turned to Daimon. It was as if, by their loose-lipped devil talk, they had summoned him. 'He's here,' said Mahvand. 'It's Jean-Baptiste.'

BELGRAVIA

Mahvand stood by the window and looked out onto the vast swathes of washing hanging on makeshift balconies on a neighbouring council estate. Even though Jean-Baptiste was more than three thousand miles away, it sounded like he was in the next room. Mahvand listened as JB regaled him with tales of the New York art scene. Waiting in the wings was Maria Rosa Rodrigo-Gonzalez, a femme fatale billionaire from Sao Paulo with an addiction to plastic surgery and overpriced light and video installations. Next to tread the boards was Sheikh Mohammed from the United Arab Emirates, who was on the brink of closing a million dollar art deal. Then there was the filthy-rich client from Moscow who was renowned for his lavish, cocaine-fuelled parties dedicated to the more wayward sexual practices of the Marquis de Sade. 'So, to cut to the chase,' said Jean-Baptiste. 'I'm staying out here a little longer than I planned.' When Mahvand put the phone down, he realised Jean-Baptiste hadn't asked him a single question about himself. But the timing of the call had spooked Mahvand enough to call it a day and get a cab back to Golden Dawn.

*

With Candy working extra shifts at Soho Books and Octavi not returning any of his calls, Mahvand decided to spend that weekend in his studio. He was applying the finishing touches to the Atlantic Ocean on the largest papier mâché sphere when Arthur phoned. 'We've found a care home for yer gran,' he'd said. 'Down in Dagenham. The doctor's confirmed what we've known for a while.' Silence. 'She lacks capacity.'

When the day came to drive Gran in Arthur's Ford Capri to the care home, Mahvand escaped yet again to the Shoreditch triangle and the confines of his studio. After drawing the curtains to blot out the late morning sun, he punch-dialled Jean-Baptiste's home-delivery guy. The pig in the vitrine looked on as he curled up in a foetal position in the armchair and sobbed. He knew he was betraying Gran just as much as Arthur. More so. But he couldn't be there when they walked away. It was too much. To leave her slumped in an unfamiliar armchair in some godforsaken nursing home. The BMW drew up outside shortly after midday. It wasn't long before Mahvand was snorting line after line of London's best, at strict half-hourly intervals, until his heart was firmly in Charlie's white-gloved grip, and the blood in his hands and feet ran cold.

In late July, with only Shiva for company, and his confidence in himself as a conceptual artist at an all-time low, it wasn't long before Mahvand got back in contact with Daimon and Jean-Baptiste's drug dealer. A week later, after a starry-eyed champagne and cocaine-fuelled evening which took in a private viewing of light installations in a disused factory south of the river, dinner in Soho at Quo Vadis, curated by

Damien Hirst, and late-night drinks at the Groucho Club, they ended up back at Daimon's flat in Belgravia.

The lift opened directly into Daimon's top-floor apartment. They walked along a winding hallway lined with bookshelves crammed with hardbacks – mostly art, photography and travel books. A Grecian statue with the classic miniscule penis guarded the entrance to the kitchen. Ganymede! Mahvand, who was a walking encyclopaedia when it came to all things mythological, knew all about Zeus shape-shifting into an eagle, abducting Ganymede and having his wicked way with him on Mount Olympus. The living room itself was an eclectic mix of ethnic trappings and pieces of contemporary and conceptual art. Sort of Tate Modern meets Persian harem. Afghan rugs and an array of cushions, that looked as if they'd been handmade in the foothills of the Himalayas, surrounded the centrepiece of the room: an enormous coffee table with a glass top that covered an intricate maze of concentric squares and circles carved out of wood like some Tibetan Buddhist mandala.

'Got it shipped over from Jaipur,' said Daimon. 'Indian rosewood. Sixteenth century.' In the centre was an opened bottle of red wine and a wine glass, and, at either end, two interlocking bronze snakes encircled two bronze candlesticks. *What is with Jean-Baptiste and Daimon's fascination with all things serpentine?* On the far wall was a Victorian fireplace lined on either side with ceramic tiles decorated with flowers that reminded him of the vine tapestries of William Morris. But in the corner, under a light fitting that looked like a model for the molecular structure of DNA, stood a urinal covered in red and black squiggles. *Very Marcel Duchamp.*

'Signatures,' said Daimon. 'Celebrity D-listers. Ageing porn stars, out-of-work children's TV presenters, wannabe pop singers with a single hit back in the eighties. You know the sort.'

A light installation mounted on the wall, flashing on and off the word 'PURPLE' in giant yellow letters, sent two contradictory messages to Mahvand's coke-addled brain.

Daimon put a CD on, left the living room, and minutes later re-emerged in nothing more than a jockstrap and a camera slung round his neck. With Jim Morrison turned up full volume urging him to 'Break on Through (To the Other Side)', Mahvand stripped down to his underpants. Daimon then proceeded to chase Mahvand round the apartment, adjusting the lens and capturing him in an array of compromising positions: falling hysterically onto the mass of Persian cushions, making lewd gestures with a fourteenth-century wood carving of a demon piggy-backing an old miser, and executing a perfect arc of piss in his bathroom. Daimon even took a photo of him completely naked snorting a fat line of coke off the glass table with a heartfelt promise to send it to a certain tabloid editor friend of his when Mahvand had achieved some semblance of fame.

Halfway through 'The End', Mahvand persuaded Daimon to hand the camera over to him. He wanted to know how it felt to be on the other side of the lens. Daimon stood as directed in front of the celebrity-signed urinal. To Morrison's trance-like exhortations to 'ride the snake to the lake, baby' – click, click, click – Mahvand pulled the shutter. Each time, the flash lit up the room and a different part of Daimon's body: the strange tattoo on his forearm; the way the supporting elastic on his jock framed his peachy, hairless buttocks; his hips. In the half-light, half-drunk and half-drugged, he became captivated by the shadows that cut across Daimon's body, with the way his lower back dipped then rose to the curved line of his buttocks, the prominence of each individual vertebra that peaked to form a mountain range of bone. All tension and anxiety had drained from Daimon's face; the mask had slipped. And, if anything, the stump near his right shoulder seemed to accentuate Daimon's natural beauty, leaving Mahvand wanting to reach out and kiss it.

Standing at the sash window with his back to Mahvand, Daimon suddenly complained of feeling cold. He took the camera and left Mahvand in the living room, reclining on the embroidered cushions like a Persian prince. Minutes later, he came back in football socks and a silk dressing gown adorned with fire-breathing dragons and Geisha girls, holding what looked like a large sketch pad high in the air as if it was a Olympic torch. He handed it ceremoniously to Mahvand.

'*The Book of Belial?*' asked Mahvand incredulously.

Daimon laughed. 'No. *The Book of Daimon*. Far more interesting.'

Mahvand put the sketch pad down on the cushions. 'Don't you think I have a right to know?'

Daimon laughed and ruffled his hair. 'You already know too much as it is.'

'So. What's in *The Book of Daimon?*' Mahvand leant back on the cushions and laid his head on Daimon's chest.

'Ideas for my next exhibition, *Death Becomes You*. I'm finally moving away from the whole light and video install-ation thing.'

Daimon opened the sketch pad. On the first page was a labelled sketch of an unmade bed with miscellaneous sex paraphernalia scattered over it – condoms, dildos, lube, a jockstrap, a cock ring, poppers, and a stash of pornographic magazines. 'It's called *Gay Man's Unmade Bed*,' said Daimon triumphantly.

'I, like, totally get that,' said Mahvand, picking up on a phrase Daimon himself had used, yet not recognising the bed as any he'd ever slept in.

'Did I mention there's going to be a huge screen erected above the bed filled with TV static? White noise. Total dissonance, man.' He got Mahvand to swear an oath of secrecy. One artist to another. After linking arms, drinking from the same glass of red wine, and sealing the oath with a kiss, Mahvand took ownership of the sketch pad.

'This section of the exhibition is called the *Holy Trinity*.'

Daimon turned the page. The first sketch was of an emaciated figure, adorned with a crown of thorns, hanging upside down with a huge, uncircumcised erection. It was cartoon-like. Mahvand couldn't make out if it was a look of agony or ecstasy on Christ's face. Underneath, Daimon had scrawled *The Erection of Christ*. The second sketch was of Christ with legs akimbo being fucked by a shepherd's crook. The effects of the cocaine served to blunt Mahvand's initial revulsion. But he couldn't help but think that there was something not only deeply sacrilegious but also inverted about the sketches. *Inversion*. He suddenly remembered Daimon referring to speed, cocaine and crystal meth as being like members of a family. *If I cross over and become a fully fledged member of Skull and Crossbones, does the*

Brotherhood replace my own family? Mahvand pushed the thought from his mind.

'So far, the third piece has eluded me,' said Daimon. He couldn't get his words out fast enough and rattled off a list of materials he intended to use, dimensions and suppliers. He even divulged the title for the second piece: *The Second Cumming*. At the back of the sketch pad was a large brown envelope. He handed it to Mahvand. Inside was a reel of film and a wad of black-and-white photographs.

'From a local funeral home,' said Daimon.

'What are they?'

'Photographs. Of the deceased.' He suppressed a smile. 'I bribed the dude who worked there.'

Mahvand said nothing. Not only was it one of the most immoral and depraved things he'd ever heard of. It was also illegal. But then who was he to judge? He recognised that he too would stop at nothing for an opportunity to create a groundbreaking piece of art that would define his career. But for Mahvand the next piece was somehow even more disturbing. Daimon told him it was the centrepiece for the show. His crowning glory. A toilet covered in a collage of 1950s' superhero figures from comic books.

'I have you to thank for that,' said Daimon, opening Mahvand's second gram of cocaine and racking up two more lines on the table.

'Me?'

'Mahvand Amirzadeh. My muse. Or, at least, one of them.'

Mahvand declined the offer of yet another line of his own coke, noticing how they seemed to have doubled in length.

'When you took your first hit of crystal in that toilet cubicle, were you, or were you not, Mr Amirzadeh, wearing Superman briefs?'

It was as if Daimon was holding up a distorted mirror of his former life. His childhood heroes had been reduced from saving the world to gazing up from the pan, rim and seat of a toilet. It was pure travesty. A new level of humiliation.

'I just put two and two together,' said Daimon.

'Why are you showing me all this?'

Daimon picked up the rolled twenty-pound note and hoovered up both lines. 'You showed me the *Mankind* exhibit.' He sniffed hard, making a grunting noise at the back of his throat. 'I'm showing you mine. Well, the ideas for the pieces, anyway. What do you think?'

Mahvand felt a pang of self-consciousness, an adolescent affliction that had lingered long after entry into adulthood. He'd never been very good at coming up with an instant, well-articulated response to any piece of artwork. Let alone one that was a parody of everything that had ever meant anything to him. But he knew Daimon was waiting for that royal seal of approval. 'I'm not sure "like" is a word I'd use.'

'Interesting,' said Daimon.

'In-yer-face. Challenging. Risqué.' Mahvand sensed that he still hadn't quite hit the mark. 'Demonic.'

Daimon's eyes lit up. 'Then, my friend, I think my work here is done.'

Mahvand was tempted to tear the page from the sketch pad, scrunch it into a tight ball and flush it down the toilet – where it rightly belonged. Then he noticed the beads of sweat on Daimon's forehead, the slight tremor in his hand.

'Who knows, Mr Amirzadeh, one day we may even collaborate on a piece together,' said Daimon, leaning in to kiss him.

And that's when Mahvand saw it. A droplet of blood trickling from his left nostril. He pulled back. 'Daimon. Your nose. It's bleeding.'

Daimon felt his upper lip, under his nose, and smiled mischievously. He looked like he'd just been caught out in some schoolboy prank. 'Occupational hazard.' He stood up, walked out of the living room and called from the hallway. 'Still, thank God for small mercies. At least one's septum's still intact.'

When the moon was but a thumbprint in the sky, Daimon led Mahvand to the bedroom. Despite all the cocaine, he was still able to perform. Mahvand had never felt more intimate with another man. Daimon managed to touch that soft spot inside him, and Mahvand began to let go. For Mahvand, the fluidity of their lovemaking, the waves of sheer, indescribable pleasure and the vocalisation of this pleasure (for both of them) came as a revelation. Mahvand gave himself to Daimon in a way he had never given himself to Jean-Baptiste. But then, Jean-Baptiste had never made love. Mahvand wasn't quite sure what they'd made. But it wasn't love.

After Daimon had cum inside him, Mahvand lay in the nook between arm and shoulder. And the silence was filled, not with the hazy, macabre image of some Amirzadeh–Mount-Stuart sex-fuelled piece of conceptual art, but with birdsong. A thrush perhaps. A thrush with eager, out-stretched mouths to feed.

For some time, Mahvand stared at the traditional tribal masks, carved from different types of wood, mounted on Daimon's bedroom wall. If they were suddenly endowed with the gift of speech, what stories would they tell? What would they make of his own life story and the tributaries that flowed into that main river? The masks were decorated with intricate patterns, images of animals, and had beautiful, elongated features and full lips. They conjured images of witchcraft, tribal ritual, initiations and magic. Mahvand gazed up at Daimon's face, the angular ridge of bone at the top of his nose, the slight curl of his eyelashes, and then glanced across at the traditional masks on the wall. He marvelled at the way the human face was represented in a myriad of forms around the world. And he found himself strangely filled with love for the human story in all its beauty, pain and tragedy – for the continual struggle to live it and retell the tale. He felt a wet trickle on his cheek. Gran had always said he'd been born with a thin skin.

They were in the spoon position before Mahvand dozed off. Daimon's arm was around him and he felt Daimon's lips brush against the nape of his neck. But for the first time since the fire, Mahvand didn't dream about trying to rescue Gran from a burning house. Nor did he find himself plunging head first at death-defying speed from the Empire State Building or Canary Wharf. He drifted into semi-unconsciousness – a sort of half sleep filled with broken dream fragments and the sensation that he was far out at sea.

When he first came round, he had no idea where he was. Or even who he was. It was a familiar, if not alarming sensation. Most mornings, on waking, he felt he was pure consciousness, unanchored, free-floating before rushing in and fully inhabiting his body and life history. But that particular morning he came crashing into his body with a particularly violent jolt and a crushing sense of guilt. At first he just lay there tuning in to the sounds of the day outside – a baby crying, the distant hum of traffic. He struggled to open his eyes, yawned, stretched and rolled over. At first he couldn't make out what the strange brown marks were on the pillow. Then he suddenly remembered Daimon's nosebleed from the night before. It was dried blood. Daimon's blood. He sat up to take a closer look. The left side of Daimon's face was caked in the same dark, brown stuff. It looked as if he'd been in some punch-up or hit-and-run. Don't panic, he told himself. It's just another nosebleed. He knelt up in the bed. 'Daimon. Wake up.'

Daimon didn't even flinch.

Mahvand raised his voice an octave. 'Daimon?'

Mahvand put an ear to Daimon's bloody nose. *Any minute. Any minute now, the soft, warm sensation of breath. A flicker of eyelids. All will be well.* He yanked the duvet off. *Oh, God. No. Not this. Please.* He mentally willed Daimon's belly to rise and fall. To feel the kiss of breath. To bear witness to a twitching of facial muscle. Then came a deal, of sorts, with a God he'd always considered borderline malevolent. *If Daimon lives, I'll do anything. Go back to the comics. Find a way to live with Gran. I'll ...*

His fingers began to tremble as he tried to shake Daimon's body back into life. Mahvand shut his eyes. He became a black seed of pure volition. *If I can will apocalyptic art into existence, I can will Daimon back to life.* He racked his brain for the correct procedure of mouth-to-mouth resuscitation. *Do I put him on his side? Press down on his chest?* He tilted Daimon's head back, pinched both nostrils, took a deep breath and poured his breath into Daimon's lungs. Nothing. He tried again. And again. At some point he gave up. Dust particles danced in the sunlight. The bird outside the window filled the moment with song. And it seemed, however fleetingly, that just then, Daimon was right there in that very room with him. Then he looked down at the inert body and bloodstained pillow; Daimon was dead.

DEATH BECOMES YOU

Sunlight stabbed Mahvand's eyes. He sat on the Persian cushions in the living room and tried to control the tremor in his hands as he snorted a ready-made white line. The light installation 'PURPLE' flashed on and off in yellow lighting. Everywhere he looked he saw Daimon: skilfully racking up a line of cocaine with his one hand, standing naked by the celebrity-signed urinal, chasing him through the apartment. *Any minute now I'll hear the screeching sound of sirens. The intercom buzzer. Footsteps on the stairwell. That knock on the door.*

He reached for Daimon's sketch pad and began to flick through the pages. In amongst a series of telephone numbers and measurements, the sketch of Christ, bent over and buggered by a shepherd's crook, stared back at him. *Then ... I think my work here is done.* Something so final about those words. As if Daimon was handing over the mantle of celebrity conceptual artist to him. *No I can't. Can I?* It was as if Mahvand had tuned in to some malevolent transmitter, as an idea, so treacherous and cunning, began to take hold, hooking itself into his brain like the pincers of a black beetle cutting into dead matter. At first, he was repulsed by it. It was gruesome, ghoulish even. But the more he felt the effects of the recently ingested cocaine, and the stronger the frequency of malevolent transmission became, the more the idea seemed to make sense. Perfect sense. It would be a fitting eulogy for Daimon. A gift from one artist to another. *God damn it. I'll do it. I'll take his sketch pad. It's my moral duty. I'll see to it that Daimon's legacy lives on.*

Mahvand went into the kitchen. Next to the oven were a set of drawers. He yanked each one out. Shoved at the back of the bottom drawer were paintbrushes, hypodermic needles, syringes, glass pipes of various shapes and sizes, and a neatly folded collection of carrier bags: Harrods, Fortnum & Mason and Harvey Nichols. He took the Harvey Nichols bag, went back to the living room, put the sketch pad and camera inside it, and then crept up the hallway to pay his last respects to Daimon.

He slowly opened the bedroom door, walked towards the bed and knelt down. He'd never seen a dead body before. It looked nothing like they say it does. There was no gently into the good night about it. No angelic smile to say I've peacefully slipped away. Just a greyish pallor to his skin. A blueish tinge to those lips that only hours earlier had expertly kissed his own. No rise and fall. But more than this, there was something almost – Mahvand couldn't quite put his finger on it, then a sepia-toned image of Great-grandfather Harbuckle in his open casket unexpectedly illuminated the fog – historical. That was it. There was already something undeniably historical about Daimon Mount-Stuart. Mahvand held his hand. Only it wasn't his, was it? The fingers were already stiff. They were cold. *Death Becomes You? Death is bullshit.* Mahvand was shot through with the significance of what had come to pass; Daimon was history.

Eventually, Mahvand did the decent thing and covered Daimon's torso in the white shroud of the bed sheet. And that's when he saw it. On the floor, in the gap between the wall and the bed headboard: *The Book of Belial*. He leant over, picked up the book and wiped off the thick covering of dust with the bed sheets. Its spine felt insubstantial in his hands, like a slim volume of poetry. The black cover bore the image of the skull and crossbones. He could hear Gran's voice. *A picture speaks a thousand words.* He deposited the book inside the bag, left the flat, got the tube and headed towards Soho Books via Soho Square. But not before grabbing a cloth from one of the kitchen drawers and frantically rubbing every surface he could possibly have come into contact with.

At the far end of the Square, he hovered by a Westminster City Council rubbish bin and three drunkards asleep on a bench, slumped like some prehistoric beast, a litter of crushed beer cans at their feet. He reached into the carrier bag and pulled out Daimon's sketch pad. Outside Govinda's restaurant, the familiar chant of the Hare Krishnas started up.

'*Krishna Krishna, Hare Hare.*'

Mahvand could deceive himself no longer. He knew exactly why he'd taken it. It wasn't to continue Daimon's legacy: to perform his moral duty – one artist to another. It was to pass off Daimon's ideas as his own. To launch his career as a conceptual artist on the back of one who would be lying six feet under.

'*Rama Rama, Hare Hare.*'

His fingers released their grip on the sketch pad. It fell amongst a half-eaten cheeseburger and a copy of *The Stage*.

When he reached Soho Books, Candy was busy advising a customer on the health and safety aspects of auto-erotic asphyxiation. She told him to wait for her at The New Piccadilly cafe.

*

Mahvand sat by the window, sipping a glass of iced Coca Cola. A pink espresso maker dominated the counter – as did hundreds of postcards, presumably from satisfied customers, from all over the world pinned to the wall behind it. Candy arrived half an hour late, flustered, in fake fur and laddered tights. Minus the wig and the thick layer of slap, she was a shadow of her former self. The absence of the perennial white mask of foundation revealed a multitude of sins: blackheads, pimples and acne scarring around the jawline. Her natural hair – a mousey-brown colour – was lank and beginning to thin on top. The last time Mahvand had seen her like this was the morning after she'd been dumped by a married Ghanaian postman from Milton Keynes on New Year's Eve.

She slung her black feathered handbag on top of the Formica-topped table, plonked herself down and immediately launched into a tirade regarding last night's escapade. She told Mahvand how she'd meant to go home after her drag act with Connie Lingus at Madam Jojo's, really she had, but, well, one thing had led to another. She'd ended up with a minor celeb (no, she wouldn't kiss and tell) and a tranny chaser from the suburbs who'd plied her with shots until the early hours, expecting a favour of a rather personal nature in return. When he'd turned nasty, she'd decked him one, before staggering out onto Brewer Street with a bloody fist and catching the night bus home.

Mahvand stared at Candy's motormouth, her flailing arms and exaggerated hand gestures. It was as if she was on speed signing for the deaf. Her bloody fist merged with an image of Daimon Mount-Stuart's bloodstained face.

After Candy had ordered the food, Mahvand told her everything. Well, almost everything. (His only omission was the fact that he was the one who'd supplied the Charlie.) Her face remained impassive. She didn't interrupt. Not once. When he'd finished, she simply leant across and rested her spatula man-hands on his. Her knuckles were scuffed, her fingers badly bruised.

'What's Mutha going to do wi' yee, eh?'

'I'm done for.'

'Sit tight, pet. Wait it out.' She wiped a tear from his cheek with her thumb.

'You don't think I should go to the police?' he asked.

'You've done nothin' wrong,' said Candy.

'I should have stayed with the body. Instead, I fled like a thief in the night.' Mahvand paused. 'I even took his camera.'

'Ah divvent think he's going to miss it. Not where he's going, pet.'

She told him she knew she was a fine one to lecture him about the evils of drugs, having been heavily into speed in her younger days (cocaine had been the strict reserve of the hoi polloi) but, well, as mother, she'd seen the error of her ways and now had every right to.

Mahvand was playing with the baked beans and yolk of his fried egg, imagining it framed by the whitewashed walls of some pop-up gallery in the East End, when the news report came on the radio.

News is just coming in from the Royal Borough of Kensington and Chelsea. Conceptual artist and London socialite, Daimon Mount-Stuart, died earlier this morning at his home address in Notting Hill. Mr Mount-Stuart's cleaner, Alejandra Hernandez, who gained access to the property shortly before midday, alerted the emergency services immediately. Mr Mount-Stuart was pronounced dead at the scene. Police are currently treating the death as suspicious, and the public are being told to report any relevant information.

Candy had stopped chewing. She placed her knife and fork down on the plate as if it were a landmine and reached for Mahvand's hand. Halfway through a mouthful of Cumberland sausage and mash, she said, 'Now listen te Mutha.' She emphasised each word in turn. 'This. Changes. Everything.'

Mahvand stared at her hands. He didn't doubt her potential bodyguard credentials.

'D'yer hear me?'

Mahvand couldn't believe that in less than twenty-four hours he'd been unfaithful for the first time in his life, supplied class A drugs to a celebrity-artist with a drug habit, and woken up next to his corpse. And, to top it all, he was now potentially a murder suspect. He pulled his hand from underneath Candy's, reached for a napkin, and proceeded to tear little pieces off it.

Tributes are already pouring in from the art world. Fellow conceptual artist Zadie Brickman has called Daimon's death 'a tragic loss.' She has told BBC News that Daimon's best work was yet to come and that it was a tragedy that his forthcoming exhibition, Death Becomes You, *will now not go ahead. 'His untimely death is a great shock and a great loss for the international contemporary art scene,' she said only moments ago from the family home in Chelsea.*

'Mahvand. Look at me,' hissed Candy.

Mahvand had seen the distress he'd already caused Candy. He'd seen it in her eyes – full of a mother's compassion. It was almost too much to bear. He stared out of the window. And that's when he saw a skeletal-looking woman in Adidas trackie bottoms lean into the open window of a Ford Capri: Crystal. *Just what I need.*

He turned to Candy. 'I'm not going to the pigs.'

'Yee have no choice. You're a prime suspect. D'yer really want an artist's impression of your handsome mug on *Crimewatch*? D'yer really need the likes of Jill Dando earnestly appealing te the nation te do everything in their power te bring yee te justice?'

He hated what he was putting her through. But if the police discovered he was the one who'd supplied the drugs … If the tabloids got whiff of his involvement …

Candy rested both elbows on the table. 'Divvent tempt me, Mahvand. I'll shut up shop and drag yee to the police station by yer earhole if Aa've te, man.'

'I'm innocent.'

'Then prove it. Or else Mutha just might start suspecting summat untoward really did happen.'

'Are you accusing me?' Candy's fairy godmother aura was fading fast. It was more like Candy – hotshot lawyer for the prosecution. 'You think I murdered Daimon?'

'Ahm saying you've got nothin te hide.'

'You think I murdered him!'

'For God's sake, man. Keep yer voice down.'

Lorenzo, the owner, called over from the counter in a thick Italian accent: 'Everything alright, Miss Darling?'

Candy grimaced and gave Lorenzo a little ladylike wave with a waggle of the fingers. 'Couldn't be better, Mr L. Best piece of Cumberland this side o' the Watford gap.'

Out of the corner of his eye, Mahvand noticed the Ford Capri drive off.

'If I hand myself in—' said Mahvand.

'Ah know such a lovely bent copper doon at Charing Cross police station,' said Candy.

'I'll be famous for one thing.'

'Oh, he's gorgeous, he is! Bent in both senses o' the word, mind. In wi' some yardie drug gang south o' the river. Handsome though. Blokeish. The type that'd give yee a reet royal seeing to if yee play yer cards right.'

'For being with Daimon Mount-Stuart the night he died,' said Mahvand.

'Reet up yer street, Ah shouldn't wonder, ye dirty bugger.'

Crystal was approaching the cafe.

'Remember, Mahvand. Mutha knows best.'

The bell above the cafe door announced Crystal's arrival. She stood in the doorway of the cafe, her face cadaverous, eyes locked on Mahvand. Her dirty, pink Fred Perry T-shirt swamped her skeletal frame and revealed a criss-cross of cuts and track marks on her spindly arms. Candy was ranting on about bent coppers and the curse of celebrity while Mahvand braced himself for the moment when Crystal would unleash a torrent of crack-fuelled abuse in his direction.

That moment never came. Instead, Crystal's bottom lip began to quiver. She looked more like a frightened rabbit caught in the headlights of an oncoming car than the tweaked-out crack addict she really was. She backed out of the door, turned, ran into the road and straight into the pathway of a speeding Volkswagen Beetle. What followed seemed to Mahvand like something out of a silent movie: a full technicoloured silent horror movie in slow motion. Crystal lost her balance, stumbled backwards and, with outstretched arms, and, face turned towards the heavens, spun round and round like a whirling dervish, as if she held the whole world in the palm of her hands. For an instant, it was as if a tear in the fabric of reality allowed Mahvand to witness her in a completely different light – as someone's daughter, friend, lover, someone like him – with her own demons to face, before a swerving screech of rubber against tarmac and an almighty thud broke the silence. Broke his vision.

Broke her bones.

And up she went, up, up, into the air, somersaulting over the bonnet, over the windscreen, before landing like a rag doll in the middle of the road. And the car – it carried on, skidding sideways, eventually smashing headlong into a street lamp. The bonnet was now a heap of crumpled metal, in part concertinaed like the bellows on an accordion, showered with glass from the shattered windscreen. Its engine hissed gas and smoke as if it knew it was destined for the scrap metal yard. And somehow, in all the commotion, a car alarm had gone off.

It took some time before Mahvand realised he was the only one left in the cafe. Candy, Lorenzo and the other customers had all gathered outside on the pavement. His only thought was to get away before Candy or someone else he knew met a fate similar to that of Crystal or Daimon. He found himself standing in the doorway of the cafe. No one turned to acknowledge his presence. He felt invisible. The words from a macabre playground game came back to haunt him. *There's been an accident. Someone's hurt. Try and lift her. It's too late.* Looking towards the wreckage of the car, he saw the driver slumped over the steering wheel, blood trickling down the back of his bald head. Her head was cricked back, eyes unblinking, glassy, still looking skyward. *She's dead.*

Mahvand ran into the road dodging cars, cyclists and pedestrians, until he managed to hail a black cab at Piccadilly Circus.

The red-faced cabbie leant towards the open window. 'Where to guv'nor?'

'Hampstead.'

Once safely inside, his trembling fingers took *The Book of Belial* out of the carrier bag and he leant back on the black leather of the passenger seat. In sprawling handwriting on the first page was a dedication to Daimon. *To my beloved Daimon. You are my New Dawn! Love, Jean-Baptiste.* Was that how a master addressed a disciple? Mahvand felt a stab of jealousy and flicked to the contents page. It was divided into six short chapters. *The New Dawn, Art and Sex Magick, Skull and Crossbones, Demonic Realms, Crossing the Abyss.* The last chapter began with the opening lines from the narrative poem Jean-Baptiste had read at Forked Tongue.

'Finding myself (I won't say how)
In that dark wood,'

Mahvand turned to the chapter on art and magic. The first page bore a strange, macabre symbol:

The chapter itself was prefaced with a quote from the Bhagavad Gita: 'Now I am become Death, the destroyer of worlds.' Mahvand tried to focus on the words on the page.

According to the Brotherhood of the Skull and Crossbones, the bloodline of true artists and magicians will be revealed to whoever smokes from the glass pipe and recites with the power of the will, the incantation to the demiurge.

Mahvand wasn't sure whether it was coming down off the coke that made the reading incomprehensible, or because it was simply a load of old mumbo jumbo. He put the book on the seat, leant back and closed his eyes. An image of Crystal lying in the road flickered into a likeness of Daimon's lifeless body. Mahvand couldn't quite shake the feeling that he might be next.

When he arrived back at Golden Dawn, two suitcases were parked by the front door like tombstones. Jean-Baptiste's black leather jacket was slung on the banister of the stairs. The plasma TV was blaring from the living room. Mahvand felt a sinking feeling in the pit of his stomach. *What's he doing back? Why isn't he still in New York?* Mahvand stuffed the carrier bag with the camera and *The Book of Belial* behind the olive tree on the front porch and closed the front door as quietly as he could.

'Is that you?' called Jean-Baptiste.

What book?! Mahvand suddenly realised. In his rush to get safely back behind closed doors, he'd left it on the passenger seat in the back of the cab.

'Mahvand?'

Mahvand walked sheepishly into the living room. Jean-Baptiste was slumped on the white sofa in his Oxblood Prada shirt, watching BBC News. Zadie Brickman was being interviewed about Daimon, perched on a chaise longue at her penthouse apartment in Chelsea. She was dressed in a vintage black dress and, just like Princess Diana when she'd been interviewed about the breakup of her marriage to Charles, had applied some heavy-duty mascara.

'Yah,' she said in a typical Sloane Ranger kind of way. 'Me and Dame were best buds. I know everyone will probably think this is a bit beyond the pale and everything, but I would simply love to do this for Dame.'

'And what's that?' asked the fawning BBC interviewer.

'Take some photographs of Dame at the morgue, of course,' replied Zadie. 'I hardly need to tell you that death was one of Dame's great themes.' Mahvand had to look away as a much younger black-and-white photograph of Daimon's face filled the screen.

Jean-Baptiste stood up and held out his arms.

Mahvand thought he looked even more beautiful. There was almost an innocence about him.

'I missed you,' said Jean-Baptiste.

They embraced.

Jean-Baptiste took a step back and wiped away his tears with the cuff of his shirt. Mahvand noticed the half-moon shadows beneath his eyes. 'Forgive me,' said Jean-Baptiste in a valiant attempt to regain composure. 'I must be jetlagged.'

'How was your trip?' asked Mahvand, trying to control the tremor in his voice.

'A two-hour delay at JFK. Not exactly what one expects when flying business class on Concorde.'

For Mahvand there were more pressing matters. Like what to do with the camera. Bury it in the back garden under cover of darkness? Remove the film and take it to a pawn shop? Throw it into the Thames?

'I wanted this to be a surprise. Then I come home to an empty house and this terrible news.' Jean-Baptiste flicked the remote control box and Daimon Mount-Stuart disappeared from their living room. He took Mahvand's hand and led him to the sofa, kicked his Gucci shoes off and laid the full length, both hands resting behind his head as if he was in some hotshot celebrity photo shoot for *Hello* magazine. Mahvand lay on top of him, watching the flames flicker silently behind the cuboid of glass, his head buried in a sea of Oxblood.

'Did you manage to get to see him while I was away?' asked Jean-Baptiste.

Mahvand hesitated. 'No.'

Jean-Baptiste gently stroked his hair. 'Pity. I always thought you two would get on like … how do the English say? A house on fire.'

In the fireplace, Mahvand saw an image of Laburnum Tree Cottage engulfed in flames. *Had Jean-Baptiste used that expression deliberately?*

'Two artists forging a common bond together.' He paused. 'Everything is alright, isn't it?'

'Why wouldn't it be?'

Jean-Baptiste toyed with one of Mahvand's black curls. 'You seem different somehow.'

Mahvand undid a few buttons on Jean-Baptiste's shirt and slid his hand in, as if doing so would put a stop to the barrage of questions.

'The trip, *mon cher*, was not quite the success one had anticipated. I auctioned some pieces from my own personal collection and ended up getting considerably less than I paid for them.'

Mahvand lifted his head. Had Daimon's death unearthed a more human, fallible side to Jean-Baptiste?

Jean-Baptiste kissed him gently on the lips. 'But I realised something much more important while I was away.' He paused. 'There's a gaping hole in my life that no amount of art or money can fill.'

Mahvand lay his head back on Jean-Baptiste's chest, ear pressed against the silk-cotton fibres of his shirt, listening to each heartbeat.

'I think ...' said Jean-Baptiste.

At that moment Shiva came into the room and locked eyes with Mahvand's.

'I'm falling ...'

Mahvand pressed his ear even closer to Jean-Baptiste's chest, as if it were the mouth of a giant conch shell and he was listening, not to the sound of his beating heart, but to the sound of the ocean.

'Never mind.'

Mahvand was stunned. He knew exactly what Jean-Baptiste was about to say. He opened his mouth to acknowledge the potential declaration of love but was silenced by an inner demon that had brought about his own infidelity and everything else in its wake. He lay curled up on top of Jean-Baptiste, immobilised. But inside he was still running. From Daimon. From Jean-Baptiste. From himself. He longed to fully let go in Jean-Baptiste's arms. To let the full horror of waking up next to Daimon's corpse wrack his body. To confess everything. He looked up at Jean-Baptiste, his eyes filled with tears.

'Perhaps you do feel the same way, after all,' said Jean-Baptiste.

SUNNY PASTURES

In early September, Mahvand, accompanied by Candy, went to visit Gran at the care home in the BNP stronghold of Dagenham. (Thankfully, Candy had had time to take stock and, all things considered, had backed off from insisting he go to the police about Daimon's death.) A plump, middle-aged woman with gold hoop earrings was waiting at reception, her hands clasped in front of her pristine white nurse's uniform. 'It's not every day we have visitors,' she said, chuckling and shaking their hands. 'Follow me.'

Brown carpet tiles, designed to withstand wear and tear, lined the corridors that turned and twisted, first this way, then the other, like the Cretan labyrinth that led Theseus to the Minotaur.

'I can't begin to tell you how much this visit means to Gracie,' said the nurse. 'She doesn't get many visitors.'

A framed watercolour of a poppy field was swallowed up by a sea of off-white wall. Mahvand feared that, if he stayed any length of time, he too would be swallowed up, washed away by the tidal wave of nothingness and all-pervading smell of disinfectant. Potted geraniums on the windowsills had been burnt to a crisp behind locked double-glazed fanlight windows. At the far end stood a Borg-like machine on wheels with a monitor and yards of convoluted rubber tubing. Mahvand imagined it placed strategically in a white-walled gallery space somewhere in East London, critics and members of the public alike clinking flutes of champagne while discussing the ethical and philosophical ramifications of the work.

He followed Candy (who clutched a bunch of lilies to her chest), who in turn followed the care worker, and seemed to descend ever deeper into the labyrinth. But another part of him was running in the opposite direction: down the corridor, out of the main entrance, through the car park and back into the street full of semi-detached, pebble-dash houses with Ford Escorts in the drive and England flags in the windows. The blaring sound of a TV set up ahead brought him back to reality as they entered the main shared living area.

It was more like walking into a high street florists or a chapel fit for a funeral. Flowers were everywhere: chrysanthemums, irises, roses, all in cut-glass vases. A framed portrait of Elizabeth II at her coronation took pride of place above the telly. And on a coffee table dotted with doilies and bone china cups and saucers decorated with English roses, was a spread Gran herself would have been proud of: scones, sausage rolls, sandwiches with the crusts cut off, a platter of dainty cakes, and a Battenberg and Victoria sponge.

'Ah could almost see mesel' living out me golden years somewhere leik this,' said Candy with a flash of perfectly manicured nails and a three hundred and sixty degree turn as if she was on stage at Madam Jojo's.

There was a slate noticeboard on the far wall. In chalk someone had written planned activities for the day: sing-song, arts and crafts, bingo, keep-fit. *At least they're not zoning out in front of the telly all day.* The care worker coughed. A silver-haired old man, in a bow tie and straw boater, gazed up from his newspaper. As if right on cue, he said, 'Welcome to Sunny Pastures, son. And may I take the opportunity to say it more than lives up to its name.'

A buxom, stocky woman with swollen ankles and crumpled brown stockings sat next to him, legs wide open, hunched over a frantic clicking of knitting needles. It was as if she was knitting away the drip, drip, moment by moment drudgery of her very existence, everything reduced to the click of two knitting needles and the emerging sleeve or front piece of some jumper or cardigan.

'This is Margaret,' said the care worker. 'Say hello, Margaret.'

Margaret stopped knitting and jerked into life. 'Hello, Margaret.'

The care worker chuckled. 'Why don't you tell our lovely visitors all about Southend?'

The elderly gentleman in the bow tie mouthed something to Margaret.

'Southend. Epping Forest. Folkestone. We get everywhere, don't we, Arnold?' said Margaret.

'Sunny Pastures. It's like the ad on the telly says. Home from home,' said Arnold.

There was something creepy in Arnold and Margaret's wholehearted endorsement of the care home. It was almost as if they were stooges who'd been planted there for his benefit.

The TV in the corner was blaring so loudly it was emitting a tinny, distorted sound. The picture was slightly fuzzy, as if the aerial wasn't tuned properly. A young woman with a child in a buggy was being interviewed by a fawning BBC royal correspondent about the recent death of Princess Diana. She'd come all the way from Penzance and had queued for more than five hours to sign the book of condolence. The camera zoomed in close as her eyes welled up with tears. 'It's true. What our Tony said. Diana was a goddess. Queen of Hearts. The People's Princess.' Her face began to crumple. 'I cried far more on hearing about Diana's death,' she sobbed, 'than I did at my own mother's funeral.'

'Here she is,' said the care worker, standing with her hands neatly clasped in front of her uniform. 'Sleeping Beauty.'

And there she was. Wigless, all the colour drained out of her, tufts of wispy white hair barely covering the crown of her head.

'Bless her. The arts and crafts activities must have taken it out of her,' said the care worker.

But what perturbed Mahvand the most were the hag hairs that had sprouted from her chin. She'd never been one to neglect her appearance.

'Gracie, love. Look who's here to see you!' The care worker crouched down and shook Gran's hand. 'Wake up, dear. You've got visitors.'

Gran woke with a start. She looked around, confused, as if she wasn't sure where she was. 'Visitors? What visitors? I never have no visitors.' She looked right through Mahvand as if he were a complete stranger. 'What are you gawping at?'

Mahvand felt a tightening inside his chest. She'd never failed to recognise him before.

'This is your grandson, Gracie,' said the care worker.

'I ain't got no grandson.'

The back of his throat began to throb.

'He's come all the way especially to see you,' said the care worker. 'All the way from?'

'Hampstead,' said Mahvand.

'Hampstead,' repeated the care worker.

''Ampstid?' said Gran, incredulously. She was staring right through him. 'Nah. Don't know him from Adam.' Then there was a spark of recognition. She reached for his hand, her eyes welling up with tears. 'Dear Lord. My Mahvand. I thought you was coming tomorrow, sweetheart.'

Mahvand knelt down and kissed Gran's cheeks. He'd forgotten how much he'd missed that familiar scent of Lily of the Valley.

'It's a lovely home, Mrs H.,' said Candy.

Gran looked as if she was about to say something then caught the care worker's eye. And stayed schtum.

'Gran, this is Candy,' said Mahvand.

'Alreet Mrs H.,' said Candy. 'What shall Ah dee wi these lilies, pet?'

'Why, who's popped their clogs?' snapped Gran.

The care worker snatched the flowers. 'I'll put them in a nice vase, shall I?' She turned to Gran. 'Where would you like Maureen to put these, dear? Shall I stick 'em near the telly? Oh, I think Lady Di would've liked that, don't you? It's as good as laying 'em at the gates of Kensington Palace, now, isn't it?'

Mahvand wondered who Maureen was and then realised the care worker was referring to herself in the third person.

'I don't give a monkey's. Fling 'em on Diana's passing hearse for all I care.'

'Gran!'

'I don't know what the world's coming to,' said Gran. Grown men reduced to tears. The flag flown at half-mast. If you ask me, Her Majesty's got the right idea sticking it out in Balmoral.'

'Gracie,' said Maureen, looking sternly at Gran.

'I'm sorry,' said Gran sheepishly. 'Yes. Of course. Maureen's right. I don't know what came over me. Thank you for the April showers.'

Mahvand turned to Candy. 'She means flowers.'

'I think they'd look lovely by the telly,' said Gran.

It was the first time Mahvand had ever seen Gran back down so quickly. When Maureen had gone off in search of a vase, Gran beckoned Mahvand to come closer. 'Come into the garden. Even the walls have ears in this place.'

Candy and Mahvand helped Gran up, each taking one of her arms as Gran shuffled towards the patio doors.

'Oh, lovely bit of fresh air,' said Gran, stepping outside. 'There's barely enough air to go round in there. Shouldn't wonder I'll be needing an oxygen mask before too long.' She looked at Candy, wetting her lower lip. ''Ere, you ain't got an oily rag, have you? Don't let you smoke inside, see.'

Candy opened her handbag and pulled out a pack of Benson and Hedges.

'Ohh, B&H. A girl after me own heart.'

They followed a winding path of crazy paving to a bench

under a tree heavy with crab apples. Concrete figurines were dotted at random about the garden. There was something faux-Edwardian about them. Something unbearably twee: one of a young girl wearing a bonnet and carrying a bunch of flowers, another of a young girl in a smock and wide-brimmed hat riding a donkey and cart. And one directly outside the patio doors that reminded Mahvand of Mary Poppins. A stone fountain in the centre of the garden, supported by a trio of chubby cherubs, released a thin trickle of water.

'A garden of young girls and cherubs,' said Gran ironically. 'They either reckon we've entered second childhood or are so bloody feeble minded we're all already away with the cherubs.' She paused. 'Suppose Arthur told you?'

'Told me what?' asked Mahvand.

'The investigation. Into the fire. What was it he said? Inconclusive. That's it.' She put on her posh telephone voice. 'The results from the investigation proved inconclusive.' She licked her lower lip. 'Whatever that means.'

Mahvand stared at the cherubs. All this time he'd hoped that they would have found the cause of the fire: an electrical fault, a cigarette accidentally dropped by Gran or Petula and left to smoulder. Inconclusive. That didn't help him come to terms with his loss nor quell a paranoid suspicion that Jean-Baptiste had somehow had a hand in what had happened.

'You're looking well, Mrs H.,' said Candy waiting for Gran to park herself on the bench.

'Am I fuck!' said Gran. 'If you only knew the half of it. That lot in there. They're trying to poison me. Keep giving me these pills.' She chuckled. 'Shove 'em down the khazi though, don't I.' Her left hand was shaking. 'They call me a troublemaker. Gracie Harbuckle – she's trouble, she is. That's what they say. All me insurance money from the house going down the drain, paying for the likes of Maureen, microwave meals and overcooked veg. This shithole costs an arm and a leg. You'd expect the five-star treatment, wouldn't you? But oh no. It's here comes Gracie, the troublemaker.'

Mahvand locked eyes with Candy then fixed his gaze on the concrete cherubs. How could he tell her they were only visiting?

Candy broke the silence. 'Ah knaa. Why divvent I gis yee a makeover, Mrs H.?'

'A makeover. At my age? Whatever for?'

'Every lass needs a decent bit of slap every noo an then. Te bring oot the inner glamour puss. What d'yer syah?'

'Go on, Gran. Candy's an expert. She spends at least two hours every day in front of the mirror putting on her face, don't you?'

'Let's just say, Mrs H.,' said Candy, raking her fingers through the acrylic fibres of her Samantha Fox wig, 'Ah divvent wake up in the morning looking leik the contender fre Miss World yee knaa see before yee.'

'Oh, go on then, dear. I'd love to see the look on that Margaret's cod and plaice when she sees me all dolled up.'

Candy opened her handbag and lined the beauty products up on the arm of the bench. Toy soldiers ready to enter into battle to beautify and push back the clock.

'Back in the day Ah always dreamed of working behind the myek-up counter in Debenhams in Newcastle city centre,' said Candy. 'Thought it wez the epitome of style an' sophistication.' She sighed. 'Sadly some things aren't meant te be.'

'Why ever not, dear?' asked Gran.

It looked like Candy was about to say something then thought better of it. She rooted through her make-up bag. 'Sensuous Rouge, Bewitching Coral, Angel Pink or English Rose?' She stood, hoisted up her black dress and knelt down on the crazy paving in front of Gran.

'Oh, English Rose. Them other ones sound like what some brass door from the streets o' Paris might wear,' said Gran, chuckling.

Candy's eyes began to well up. 'A perfect choice, Mrs. H.' She turned to Mahvand. 'That's what Ah always called our Lady Di. England's rose. When she shook hands wi' those young lads dying of AIDS, dressed in Catherine Walker …' Candy wiped a tear from her eye with the back of her hand. 'Just gissies us a mo, Mrs H.,' said Candy. 'Mutha's still in shock.'

'Who's mother?' asked Gran.

Mahvand interjected. 'What did we agree, Candy?'

'Well, if it upsets you that much, dear, I suppose I could try Angel Pink,' said Gran.

'You're our English Rose, Mrs H.,' said Candy, sniffing. 'And once I've waved me magic wand, you'll be the bloom of Sunny Pastures.'

It wasn't so long ago when Gran would wave at him in her wide-brimmed straw sunhat, clutching a pair of secateurs and a thorny stem. Before the arthritis took over. Before she started to forget things. When they still had a home. Mahvand looked at the neat rows of marigolds and the hydrangeas with ugly pink and blue flowers. Like old dears' rinses. Not a rose in sight.

Candy clipped Gran's hag hairs one by one then applied some lip balm to moisturise her lips. She showed her how to apply the lipstick to a brush and work outwards to the corners of the mouth then used another brush to apply lip liner and give Gran's lips definition. When she was finally done, she gave her hand mirror a good wipe and handed it to Gran.

'Noo gandie in the mirror' – Candy held up her own hand so the palm was facing her – 'an repeat after me. I have beautiful lips.'

'Candy, you're not behind the make-up counter in Debenhams now, you know,' said Mahvand.

'I want to go home,' said Gran.

Mahvand couldn't bear it. She reminded him of a baby fawn that needed its mother.

'Go on, Mrs H. Gandie in the mirror an' say "Aa've got very beautiful lips."'

Gran handed the mirror back to Candy. 'Can we go now?'

'I have very—' said Candy.

What is she playing at? 'Leave it, Candy,' said Mahvand.

Candy shrugged her shoulders and stood up. 'Jesus, man, I've laddered me tights!' She brushed herself down and rubbed her knees. 'That's what comes frem wearing thirty denier Pretty Polly stockings frem M&S.' She began to pack away her beauty products.

Mahvand placed his hand on top of Gran's. 'You can't go home, Gran,' he said softly.

'What you going on about?' said Gran.

'Don't you remember? There was a fire.'

'Stop confusing me. The pair of you. You think I don't know me arse from me left elbow.' Gran used the arm of the bench to push herself into a standing position. Her dowager's hump seemed even more pronounced. 'If you won't take me home, I'll–I'll bloody well take meself. You see if I don't.'

The patio doors opened. A sing-song voice called out, 'It's three o'clock. Time for tea and biscuits, Miss Harbuckle.'

Gran gripped Mahvand's arm. 'Get me out of here!'

'Gran, calm down. It's only tea and biscuits.'

'Is it fuck!' Gran turned to Candy. 'It's all your fault. Turning my own grandson against me. You're nothing but an evil cradle snatcher, you are.'

'Gran, stop it. Candy's gone out of her way to give you a lovely makeover.'

'Call a cheap bit of lippie a makeover?' Gran turned to Candy. 'Can't find someone your own age? That it?' said Gran.

'Mrs H., Ah can assure yee–' said Candy.

'For heaven's sake, Gran,' said Mahvand. 'Candy's not my girlfriend.'

'Don't tell me,' said Gran. 'You're already engaged. Well don't bother sending us an invite to the wedding. I shan't come.'

'Gran, don't you remember? I'm gay.'

A look of confusion crept across Gran's face.

'And I'm a transsexual,' said Candy.

'A trans what?' asked Gran, incredulously.

Candy articulated the word loudly and slowly. 'SEX-U-AL.'

'Wash your mouth out,' said Gran. 'You should be ashamed of yourself. Talking filth in front of a defenceless old lady.'

Maureen called from the patio doors. 'Maureen's got custard creams and bourbons, Mrs Harbuckle. Gracie's favourite.'

Mahvand thought he detected a sinister undertone in Maureen's sing-song voice. *Could Gran be right? Is Maureen really planning to poison her? And what about the Victoria sponge and Battenberg? Is it all merely for show?*

A crackled recording of Vera Lynn's *We'll Meet Again* started up from inside the care home. As if Gran needed reminding of German Messerschmitts bombing her two-up-two-down in Bethnal Green. 'I live with Jean-Baptiste now,' said Mahvand. 'The art dealer from Hampstead.'

Gran looked at Mahvand as if she'd forgotten who he was again.

'The one Petula fancied her chances with,' said Mahvand.

There was a glimmer of recognition in Gran's face. 'The sheep in wolf's clothing?' She paused. 'The tea leaves never lie, Mahvand.'

'He's helping me make a name for myself.'

'He who sups with the devil should have a long spoon.' Her face softened. 'You may think I'm the one who needs looking after. But really, sweetheart, it's you.'

'I have a big exhibition coming up, Gran. Two months' time. I want you to be there. If it wasn't for Jean-Baptiste—'

Maureen was walking down the path towards them, gold hoop earrings glistening in the sunshine, bingo wings mottled with the split and splat of English skin. 'There you all are. Isn't this lovely, all out in the garden together.' She paused. 'Ohh, Mrs Harbuckle,' she crowed, 'look at you! Don't you look a million dollars?'

Why can't she leave us alone? There was a strained jollity to Maureen's voice that Mahvand hadn't detected before. Would it vanish without a trace once they'd all gone?

'I won't be fobbed off with the promise of PG Tips and custard creams,' said Gran, her voice sliding from cockney to an embarrassing attempt at Received Pronunciation. 'Gracie's got more important things to do.'

Mahvand felt a lump in his throat at hearing Gran adopt one of Maureen's mannerisms and refer to herself in the third person.

'And what's that, dear?' asked Maureen.

'Wouldn't you like to know?' said Gran.

'I think it's high time we got Gracie Harbuckle indoors,' said Maureen sternly. 'Someone's getting a little bit tired and beginning to show off.'

'My Mahvand's come to take me home. That's what,' said Gran.

Mahvand exchanged a look with Candy.

Maureen put an arm around Gran and began steering her towards the patio doors.

'Get your thieving hands off me!' shouted Gran, showering Maureen with spit.

'Now, what have we said before about these little out-bursts, Mrs Harbuckle?' said Maureen.

'Don't think I don't know you're trying to bump us all off,' said Gran, her fingernails digging into his arm. 'Please. Don't go. Don't leave me to rot in this hellhole.'

Maureen grabbed Gran by the elbow. 'It's heartbreaking, I know,' she said to Mahvand with a well-worn look of sympathy. 'But it's probably for the best if you made yourselves scarce.'

Best for who? Mahvand looked into Gran's rheumy eyes, filled with tears. She'd lived through the Second World War, fought her own battles with yobs and drug dealers from the fourteenth floor of an East End tower block. Brought him up singlehandedly. And look where she'd ended up.

'She's better off here, love,' said Maureen. 'Where we can look after her. Properly.'

'This is your home now, Gran,' said Mahvand. The word 'home' stuck in his throat like a piece of grit.

Gran clung to him with a look of terror in her eyes. 'I'm begging you. Take me with you. Please, love. I can't bear it much more.'

Mahvand had asked Jean-Baptiste if Gran could move in with them. On more than several occasions. Each time, JB had smiled and said there's no more room at the inn.

'I would,' Mahvand said. 'But I can't. It's ... We'll visit again soon. I promise.'

Gran relinquished her grip. 'I love you, Mahvand. I've always loved you.' She paused. 'And your mother. She loves you. We both do.'

It was as if she was saying goodbye for the last time.

Mahvand wanted to say he loved her too, that she'd been more than a mother to him. That he didn't mind her funny ways, the dementia, nor the fact that she'd never really understood his devotion to comics. None of that mattered. Love. That's what mattered. That's all that mattered. But what he was doing felt like the most unloving thing in the world. Candy put an arm around his waist, and the painful constriction inside his chest and throat gave way to tears. As she led him down the side entrance of Sunny Pastures, he could hear Maureen saying, 'You're nothing but trouble, Gracie Harbuckle. Trouble by name. Trouble by nature. And when you get in, you can wipe that muck off your face for starters.'

MOON CHILD

When Mahvand arrived back at Jean-Baptiste's (he still couldn't call it home) his ears were assaulted by an onslaught of screeching violins coming from the surround sound system. *Threnody to the Victims of Hiroshima*. Jean-Baptiste had been playing a lot of modern classical music recently. Swirling the last of a rather expensive French red, he'd wax lyrical about the link between artistic genius and the diabolical. 'For the ancient Greeks,' he'd say, 'one's daemon was one's spirit of tutelage. One's inspiration. One's genius. Listen to your daemon, Mahvand. Let it show you the way.' If that particular piece of music was anything to go by, Mahvand thought it perhaps best not to follow his 'daemon'. It was like listening to a swarm of bees, thrumming against the inner chamber of your ear, while you wait in agony for the moment of climax when their fluid-filled abdomens curl and spasm, releasing the venom along the barbed shaft in one death-defining squirt.

The sliding glass doors were open at the rear and a cool breeze was blowing through the house. A breeze that seemed to blow a chill right through Mahvand's soul. On the glass table near the fireplace, a cut-crystal wine glass still held a few drops of Château Haut-Brion. The rim was marked with Jean-Baptiste's lip imprint. Next to it, on a hand mirror, was the drug paraphernalia for Jean-Baptiste's spiralling methamphetamine habit: a glass pipe blackened around the bowl, a butane gas lighter, and a sachet filled with shards of white crystals. *Strange that he never seems to get a come-down from meth. If anything, he seems in even better health now than when I first met him.* Further down on the exposed brickwork, next to Warhol's *Marilyn Monroe*, was a flashing light installation. 'PURPLE' flashed on and off in yellow light. Daimon's light installation. *What's it doing here?* Mahvand was hit by a wave of nausea and reached out to a section of the fibreglass sculpture of a human heart near the fireplace.

He'd worked hard trying to convince himself he'd never been at Daimon's apartment that night. Never woken up to a corpse and a bloodstained pillow. Never dreamt of washing his hands, only to discover his own palms were bleeding like the stigmata of saints of old. The word on the installation changed from PURPLE to MURDERER. The colour from yellow to red. Mahvand looked again. It had changed back to PURPLE.

'How was your grandmother?'

Mahvand took a step back and nearly lost his balance. Jean-Baptiste was at the top of the spiral staircase, dressed in a Paul Smith pinstripe suit, his face in shadow.

Mahvand felt a surge of adrenaline and tried to control the tremor in his voice. 'I didn't think light installations were your kind of thing.'

As Jean-Baptiste took the Perspex steps one at a time, the screeching violins faded away. He seemed to glide across the white marble flooring. Mahvand noticed the beads of perspiration on his forehead.

'Daimon left it to me in his will. Along with the celebrity-signed urinal. It was delivered this afternoon.' He paused. 'Thought it might be more suited to the bedroom. What do you think?'

It will be the last thing I see before falling asleep. The first thing I see in the morning.

'There's something else,' said Jean-Baptiste, grinding his teeth, 'you should see.'

Mahvand knew that he knew. Just not how much he knew. Jean-Baptiste grabbed Mahvand's wrist and led him into the hallway. His hand felt clammy. Mahvand was tempted to pull in the opposite direction but feared it would turn into a tug of war. And he knew who'd win that. A psychopath on meth was no fair contest. He scrabbled around in his brain for an excuse. Any excuse: Gran. A headache. His asthma. But he feared whatever excuse he came up with would be taken as an admission of guilt. They stopped outside the door that led to the basement. Jean-Baptiste removed the bunch of keys from his shorts pocket and caressed each key in turn as if they were beads on a rosary. He stopped at one, locked eyes with Mahvand, placed it in the lock and slowly turned. The door opened.

'I'm not feeling so good,' said Mahvand.

Mahvand eyed the keys, the beads of sweat on Jean-Baptiste's forehead, the dark descent to the basement. He imagined himself charging at Jean-Baptiste head first like a bull towards its matador, but his survival instinct kicked in a moment too late. His head was already ducking down in supplication, his fingers felt their way along the rough surface of the brick wall, a cobweb caught his face and he carried bits of it down with him in his mouth. He resigned himself to his fate.

When Mahvand reached the bottom of the staircase, the bright glare of a single light bulb lit up a series of enlarged black-and-white photographs. Each photograph seemed taken at an odd angle or was out of focus. They were all pegged onto a piece of wire that stretched from one end of the basement to the other. The young man in the photographs looked half-demented – grinning inanely with a manic look in his eye. Or else his face was creased up with laughter. Or was it pain? Mahvand stepped closer and examined the photograph with the strange object. Only then did he realise. He was the young man in the photograph. He'd come face to face with a blurred and intoxicated version of himself. And all the memories of that last night spent with Daimon came rushing back.

'Something the matter?' asked Jean-Baptiste.

There he was in black and white, strung up like pieces of meat in Jean-Baptiste's basement abattoir. The camera never lies. And there, half-naked, making a lewd gesture with that fourteenth-century wooden carving, peeing in Daimon's bathroom. And most incriminating of all, snorting a big fat line of cocaine off Daimon's antique Indian table. There were photos of Daimon too. The ones he'd taken. Images he'd felt that at the time had captured that unsettling yet undeniably erotic blend of vulnerability and defiance. Now they just seemed ghoulish. Daimon brought back from the dead with the aid of film-developing chemicals and the womb of a darkroom.

'Who knew?' said Jean-Baptiste. 'A natural talent behind the lens. Well, you certainly capture the interplay of light and dark in a unique way.'

'How could you?' said Mahvand. 'Have you no respect for the dead?'

'I think you'll find, *mon cher*, that the question is – did he?'

How had he missed them? Interspersed with the photographs of himself and Daimon were ones of complete strangers. Eyes closed. Some encased in zipped body bags. They were mostly old folk, but one stood out from the rest; it was of a young child in an open casket clutching a teddy. Corpses all, awaiting a falling clod of earth or temperatures hot enough to incinerate bone, destined for much greater things than a morgue or a crematorium just a slip road off the M25. If Daimon had lived, they were to form the backbone of his much-hyped exhibition, *Death Becomes You*. Mahvand looked at the one of the young girl with her soft toy, eyes closed, hands crossed on her chest as if in prayer. *Is nothing sacred?* Mahvand snatched at the photographs, pulling them from their pegs.

Jean-Baptiste grabbed him just above the elbow. 'Granted, the photos of the dead are a bit... what's the English expression?' He paused. 'Beyond the pale. But the photographs of yourself. They'd make a marvellous addition to your own exhibition, don't you think?'

Mahvand was finding it difficult to catch his breath. 'I–I can explain.'

'Shame there's not one of you and Daimon doing it doggy-style just before he died. Death. Sex. Celebrity.' He ran his forefinger along the edge of the mirror and examined the dust. 'If I could distil the essence, I'd bottle it and bring out my own perfume.'

Mahvand broke away. 'How did you—'

'Find the camera?' He laughed. 'Let's just say Shiva must have smelled a rat. I caught him scratching at a small mound of earth in the garden this morning.'

'I was going to tell you,' said Mahvand.

'No need. I understand. It was a meeting of minds. Two artists forging a common bond. Nothing more.'

Jean-Baptiste unpegged the photograph of Mahvand half-naked, making the lewd gesture with the fourteenth-century wood carving.

'He was high,' said Mahvand.

'And you weren't?'

'You know he's a cokehead.'

'Was,' said Jean-Baptiste.

'Sorry?'

'Was. As in he is no longer. As in he's dead.' A pause. 'He doesn't have a say in the matter, does he?' He paused. 'But really, it all boils down to one very simple question.'

'Can we go back upstairs and discuss this civilly?'

'Who supplied the cocaine?' Jean-Baptiste had begun to take small steps towards Mahvand, who was backing off towards the rubber cast of the fallen angel.

Mahvand could smell the toxic fumes of meth on Jean-Baptiste's breath.

'Cause of death,' said Jean-Baptiste. 'Heart attack. Large amounts of pure cocaine ingested. Underlying atherosclerotic heart disease.'

'He's an addict.'

'With a heart condition,' said J.B

'I didn't know,' said Mahvand.

'Would that have made a difference?'

'To what?'

'You tell me,' said Jean-Baptiste.

'Why ask if you already know the answer.'

'I want to hear it. From you.'

'He'd have got it from someone else,' said Mahvand.

'But he didn't, did he?'

'What?'

'Get it from someone else,' said Jean-Baptiste.

'Where there's a will, there's a way. Isn't that your dictum?'

'Say it.'

'If I'd known he had a heart condition—'

'Say it.'

'If I could go back. Right what's wrong.'

'Say it!'

'Fine,' said Mahvand, his back pressed against the rubber cast of the fallen angel. 'I supplied the coke. I called your dealer when you were in New York. Satisfied?'

Jean-Baptiste smiled. 'I knew all along you had it in you.'

Mahvand wanted to lash out, hit him hard, but his fingers refused to do his bidding and curl into a fist. So he used his tongue instead. 'At least with Daimon it was more than just a fuck.'

Mahvand didn't see Jean-Baptiste's hand coming as it struck him hard across the face.

'Forty-five thousand,' said Jean-Baptiste.

Mahvand cupped his hand to dull the stinging sensation across the right side of his face, the ringing in his right ear.

'*Mankind as a Cancer on the Face of the Earth*. Forty-five thousand. I sold it to a buyer from New York. Thought you'd like to know.'

Jean-Baptiste grabbed Mahvand's wrists and pulled him across the basement until he was standing in front of an oval-shaped mirror. The ceramic frame was adorned with bare-breasted nymphs and mermaids writhing like lustful goddesses in a Hindu temple. A faint crack ran diagonally across the glass. Mahvand stared at his own pale reflection, tears welling up in his eyes. Jean-Baptiste's fingers had left their mark across his cheek and they now held Mahvand firmly in an arm lock. The mirror misted over with the warmth of his breath. He gripped Mahvand's jaw with the other hand and leant forward, his head level with Mahvand's, pressing hard against it so they appeared like some weird aberration of Siamese twins. Mahvand stared at Jean-Baptiste's reflection in the mirror: the clenched jaw, gritted teeth, and sallow cheeks. Two shining glints of light in his dark, unshaven face, in turn, stared back at him.

'A prophet of the new dawn. That was your destiny. It was foretold me in a sacred ritual.'

Mahvand wrestled against Jean-Baptiste's firm grip. 'You're hurting me.'

'"*He shall come from humble beginnings*" the voice said.' Then Jean-Baptiste uttered some words in a language completely unfamiliar to Mahvand.

The mirror remained shrouded in mist, but it seemed to Mahvand that the ceramic border was undulating with movement; the nymphs and mermaids were breathing, breasts heaving, and lips mouthing sweet nothings. As with sailors of yore, they toyed with their Pre-Raphaelite locks and whispered of silver bells and cockle shells and a life lived full fathom five. *Has Jean-Baptiste put a spell on the mirror? On me? Is the basement—?* A moment later and he simply didn't care. He felt a familiar sensation of falling and wanted more than anything to succumb.

'"*He shall dabble in the ancient art of words and images.*"'

Mahvand began to make out the shape of a skull and crossbones in the misted pane of glass.

'"*He shall hail from that part of the world formerly known as Persia. And his name shall mean Light of the Moon.*"'

The more Mahvand kicked and struggled, the more Jean-Baptiste tightened his vice-like grip.

'*La lumière de la lune*! You were my moon child. Through me, you were to create a piece of art so divinely diabolical that whoever witnessed it would fall head over heels in love with the realm of dark and shadow.'

The mist gradually began to clear. The glass wobbled like water. Scales on the mermaid's tails swished this way then that, emitting a rainbow spectrum of light, like oil on water. The nymphs seemed to writhe rhythmically, bewitching him with a gentle pelvic thrusting. 'Mahvand,' they called. 'Light of the moon!' *Am I slowly losing my mind?* The liquid mercury suddenly turned back to glass. Once again, Mahvand found himself looking at himself, looking at Jean-Baptiste, looking back at him in the looking glass.

'Do you think I give a fuck that you were unfaithful?' said Jean-Baptiste. 'It has nothing to do with sex. Nothing. You weakened the transmission. Diluted the alchemical relationship between master and disciple.' He suddenly yelled. 'You're nothing! Nothing without me.'

Their reflection became fainter and fainter, until it was nothing more than a ghostly imprint on the glass. Fearing his actual physical demise, Mahvand glanced down to check he was still all there. He received the sight of Jean-Baptiste's nicotine-stained fingers, still pressing firmly against his mouth, with mixed blessings. Glancing back at the mirror, an image began to form. Mahvand shut his eyes tight and, just as he used to do as a child, wished he was in the teleportation machine from Star Trek.

'Open your eyes!'

Mahvand stared at the mirror with a mixture of horror and fascination. An aerial view of London dissolved back into the ripples of water to give birth to a strange dome-like structure. It looked like some huge alien spaceship had landed somewhere south of the river. Then, as if a camera was panning back, he saw it all from a distance: the jubilant throngs of people waiting in the cold on the banks of the Thames, crammed along the length and breadth of Tower Bridge, dancing in the fountain at Trafalgar Square. It suddenly dawned on Mahvand what he was witnessing – New Year's Eve celebrations at the completed Millennium Dome. The hands of the clock face on Big Ben chimed twelve and an explosion of fireworks lit up the sky. Then, gradually, the image of the Millennium Dome superseded the comets, shooting stars and Catherine wheels. Inside, trapeze artists and spinning acrobats with reams of brightly coloured ribbon pirouetted and did the splits in mid-air. Mahvand saw himself sitting high up in a box, surrounded by a host of New Labour politicians, minor royals and celebrities that he recognised from Saturday night light entertainment shows. He was wearing a shredded T-shirt bearing the symbol of the skull and crossbones. There was no sign of Jean-Baptiste.

'Ever since I came back from New York I could never fuck another vision out of you. Why is that, do you think?'

'I don't need you to fuck another vision out of me. On that score, you are clearly surplus to requirement.'

A cheer rose from the crowd as giant sparklers inside the dome lit up the number 2000.

'I'll tell you why!' he yelled. 'Because you were too busy whoring your way around London's art scene to even think about the gift you were squandering.'

The looking glass, once again, began to wobble like water, partially obscuring Mahvand's final and enduring image: a black fibreglass sculpture of some alien-like being whose egg-shaped head touched the roof of the dome and glistened with particles of black light. Jean-Baptiste released his grip. Mahvand fell to the floor gasping for air. But now he fully understood; all had been revealed. Jean-Baptiste was right; this was his destiny. He would be commissioned to produce a piece of art for the Millennium Dome. And in the process, there was no doubt that he would lose everything he had ever held dear.

Jean-Baptiste's expression softened. He hesitated. A look of confusion came and went, like a passing shadow, before his face assumed that taut, mask-like quality. 'You know, I think I'm done here.' He stood up and wiped his hands on his trousers as if he was wiping away his part in the relationship. 'Consider the exhibition cancelled. Find your own gallery space, curators, PR men, sponsorship. Oh, I forgot. You don't know anyone, do you? Or rather you did. But, well, thanks to you, now he's dead, isn't he?'

Jean-Baptiste turned his back and climbed the rickety staircase, ducking to avoid the swinging light bulb on the piece of cable wire. At the top of the stairs, he called out. '*Bonne chance!*' The way he said it felt like a curse.

Mahvand stared vacantly at the rubber cast of the fallen angel at the far end of the basement and, for the first time, felt an unexpected tenderness towards it.

BELIAL

A few weeks later, Mahvand moved out of Jean-Baptiste's and into Candy's spare room in some nether region of Wood Green. To take his mind off things, he'd gone to an alternative comics convention near London Bridge, thinking he might bump into Octavi. Instead, he'd ended up wandering around by himself, feeling like the artist he'd been had fallen by the wayside. RIP. Here lay comics artist Mahvand Amirzadeh. Died 1997. Cause of death: lack of artistic integrity. But who was he now? A conceptual artist? Papier mâchéist? Some Nostradamus freak who relied on sex-induced visions of the apocalypse to create anything? He had a month to vacate the studio in Shoreditch, the forty-five thousand pound deal on *Mankind as a Cancer on the Face of the Earth* had somehow fallen through, and now that Jean-Baptiste had dropped him, not a single gallery owner was interested in showcasing his work.

Still, despite his initial deep-seated reservations, he clung to the prophetic vision he had witnessed in that mirror in Jean-Baptiste's basement, in the hope that it signified a potential shift towards greater artistic recognition. He even managed to begin work on a new artistic project: a triptych of papier mâché superhero sculptures committing heinous crimes. Two stood half-finished in his studio like albatrosses about to jump off the edge of a cliff. The third stood propped up at the back of the sex shop next to the blow-up doll of Brad Pitt – a five-foot-high papier mâché sculpture of a red-eyed, leather-clad-fisted Batman in the end throes of strangling Robin.

It was Tuesday afternoon in early October. Mahvand had finished his early shift in the bookshop (Candy having threatened the manager with walking out herself if he refused to take Mahvand back), nibbled his way through his ham, mustard and tomato sandwiches on a wet bench in Phoenix Gardens and come back to help Candy with a new delivery of penis pump enlargers.

A middle-aged man in a suit, with a port-wine birthmark across the left side of his face, was lurking in the watersports porn section. Mahvand just hoped he wasn't Soho's infamous small-dicked phantom flasher Candy had said was doing the rounds yet again, and passed her a Big Boy Penis Pump. She scanned it in at the till.

'D'yer want Mutha te touch up those dark circles for yee, pet?' Candy reached for her Hermes handbag that she'd got for a fraction of the price from an old friend who was now serving time for armed robbery in Pentonville prison. 'Ahm not sure the heroin-chic look is quite what gets our customers parting wi' their hard-earned cash.'

'Well if it's one of those buff, Barbie doll Brazilians you're after, you should save me the bother and just scour the escort section of *Boyz* or *QX* magazine,' said Mahvand. He slid a pair of scissors along another brown box, peeled off the brown tape, took out a small pot of 'Miraculous

Penis Enlargement Oil', and slammed it down on the counter.

'Look, Ah knaa you're in mourning for what never wez but' – she clasped her hand on top of his – 'yee need te move on, pet.'

'Maybe if I hadn't been kept awake by your bedhead slamming against the bedroom wall for the last four nights, I might just be able to.'

Candy put the scanner down on the counter and placed her hand on top of his. 'Yee knew aal aboot Trevor before yee moved in.'

It was true. She'd told him about Trevor, the Nigerian taxi driver from Lewisham. How he'd write sonnets to her in strict iambic pentameter on lavender-scented paper in his black cab, serenade her on the ukulele his grandfather had passed down to his father and so on down to him. She just forgot to mention Trevor'd be round her gaff in Wood Green most nights of the week. And that in between the intermittent creaking of bed springs, banging of metal bed head against the wall, Candy's wailing, and Trevor's foul-mouthed expletives at the moment of climax, he'd lie wide awake on his blow-up mattress in the front room ruminating on what might have been.

'Anyways, who wez it once said tha' celebrity is the mask tha' eats away at the face? If yee ask me, you're better off oot of it, pet. Yer handsome profile's still intact. Not even a slight wearing away of earlobe or nose cartilage. And no sign yet of any skull showing through.'

'Great. Penniless. Stuck in a dead-end job. With my one and only dream of achieving a modicum of success as an artist gone up in smoke.' He handed Candy another penis pump. 'Give me the flesh-eating mask any day.'

Candy reached for her flask of gin under the counter and took a swig. 'Oh, Mahvand, if Ah could adopt yee reet here an now on this very spot, believe me, Ah would.' Her eyes filled with tears. 'You're the son Ah always dreamed of having. Me aan flesh and blood, queer through an' through. I'd fight tooth and nail fre yee te become the artist yee want te be.'

Right then he wanted Candy to take him to her silicon-implanted breasts. To tell him everything would be alright. That a mother's love could conquer all.

'When Paul O'Grady made it on te *Woman's Hour* then went on to win that award for *An Evening with Lily Savage*, divvent think fre just one minute tha' Ah wasn't screaming inside. Tha should hev been me!' She pulled a pack of Benson and Hedges out of her cleavage, lit one and inhaled deeply. 'Aal those working men's pubs, gay bars, hecklers, missiles thrown on stage, picking mesel' up and dusting mesel' doon. Aal in the hope tha' one day *this* Candy Darling, just like the Warhol superstar, would be a household name.'

'But you have made it! Candy Darling. Sex shop impresario. Cabaret artiste. Entertainer extraordinaire. You said so yourself.'

Candy let out a deep sigh. 'Yee know, pet, the secret te success is redefining it fre yourself. Divvent let anyone else call the shots. Ah look at mesel' now in the dressing room mirror, an' d'yer know what? Ah leik what Ah see, man. Warts an' all. Slap o' no slap.' She laughed. 'Aye, wish Ah could have said the same a few years back.' She paused. ''Ere, hand Mutha another one of them penis pumps.'

'Excuse me.' The man with the birthmark had sauntered over. His clavicle jutted out from the open collar of his shirt, reminding Mahvand of the hooked wishing bone Gran would pull from the turkey each Christmas.

'If I could have a word,' he said.

Candy looked up. 'What can Ah get yee, pet? One o' them watersports videos wez it? Vintage, aal American or British beef? Te my mind, piss is piss, but some punters are quite particular when it comes te the nationality o' the pissee, while others are into what you might call "Period Piss", if yee catch my drift.'

The man cleared his throat.

'By the way, Ah can't do "Buy One Get One Free" – tha' offer wez up Friday last – but there's a discount o' ten per cent if yee purchase it alongside a twelve-inch rubber truncheon.'

'It's nothing like that, madam.'

'Wheyaye. Come on, yee can tell Mutha. Ne need te beat around the bush, man.' She raised her hands to the ceiling, bangles jangling, as if she was on stage at Madam Jojo's, and laughed. 'Everything's all oot in the open doon here. Wouldn't yee say, Mahvand?'

Mahvand blushed. Whether it was Candy's over the top theatrics, or her rap on all things that by rights should be flushed down the loo, he couldn't tell.

'Are you Mahvand? Mahvand Amirzadeh?' said the man.

Mahvand could feel his heart pounding.

'Who wants te knaa?' asked Candy, placing both hands on the counter.

'Detective Inspector White, madam. Just making routine inquiries.'

Mahvand nodded and averted his gaze. Floaters appeared in his field of vision. He was struck by a wave of nausea. This was it. The moment he'd dreaded, ever since fleeing Daimon's apartment, had arrived. He'd be handcuffed, escorted out of Soho Books and bundled into the back of a police van.

'Mr Amirzadeh, are you aware of the death of conceptual artist and well-known socialite, Daimon Mount-Stuart?

Mahvand made the mistake of looking up at DI White. Two grey eyes stared back at him. Eyes that reduced him to part of a puzzle that needed to be solved.

Candy cleared her throat. 'What's tha got te dee with our Mahvand, Constable?'

'Detective. And you would be, Miss …?'

'Darling.' She extended her right hand. 'Candy Darling. Cabaret artiste. Sex shop impresario. Entertainer extra-ordinaire. Pleased te meet yer acquaintance.' Her hand hovered awkwardly in mid-air. 'Who wez it yee said had popped his clogs, Inspector?'

'Daimon Mount-Stuart.' He turned to Mahvand. 'Where were you, Mr Amirzadeh, between the hours of 8 p.m. on Saturday 26th July and midday on Sunday 27th?'

Mahvand stared blankly back at White. Part of him wanted to admit to everything right there and then. The guilt and deceit was exhausting.

'If truth be told, Inspector,' said Candy, 'this one can hardly remember what he had fre breakfast. Memory leik a sieve.'

White scratched at his birthmark.

Candy placed a perfectly manicured hand on her cleavage. 'How could Mutha forget?' She turned to Mahvand. 'Yee were wi' me. Remember? Saturday night. At Madam Jojo's. Diva night. Then we got the night bus back te mine.'

'Madam. Would you kindly stay out of this.' White took a notepad from the inside pocket of his trench coat. 'You can vouch for that can you, Mr Amirzadeh?'

The events that had led up to Daimon's death came crashing back. 'Yes. I was there,' said Mahvand. 'I was at Madam Jojo's.'

Candy interjected. 'I wez impersonating Shirley Bassey. *The* Miss Dame Shirley Bassey. No one ever forgets Mutha's Shirley Bassey impression, Inspector. Mahvand here's been a leiflong fan, haven't yee, pet?' She lifted the latch and came out from behind the counter. She placed both hands on her hips, sauntered over to White and draped an arm over the detective's shoulder as if it was a feather boa. 'Ah may not be Mystic Meg, but me female instinct tells me you're not particularly enamoured o' the Welsh diva, Inspector.'

'Can't say I am, Miss Darling. But please, will you allow Mr Amirzadeh to speak for himself. Or, if you'd rather, we can conduct the investigation at West End Central Police Station.'

'Who did you say had died?' asked Mahvand.

'Daimon Mount-Stuart. One of London's finest conceptual artists, by all accounts.' He cleared his throat. 'Prefer a nice Monet or Turner myself. Still, each to his own.'

'Ah knaa what yee mean, Inspector. *The Poppy Field Near Argenteuil. Water Lilies. The Grand Canal, Venice.* It's enough te bring tears te yer eyes, man.'

Mahvand somehow doubted Candy's blatant attempt to appeal to the detective's conservative taste in watercolours and landscapes would be enough to win him over.

'As fre that filth they pass off as modern art,' said Candy. 'The portrait of Myra Hindley painted wi' little children's handprints, upside doon Christmas trees, a dog's turd in a white-walled room. Pure filth. What's the world coming te, eh?'

White pulled a book from another inside pocket: a little black book with an image of the skull and crossbones symbol on the front cover.

'A few days ago a cabbie dropped it off in a large brown envelope at a police station in Farringdon. Gibbering wreck, he was. Mumbling something about demonic entities, with a crazed look in his eyes.'

Mahvand knew exactly who he was talking about.

'Seems he'd been holding onto it for quite some time. We interviewed its author yesterday morning. A Mr Lebeau-Chevalier. Residence: Golden Dawn, Frognal, Hampstead.'

So that's how they tracked Jean-Baptiste down so quickly. Has Jean-Baptiste told them everything?

'Mr Chevalier has been ruled out of the investigation. Passenger information released from United Airlines clearly shows he was flying back from New York at the time.'

'Ah hardly see how anything o' this has te dee wi' the employees at Soho Books, Inspector,' said Candy haughtily.

'Mr Amirzadeh, Monsieur Lebeau-Chevalier has already confirmed that you did indeed have relations' – White cleared his throat – 'of a sexual nature with him. And until quite recently, lived with him as his' – He paused – 'homosexual lover at his residence in Frognal.'

'What has any of this to do with a murder enquiry?' asked Mahvand.

'Who said anything about a murder enquiry?' said White.

'Let's call a spade a spade, Inspector. You'd hardly be questioning his lordship 'ere if Mount-whatever-his-name-is had snuffed it in his sleep,' said Candy. 'Now, would you?'

'Mr Amirzadeh, did you also, at any time, meet, or indeed have sexual relations with the deceased, Mr Mount-Stuart?'

'This is preposterous, Inspector,' said Candy. 'You can't go willy-nilly accusing upstanding pillars of the community of necrophilia.'

Mahvand looked the detective in the eye. He thought about point-blankly denying he'd ever met Daimon. But what if they'd been papped at a gallery or restaurant by the paparazzi? What if, despite his frantic attempts to wipe his own fingerprints from Daimon's apartment, the police had still managed to find some? Or they asked to test his DNA? 'I'm familiar with some of Mount-Stuart's work, yes.' He paused. 'I recall that we did meet up on a couple of occasions. Purely on a professional basis. To discuss art. I must say, I'm shocked to hear of his passing.'

'Then you are aware, Mr Amirzadeh, that the deceased was …' he paused for dramatic effect, 'an amputee?'

'Does a young lad who's devoted to his gran and toils away in a second-rate bookshop look leik he'd be rubbing shoulders wi' amputated celebrities from the London art scene, Inspector?' said Candy.

'Were you also aware that on his remaining forearm Mr Mount-Stuart bore the exact same tattoo that appears on Mr Lebeau-Chevalier's lower back?'

'He did?' asked Mahvand, who figured Jean-Baptiste must have been subjected to a full strip search and hoped the same fate didn't await him.

'Commonly known as an astrological symbol, the tattoo is also used in occult circles to denote the misuse of drugs and sorcery,' said White. 'Would you please unbutton both shirt sleeves, young man, and roll them up to your elbows.'

'Detective, this is preposterous,' said Candy. 'Are yee suggesting my employee, who Ah hasten te add is one o' the most ordinary, conscientious an hard-working employees I've ever had the good fortune o' hiring, is part of some bizarre underground cult?'

'Just pursuing a line of enquiry, madam.'

Mahvand rolled up both sleeves.

'Now, would you mind bending over and lifting up your shirt?' said White.

Mahvand complied but couldn't help thinking this gave a whole new meaning to the word 'shirt-lifter'.

'There goes tha' line of enquiry,' said Candy smugly.

White opened his mouth as if to say something. Then it seemed he thought better of it. He snapped his notepad shut and placed it back in his inside pocket. 'Well, Miss Darling. Mr Amirzadeh. That's all for now.' He pressed his business card firmly in Mahvand's palm. 'If anything else comes to mind, call me.' He nodded his head towards the rear of the shop. 'By the way. The papier mâché sculpture. Local supplier is it?'

'Oh, tha',' said Candy breezily. 'Just summat we're trying oot. Seeing if we can muster up some interest before launching a new superhero fetish wear line. Yee knaa, spandex underwear, men's tights, face masks, tha' sort o thing.'

'Bit macabre for a sex shop, don't you think,' said White, his eyes narrowing perceptibly. He exaggerated each syllable of the next word. 'STRANG-U-LA-TION.'

'Niwor heard o' breath control, Detective?' replied Candy tartly. 'Edge play, BDSM? At Soho Books, we pride ourselves on catering fre every erotic fixation, every repressed dark desire.' She paused. 'An what is it tha' floats yer boat, Detective? Simulated interrogation scenes?'

White visibly stiffened. 'Thank you for your time,' he said, and made his way up the staircase.

Mahvand went upstairs to check that the detective wasn't lurking somewhere in the bookshop then came back down. Candy was on the phone to the manager of Madam Jojo's, alerting him, in hushed tones, of White's imminent arrival.

'There's something untoward about tha' copper,' said Candy. 'He gives me the creeps.'

'A pig is a pig,' said Mahvand. 'They're all creeps. But Mutha, you were brilliant back there. You deserve an Oscar.' He paused. 'You don't think I should hand myself in?'

'Too late for tha' now, sweet pea. I'd be done mesel'. For perverting the course o' friggin justice.' She paused. 'Then we'd both be looking at a hefty stint behind bars at Her Majesty's pleasure.'

'I'm sorry, Candy.' Mahvand began pacing up and down.

'Yee knaa what this means, divvent yee?' she said.

'I don't know what anything means anymore.'

'Ahm gonna have te get Connie Lingus te dee yer shifts upstairs for a while.'

'You mean I'm a fugitive?'

'Now did Ah say tha'?'

Mahvand was on the verge of tears.

'Will yee quit with the theatrics, dowtah. Look, yee can keep house. Be me seamstress. I'll teach yee te sew sequins.' Candy took a flask out from under the counter, unscrewed the top and took a swig.

Mahvand heard footsteps on the stairs. *Has White reconsidered? Does he intend to take me to the local police station for further questioning?* Mahvand wasn't willing to find out. His eyes darted from the changing room to the exit door and then to Candy behind the counter.

'Quick!' he hissed.

Candy instinctively seemed to know what he meant, lifted up the latch door to the counter and Mahvand pushed his way past her and ducked down. He was face to face with a shop mannequin's head and something that resembled a furry ferret – of course, the Samantha Fox wig – a stash of porn, currently banned under customs and excise regulations, and Candy's flask of mother's ruin. All he could hear was the sound of his own breathing and those heavy footsteps on the stairs. All he could think of was the drone of White's voice, the penetrating gaze of those grey eyes.

'Can Ah help yee?' It was Candy's voice, guarded, disdainful. *Why isn't she trying to win him over with her wit and charm?*

'I don't think we've been introduced,' said the other voice.

Mahvand pictured the diamond cufflinks and that vintage watch, which he had only recently discovered was made by Breguet (the founder of whom made pieces for both Louis XVI and his queen, Marie Antoinette). He was tempted to spring up and jump the barricade with all the zeal of an eighteenth-century French revolutionary. But, for now, he would remain behind the counter and let Candy do the dirty work.

'There's no need,' said Candy. 'Ah knaa who yee are. Mutha never forgets a voice.'

'You must be Miss Darling,' said Jean-Baptiste. 'Mahvand always spoke most highly of you, *mademoiselle.*'

'Be tha as it may. You've no reet coming here after what yee did te him.'

'There's two sides to every story, Miss Darling.'

'Taking the lad in. Filling his head wi' fantasies o' artistic grandeur. Then leaving him destitute an' heartbroken. Yee ought te be ashamed of yourself. A man of yer age an' background.'

'Mahvand is a grown man,' said Jean-Baptiste. 'There's no need to play Mother Hubbard, Miss Darling.'

'There's every need. Especially when a Great Dark Man is on the prowl.'

Mahvand couldn't resist it and peeked above the counter top. Jean-Baptiste had his back to him but he recognised the Saville Row suit, Prada shoes and slicked-back hair.

'I came to warn the boy,' said Jean-Baptiste.

'Well, as yee can see. His lordship's not 'ere, is he?' said Candy.

'Just tell him. Tell him I need to see him.'

Mahvand stood up. 'You can see me now.'

'I owe you an explanation, *mon cher*,' said Jean-Baptiste.

'Stay away from me,' said Mahvand.

'Yee heard him, Casanova,' said Candy, hands on hips. 'Go on. Sling yer hook.'

Mahvand came out from behind the counter, his hands beginning to shake, and stood in front of the *Men in Uniform* porn videos. Candy put an arm around his shoulders.

'Please. We need to talk.' Jean-Baptiste looked suspiciously at Candy. 'But not here.'

'What you've got te say te his lordship, yee can say in front o' me,' said Candy.

Jean-Baptiste gazed up at the ceiling. 'Is that what you want for him? Selling hardbacks on film stars, famous artists and celebrities above a glorified Ann Summers? Pissing his life away, all the while regretting that he'd blown his only chance of becoming a celebrity himself.'

'And what is it yee want fre him?' asked Candy. 'Discarding friends an' family leik the wrapping on a McBurger while he tramples on the backs of others te get te where yee want him te be.'

Jean-Baptiste held out his hand to Mahvand. 'Let's discuss this civilly. Over lunch. I've reserved a table at The Ivy.'

'His lordship's already eaten,' said Candy. 'His usual. Ham, mustard and tomato sandwiches. Ne butter. White bread. Mother's Pride. All washed down with a couple o' cans o' Coca Cola on a park bench in Phoenix Gardens. But yee probably wouldn't knaa aboot any o' that. You're not interested in the real Mahvand. Never have been, have yee?'

'Candy's right,' said Mahvand. 'I'm not going anywhere. You wouldn't listen when I tried to explain about Daimon. Why should I listen now?'

'I kept things from you with good reason,' said Jean-Baptiste.

Mahvand stepped back.

'Please,' said Jean-Baptiste, holding out his hand. 'Let me make amends.'

'Yee heard what he said,' said Candy. 'Ah think you'll find, monsieur, the exit is on street level.' She gestured towards the staircase. '*Au revoir.*'

'You leave me no alternative then. *The Book of Belial.*' Jean-Baptiste paused as if about to regret what he was going to say. 'I wrote it. And didn't write it.'

'What stands on four legs in the morning, two legs at midday an' three in the evening?' said Candy.

Jean-Baptiste glowered at Candy.

'Look, if Ah need a riddle, I'll gan te Giza an ask the friggin' Sphinx,' said Candy.

'So who wrote it?' asked Mahvand. 'The Holy Ghost?'

Jean-Baptiste's eyes had glazed over. 'Belial'

'Your alter ego?' asked Mahvand.

'A fallen angel.'

'You expect me to believe that you co-authored *The Book of Belial* with a demon?' asked Mahvand.

'A fallen angel. There is a world of difference. The latter are infinitely more powerful.' Jean-Baptiste paused. 'You could say I channelled the entity.'

'OK, Monsieur Lebeau-Chevalier. Or whoever yee are. The show is ower,' said Candy. 'So the muse fre yer own stream o' consciousness is a fallen angel. Go figure. An' while you're at it, go hoodwink some other gullible kid wi' yer mumbo jumbo an' psychic showman bullshit.'

'Have you ever considered, for just one moment, Miss Darling, that all three of us share something in common with the Prince of Darkness?'

Candy turned to Mahvand. 'Ah knaa you've always had a penchant fre dark, mysterious men, but divvent yee think dating a satanist is taking it a tad too far, even fre yee?'

'Are we, or are we not, all three of us, in our own unique way, outsiders in some sense?' said Jean-Baptiste.

Candy opened her mouth but Mahvand got there first. 'Why are you telling me all this now?'

'So you understand,' said Jean-Baptiste.

'What? That you have connections in the underworld?' asked Mahvand.

'Who I am.' Jean-Baptiste paused. 'Who you are.'

'Am I meant to fall at your feet and say all is forgiven?' asked Mahvand.

'Have you ever asked yourself,' said Jean-Baptiste, 'who, or indeed, what, was your muse for *Fallen Angels of Homo Heaven*?'

'… now we're both on the guest list at the latest club in Pandemonium?' said Mahvand.

'We're alike. You and I.' Jean-Baptiste paused. 'Birds of a feather.'

'Divvent listen to a word,' said Candy. 'Ahv met his sort before. Pure poison, pet.'

Mahvand edged towards the shop floor mannequin – the one sporting the mouth gag and rubber face mask. 'The weird symbol inside *The Book of Belial*. What's that about?'

'A sigil. Each fallen angel, of any significant ranking in the infernal hierarchy, has their own pictorial signature. Their sigil.'

'Belial?' said Mahvand.

'*Oui.* It was Belial who told me of my changed nature. I am a hybrid.' He paused. 'Part human. Part fallen angel.'

Candy marched over to the counter and picked up the telephone handset. 'OK, sunshine. As Donna Summer 'erself once said. Enough is enough. If it's not New Age con artists channelling cherubs or sixteenth-century Franciscan monks fre a pretty penny, it's unhinged, self-deluded occultists of a certain age in the grip of an identity crisis jumping on the bandwagon. Now if yee divvent get the hell oot of me shop right now, Ahm calling the police.'

'I hardly think, Miss Darling, under the current circumstances, that would be a wise idea, do you?' said Jean-Baptiste.

'Fine. The men in white coats then,' said Candy.

Jean-Baptiste cocked his head to one side. 'I thought you, of all people, *mademoiselle*, would understand what it means to endure a hybrid identity.'

Candy put the receiver down, marched over in her killer six-inch heels, and swung her arm back into position. Jean-Baptiste lifted his hands to shield his face. But not quite in time. Candy's fist, still bruised from her last escapade in Soho, smashed right into Jean-Baptiste's perfectly proportioned Roman nose. He stumbled backwards, lost his balance and crashed into the newly erected display of Mother's Big Boy Penis Pumps, sending them flying in all directions into the air.

Mahvand stood there dumbfounded, staring at Jean-Baptiste splayed out on the shop floor. Blood trickled from his nose onto his white shirt. It unearthed another image: that of Daimon sitting on the Persian cushions in Notting Hill with blood streaming from his left nostril. He'd been too late to help Daimon but maybe with Jean-Baptiste he still had a chance. He came rushing to Jean-Baptiste's aid and knelt down in amongst the scattered pumps.

Jean-Baptiste reached for Mahvand's hand. 'After the Sons of Light waged war with the Sons of Darkness, the fallen ones came into the daughters of men and taught them charms and spells and showed them the cutting of roots and stems.'

'He's got concussion,' said Mahvand.

Towering above him, Candy began to stroke Mahvand's hair. 'It's more than that, pet.'

Mahvand pulled away. 'You're right. Thanks to you his nose will never look the same again!'

'Two branches diverge on the Tree of Life,' said Jean-Baptiste. 'To the right grows the Yahweh/Adamic branch. To the left – the way of the old serpent. By my own volition, I allowed my skin, my soul – my everything – to become grafted onto that leftward leaning—'

'Dowtah, what are we gunna dee wi yee?' said Candy.

'—Twisted bough.'

'Face facts,' said Candy. 'Yee were going out wi' a paranoid schizophrenic.'

'Get an ice-pack!' shouted Mahvand. 'You have no idea!'

'Divvent tell me you're going te take him back. After everything that's happened. Divvent—'

'Just do it!'

Jean-Baptiste lifted his head. Mahvand looked into his

eyes. 'Channelling Belial. I don't expect you to believe me. But it changed my DNA.'

'Get a grip, man,' said Candy, hands on hips, standing at the foot of the stairs. 'It's that shit you smoke that's changed yer DNA. It fried yer friggin' brain.'

'I am a genetically mixed human-fallen-angel. A hybrid. Every bit a cross-breed as the Nephilim.'

'Where angels fear to tread,' said Candy, raising her forefinger to Mahvand. 'You go rushing—'

'I'm done for,' said Jean-Baptiste.

'Ice!' shouted Mahvand.

But as Mahvand sat astride Jean-Baptiste and locked eyes with him, he felt a familiar uncoiling sensation at the base of his spine and found himself swaying, involuntarily arching his lower back. A sudden surge of high-voltage energy shot up to the back of his skull, forcing his eyes to roll inside their sockets. This was followed by the aftershocks – uncontrollable spasms and contractions all over his body. As the contractions gave way to a tingling in the tips of his fingers, an overwhelming sensation of falling came upon him and he telepathically gave his consent to the descent. Deeper and deeper he fell, echoing our First Mother's primal fruit-theft, before finding himself in Jean-Baptiste's warm embrace and a deliciously dark kind of paradise.

SMOKE AND MIRRORS

'He who fights with monsters should be careful lest he thereby becomes a monster. And if thou gaze long into the abyss, the abyss will also gaze into thee.'

Beyond Good and Evil, FW Nietzsche

The sweat of mid-afternoon sex clung to Mahvand's skin like ectoplasm. He lay naked under the silk sheets, propped up on one elbow with a copy of *The Book of Belial*, pondering Nietzsche's opening quote. Jean-Baptiste lay next to him, his face cast in shadow like the other side of the moon. Abyss. The word itself filled Mahvand with existential angst, tortured him with a feeling that gripped his soul. But the more he re-read the words of that final chapter and studied those strange symbols on the pages, the more he zoned out to Jean-Baptiste's way of seeing things. Maybe, just maybe, JB was right in thinking that the abyss would act as some kind of metaphysical womb. The book fell from Mahvand's hand and he curled himself into Jean-Baptiste's outstretched body, secretly thrilled at the prospect of the abyss giving birth to that long-awaited masterpiece: a single defining piece of conceptual art that would make all the pain of the last few months more than worth it. An Amirzadeh–Baptiste collaboration.

In the weeks leading up to the initiation ceremony, it was as if someone had flicked a switch in Mahvand's brain. He applied himself with a disciple's dedication and fortitude to the exercises Jean-Baptiste promised would prepare him for the perilous nature of the abyss: amongst other things, meditating on death and impermanence, viewing facial profiles for any indication of past life material (apparently the frontal view did not offer up such information as readily), reviewing key events in his life backwards (again to promote recollection of past-life experiences) and, hardest of all, going a whole week without using the pronoun 'I' when talking (to break the hold on him of his ego). In the second week, he finally accepted that he and Jean-Baptiste were, in some way, karmically connected. For when he viewed Jean-Baptiste's side profile, an image began to form of a somewhat unattractive young man wearing a typical late-eighteenth-century powdered, white wig.

On the night of the ceremony, they dined in style to a sumptuous meal of lobster and champagne followed by braised venison seasoned with herbs from the garden. Jean-Baptiste cracked open a vintage bottle of Chateaux Margaux to celebrate the occasion. Mahvand gazed at the flames that flickered from candles on the candelabra, casting shadows on the bare walls. (Those beloved framed posters of comicbook magicians and sorcerers were long gone.) As too was the boy who would regularly prune his gran's unruly rose bushes, self-publish his own autobiographical comics and drink nothing but Coca Cola.

Jean-Baptiste took a sip of red wine. 'All magicians, you know, in all the great spiritual epochs throughout history, have desired one thing. To create a messiah by some adaptation of the sexual process. Mary, of course, had God impregnate her.'

'Some adaptation,' said Mahvand, with a conspiratorial smile.

'*Mais oui.* Personally I'm still baffled by how the Blessed Virgin ever managed to accommodate his Lordship's celestial member.' He dabbed his lips with the white linen napkin. 'In Assyria they tried incest. Medieval philosophers, I hear, attempted their own alchemical experiments with the sacrament of semen.' He rested his hand on top of Mahvand's. 'And I have you. My moon child.'

Moon child. Mahvand thrilled to hear his new name. His new identity. He was more than ready. The weeks of meditating at dawn and sunset with eyes half-open in front of a makeshift shrine composed of wilting black roses and the skull of a dog had clearly worked their magic.

Jean-Baptiste produced a red silk scarf from his trouser pocket and wound it around his left hand. 'Tonight you will see the world behind the world. I have every confidence that you will endure the birth pangs of the abyss to give birth to our most magnificent magical child. A piece of art so deliciously dark, a concept so damningly erotic, it will fill the heart with a longing,' He paused. 'Without hope.'

The words scrawled on the wall of the cubicle toilet in Kaos suddenly came back to Mahvand: *There is no God but You.* There was a moment's hesitation before he reached for Jean-Baptiste's hand, unwound the scarf, and proceeded to blindfold himself.

'Good man,' said Jean-Baptiste.

Mahvand felt Jean-Baptiste's fingers interlace with his own and, following Jean-Baptiste's lead, he took his first few steps. He stretched out his other hand like the victim in blind man's bluff. His fingertips came into contact with the smooth surface of a wall, Jean-Baptiste's trouser leg, and several spiralling, Perspex steps. Why, thought Mahvand, who'd anticipated a rather arduous descent to the basement, is he taking me to the top of the house?

After what seemed like an eternity, there were no more steps to climb. Mahvand envisaged the enormous door, made from slats of mahogany, maple and pine, standing before them. The door that, Jean-Baptiste had assured him, would never open. A piece of conceptual art designed by an up-and-coming conceptual artist from Buenos Aires who, Jean-Baptiste had explained at great length, was interested in questioning the functionality of everyday objects. Jean-Baptiste's hand slipped from Mahvand's. Every sound was magnified: his own erratic breathing, a jingle-jangle of keys, the lock turning, door creaking. Jean-Baptiste had deceived him. There was no Argentinian conceptual artist. This was no conceptual door. Part of him regretted having reached out for that blindfold and wanted to tear it off. The other part felt the transgressive pull and allure of that which Jean-Baptiste enigmatically referred to as 'the abyss'.

'Mind how you step,' said Jean-Baptiste.

After Mahvand has crossed the threshold and Jean-Baptiste had lifted the blindfold, Mahvand squinted as his eyes adjusted to the light inside the tomb-like attic. There was something theatrical about it all, which, foolishly, made him drop his guard. Candles flickered in the darkness like hundreds of eyes. A shrine had been erected at the far end. A stone figure of a pharaoh, with a snake writhing from the centre of his forehead, stood in pride of place behind a human skull. Other ancient Egyptian figures were arranged strategically around a glass pipe and seemed to form the points of a pentacle or star. Mahvand recognised the goddess Isis suckling the god Horus, and Osiris, god of the afterlife, underworld and the dead. From the ceiling, a giant image of Belial's sigil printed on cloth hung above the shrine like some satanic halo. It reminded him of a stage set. *All I have to do is play my part.*

As Jean-Baptiste undressed, Mahvand tried to avoid eye contact with the scrying surfaces of the oval-shaped mirrors, which hung from the walls, and reflected back the flickering eyes of burning candles. He eyed a horned statue, with an enormous phallus and hind quarters of a goat, suspiciously. It stood in the far corner playing the pipes and looked as if he might come to life at any minute.

Jean-Baptiste kissed Mahvand on the forehead and proceeded to undress him. 'Be ruled by me.'

Mahvand sat down and crossed his legs, the dusty floor-boards hard and cold against his bare buttocks. He closed his eyes and tried to envisage the magical child that would manifest in the void. The masterpiece that would surpass all their previous magical children. But try as he might, his visionary powers failed him. Naked, Jean-Baptiste walked to the shrine, picked up the human skull and held it up to the sickle moon that appeared through the gap in the open window.

'Hail Lord Horus, Great God, I invoke Thee!
  Son of Osiris and Isis, who was nursed by Nephthys,
I invoke Thee!
  O Divine Falcon
  Whose right Eye is the Sun and Thy Left Eye the Moon
  O Glorious Eye, open at Thy command!
  I welcome Thee!'

Why isn't he invoking the spirit of Belial? Or is that yet to come?

Jean-Baptiste ceremoniously replaced the skull on the table, picked up the glass pipe and warmed it with a blue flame from his lighter. He inhaled several times until the attic was filled with yellow toxic smoke. When he walked back, Mahvand thought it strange his knees were bent and he was walking on tiptoe. He held the pipe to Mahvand's lips and applied the blue flame again. The smoke encircled the shaft, filled the bowl and billowed over the top. *Like a bubbling cauldron.* Mahvand took hit after hit.

Is it a coincidence that methamphetamine shares the same name as the demon, Mephistopheles?

Jean-Baptiste walked back and replaced the glass pipe on the shrine, still walking on tiptoe. He came back carrying a silver bowl in both hands, placed it on the floor and crouched down. Mahvand peered into it but couldn't make out what it was. Jean-Baptiste dipped his hands into the bowl, sending a puff of acrid-tasting smoke into the air. Mahvand began to cough.

Jean-Baptiste held up his palms. They were covered in a greyish white powder. He proceeded to rub the powder over Mahvand's body. First his chest and belly, then each arm, just like Gran when she used to soap him all over with Palmolive in the bath.

'Ash,' said Jean-Baptiste.

Please God. Not Ashraf's ashes.

'Don't worry,' he said in a hushed tone, as if reading his mind. 'It's wood. Or rather, it *was* wood. From the bonfire.' Mahvand wasn't so sure. Jean-Baptiste worked his way up from Mahvand's feet, covering his legs, genitals and buttocks with the ash. 'I first saw it done when I travelled to Varanasi in India. Aghori sadhus hanging out in crematoriums, smearing the ash of the deceased all over their emaciated bodies.' He asked Mahvand to close his eyes as he smeared his face in it. 'The principle is still the same. But instead of taking on the power of dead bodies, you take on woodland spirits.'

Mahvand spluttered as some of the ash got inside his mouth and began to mix with a strange bitter taste dripping down the back of this throat. When he opened his eyes, he had the strangest feeling that the room was a living and breathing organism. The walls seemed less solid and seemed to contract and expand like a pair of lungs in synchronicity with his own breathing.

'Something's not quite right,' said Mahvand.

'Go with it. Just remember to breathe and you'll be fine.' Jean-Baptiste held him from behind and Mahvand let go like a rag doll in his arms. Jean-Baptiste's words echoed in Mahvand's mind, and he found himself swaying to the cadence and rhythm of the message until it became nonsensical and sunk without trace. When Mahvand opened his eyes, everything was pulsating, breathing: the floor-boards, mirrors, the human skull.

Jean-Baptiste walked low on his haunches, slowly, in a circle around Mahvand, still on tiptoe, dropping what looked like white crystals onto the bare floorboards. It was then that Mahvand realised what Jean-Baptiste's movements reminded him of – those of a goat's. Mahvand's stomach lurched. His head didn't feel like it belonged to his body. He reached out and grabbed fistfuls of air.

'Salt. It will also protect you from demons and other entities. Just remember to stay in the circle at all times.'

Mahvand decided to reach out to try and break the circle but was held back by some kind of invisible force field.

Jean-Baptiste dropped the salt on the floor in front of the shrine. He then stepped inside the salt-marked perimeter of the triangle and began to sway. It was as if an umbilical cord stretched from the circle to the triangle attaching Mahvand to Jean-Baptiste. As if the air hummed with high-voltage electricity. The swaying turned into larger undulating movements, as Jean-Baptiste sculpted the air into strange shapes around him. His fingers formed into an ever-changing flow of mudras as if he was an Indian kathak dancer telling a familiar and well-rehearsed story. Jean-Baptiste began to stamp his feet. His eyes rolled back, the whites like two moons in the sockets of his skull. Mahvand was transfixed as he witnessed a constant flow of archetypal figures rise into being, and, with unswerving passion and conviction, claim the territory of the triangle then sink without trace into the nothingness from whence they came. There, Jean-Baptiste sank low on his haunches and clenched his fists as he became a tribal warrior then shape-shifted into a warrior of a different sort as he pulled back one arm and seemed to release an arrow from his bow. Here, his hands twisted, contorted, fingers extended and began to form an ever faster criss-cross of lines in the air. But what gave the drama the depth and the edge were the supporting cameo performances of ordinary men and women: a man crushed by his own life experiences, hands held above his head as if shielding the all-too-familiar debris of broken relationships, ill health and disappointment; a mother holding a baby in her arms, gazing lovingly into its eyes; a monk in prayer; another stepping off a step with a noose around his neck. Mahvand marvelled at each gesture, each smooth transition to a new iconic image of mankind. But he also felt a growing sense of unease. It was as if he, and the cosmic drama he was watching unfold, were part of some great conjuring trick. As if, were he to pull a stitch at any point in the fabric of the storytelling, the individual drama would unravel and reveal the impersonal forces at work: the cycle of birth, death and rebirth. Something rising out of nothing and returning to the nothingness from which it came and so on until the end of time. Mahvand gasped in horror. The final and enduring image was Jean-Baptiste's final conjuring trick: a snake eating its own tail.

Jean-Baptiste suddenly stopped and raised both hands into the air.

'*Hail. Belial! Lucifer of the Twilight.*
I humbly invoke you. King of the Earth;
I invite you to come forth from the sky.
To come forth from the ends of the earth
To come forth from the depths of the underworld!'

Mahvand half expected the fallen angel to rise from the floorboards and drag him kicking and screaming to the gates of Hell. Instead, a cool breeze blew through the attic room, snuffing out the candles nearest to the open window. Jean-Baptiste's frenetic movement came to an abrupt stop and he fell like an empty sack to the floor. The darkness glistened like night on the water's edge. The air grew pregnant with a bewitching yet malevolent presence. The same presence Mahvand had felt all those months ago when he had put pencil to paper and filled the blank page with a fiend-like image of Jean-Baptiste.

'One small step for man,' it whispered, 'one giant leap for mankind.'

Mahvand felt his legs wanting to go from under him.

Jean-Baptiste slowly came to a standing position, as if he were nothing more than puppeteered flesh. Then, with no warning, as if a great force were pushing him from behind, he lunged forward with a look of terror on his face and collapsed outside the triangle. Mahvand yelled, but no sound came. Some invisible umbilical cord had been severed. Jean-Baptiste rose puppet-like from the floor and, in a husky East End accent, said, 'Why did you abandon me? Why did you leave me to rot in that fucking hellhole?'

This is not real. JB was standing with a stooped back, arms folded across his chest. *It's the work of the devil.* As if by magic, JB's flesh seemed to fall away from the bone until all that remained was Gran in the forget-me-not nightdress he'd bought her last Christmas, a look of hurt and betrayal in her eyes. *It's an hallucination.*

'My own flesh and blood abandoning me to Filipinos and thugs on a minimum wage,' said Gran.

Mahvand's eyes filled with tears. Suddenly, he couldn't remember where he was. Nor what had happened in the moments leading up to this moment. All he knew was that Gran was standing before him and he was in-the-dock. 'You needed looking after.'

'Do you know how many times you came to visit?' said Gran. 'Once. With that floozy on yer arm. My own grandson. Not good enough for you now, am I? That it?'

Tears streaked down Mahvand's white-powdered cheeks. 'What could I do?'

'Keep to the straight and narrow,' said Gran. 'I warned you. But you never listened. In one ear and out the other. Like mother, like son. But you can 'elp me now. We can 'elp each other.' She pressed her face up close to the invisible force field of the circle as if she was pressing up close to a pane of glass. ''Elp each other escape our own hellholes.'

Mahvand became aware that he wasn't looking at Gran anymore but into the face of Jean-Baptiste. All his energy was sapped. For a moment he felt confused and completely lost. *How on earth have I ended up in this godforsaken pocket of the universe?* Then he suddenly remembered: the drugs they had both ingested, Jean-Baptiste's demonic invocation and his mission to cross the abyss with one sole purpose in mind. It was like waking up into a full-blown nightmare.

'Come wiv me. Downstairs. It will be dawn soon. We can go for a walk. Across the heath. I know just the bench. One wiv a rather special plaque. *In loving memory of Gracie, my beloved grandmother.* My Mahvand. You always did 'ave a lovely way with words.'

Jean-Baptiste's warning not to leave the circle was drowned out by the very distinct possibility that his gran might actually be dead. He reached for her hand and crossed INTO THE ABYSS.

As soon as he did so, Jean-Baptiste took his hand and led him towards the shrine. Only, when Mahvand looked down at his hand, it didn't belong to Jean-Baptiste. He had no idea who or what it belonged to. It was in the shape of a human hand, but the palm and the fingers had no discernible features, and they lacked skin, human or otherwise. They glistened with an other-worldly dark light that radiated along the inner aspect of Mahvand's arm and penetrated his very soul.

'We meet at last,' it said.

Mahvand looked up into an egg-shaped head with no human features. He tried to pull his hand away but found that the harder he pulled, the tighter the hand grip became. It had no mouth to speak, nor eyes to see. But it had no need of either as it eavesdropped on the thoughts emerging in Mahvand's head, saw into the very depths of his soul.

'Belial?' asked Mahvand.

'Identity. It's more fluid than humans often give it credit for.'

'It's not what—'

'You expected?' said Belial.

Belial seemed to understand him implicitly. Like some long-lost twin. 'Things often aren't, are they? What you expect them to be.'

His words were like pebbles that skimmed the surface of Mahvand's mind before sinking to an ever-increasing ripple of concentric circles.

'What exactly did you expect?' asked Belial. 'A bottomless pit? Black hole? Primordial chaos? Like the after-death state, the abyss is unique to each entrant. It's your own self-styled creation. The end result is the same. Death of the ego. Death to what you hold dear. Death of yourself.' He paused. 'You have no idea, *mon enfant*, how long His Infernal Majesty has been waiting. And preparing. For your homecoming.'

It wasn't long before all his resistance had evaporated and Mahvand finally gave his consent for Belial to enter and possess his body. A dark light now glistened under the surface of his ash-covered skin and filled him with an incredible sense of power. Eve, so they say, succumbing to temptation in that garden of heavenly delights, had taken but a mere bite of the forbidden fruit. This was more akin to devouring the flesh, core and pips in one greedy mouthful. Intoxicated, Mahvand looked out into the room with eyes that were not his own and, like a newborn, took his first breath. Belial no longer stood at his side.

From the waist down, Jean-Baptiste lay outside the triangle, coughing, with a look of bewilderment on his face. Mahvand held out his hand and helped him up. Jean-Baptiste was shaking, beads of sweat had broken out on his forehead and he was covered in dust, bruised and cut on one side from having fallen so many times onto the floor.

Jean-Baptiste looked over to the empty circle. 'You broke the circle!' He shook Mahvand roughly by the shoulder. 'What were my instructions?'

Mahvand smiled. 'The circle. The incantation. In the end it didn't offer Mahvand much protection, did it?'

'Mahvand?' said Jean-Baptiste.

'Oh come now, *mon cher*,' said Mahvand. 'You're not telling me you don't recognise the muse for your little black book? Your daemon?'

Jean-Baptiste's fingers were trembling. 'Mahvand. I know you're in there. Just tell me. Did you visualise the blueprint for our magical child?'

'No. But I received further instruction. You were right. It involves an adaptation of sexual practice.' An iron rod between his legs, angrier than ever, Mahvand said, 'Well, an adaptation of *our* usual sexual practice.'

Jean-Baptiste lay on his back on the bare floorboards under Belial's sigil, his head in line with the human skull on the shrine, his arms stretched out like Christ on the cross. 'There's a sachet of lube. Inside the skull.'

Overseen by the statue of Pan and Belial's sigil, Mahvand opened the jaws of the skull and reached inside. He pulled out a sachet of lubrication and tore it with his teeth. He then smeared the sticky gel on his erect penis and Jean-Baptiste's arsehole. It was at that moment that the words of Jean-Baptiste's epic poem came back to him:

> '*Well hear this, wolf-king lover*
> *Does your rosebud pucker?*'

Holding Jean-Baptiste's ankles, he spread his legs wide apart and masterfully entered him. *Who's the wolf-king now?* With each thrust, Mahvand erased every last trace of his own virginity. He slid a little deeper along the velvet-soft passageway, a little deeper into Jean-Baptiste, a little deeper into himself, each moment an intimate revelation of self and other, until he did not know, nor could he feel, where he himself ended and Jean-Baptiste began: a communion of flesh. Shadows danced across Jean-Baptiste's face like Salome in the Dance of the Seven Veils. Mahvand took his place as King Herod at the head of the table. He began salivating, masticating, feasting on Jean-Baptiste's face, gorging on eyeball, biting the curl off his upper lip, licking each earlobe into oblivion. Only, at some point it wasn't Jean-Baptiste's face he was kissing. It was the severed head of John the Baptist; it was his own.

A voice said, 'In the beginning was the deed.' Although his lips weren't moving, Mahvand recognised the voice as Jean-Baptiste's. The moment surpassed all understanding; the veil had been lifted.

Other faces came in and out of being. And still he kept fucking. Familiar faces. Faces he himself had once inhabited and grown to a certain age with: an old woman, renowned for her skill in herbal medicine and midwifery, shunned and vilified and eventually burned at the stake for being a witch; a slave boy in the land of the free who worked on a cotton field by day and performed favours of a sexual nature to his elderly white master by night; a devastatingly handsome yet troubled young painter in residence at the Palace of Versailles.

At some point, Mahvand became aware that the painter's face was morphing into Belial's egg-shaped head. It began to glisten with the same particles of black light that moments before had penetrated the blood-air barrier of his own being.

Mahvand's pelvic thrusting gathered pace as the black light gave way to an image of his own father humping his way towards conception. Then it was all of them: the old woman, the slave boy, the artist, Belial, his father, himself, Mahvand (in his current incarnation). All of them. Coming into being. Out of being. Into. Being.

Just before the moment of climax, Mahvand felt something, or someone, leave his body. *What am I doing?* He looked deep into Jean-Baptiste's eyes. Two horizontal black slits stared back from a bed of aqueous yellow. *Dear God.* Mahvand shuddered as he realised he was no longer holding the flesh and bone of human feet but the sharp claws of cloven hooves. *Forgive Me.* When he glanced back up at Jean-Baptiste's face, two enormous horns had sprouted from the sides of his head and curled majestically towards the ceiling. Mahvand felt a cool breeze and the soft embrace of feathers, each one as black as sin. He recoiled in horror as the nature of what he was doing became crystal clear; he was rutting Baphomet, the Sabbatic Goat. He tried to pull back. But it was too late; he had reached the point of no return. As Jean-Baptiste's designer stubble was miraculously transformed into the beard of a billy goat, Mahvand's whole body spasmed. Both eyes rolled up towards the psychic third. He felt the contortion of facial muscle; he was cumming. Jean-Baptiste was cumming. Coming together in a high-voltage moment of sex magick that obliterated any residual will, for either partner, to visualise magical children.

Mahvand collapsed on top of Jean-Baptiste, quite spent, and rested his chin on his lover's chest, which was splattered, Jackson-Pollock-like, with jism. He realised the magick was still at work when JB's throat was adance with flecks of dark light. Each one exploded in a tiny puff of smoke before giving birth to its very own pair of black paper-thin wings. A cool breeze snuffed out the remaining candles and Mahvand witnessed a host of black butterflies make their way to the open window and towards a sickle moon in a sky now stained red by the early morning sun.

As the last butterfly disappeared into cloud, he felt something small and pricking lodged inside his hand. He uncurled his fist. Whatever had transpired between them, it had worked; it was real. For there, in the womb of his palm, where his lifeline crossed the line of destiny, was the tiny miracle of something born from nothing, their magical child: a beautiful, glistening black seed.

BLACK SEED

When Mahvand had recovered from witnessing the miracle of that Virgin Birth, his thoughts turned to Gran. With the black seed firmly stuck to the palm of his hand, he ran down three flights of stairs and phoned the care home. He'd never been so relieved to hear her voice. After that, he made sure he phoned each day. Gran would often lose the thread of the conversation or even completely forget who he was. But on the rare occasion when she was compos mentis, there was always a strained jollity to her voice, as if she were trying to reassure him that life at Sunny Pastures wasn't that bad. The right thing to do would have been to go down to Dagenham in person. But ever since crossing the abyss, the thought of visiting that care home somehow filled him with dread.

Mahvand kept the black seed on a bed of cotton wool inside an empty matchbox, in a a storage trunk, in one of the many spare bedrooms in the western wing of Golden Dawn. He'd grown to love that little black seed, and would sneak into the bedroom when Jean-Baptiste was out, open the top drawer, reach for the back corner, and take it out. And just as Belial had telepathically communicated with him, so too did the black seed. It didn't want to be planted in the grounds of the house like all the other seeds; to suffer the indignities of water, wind and rain; to blossom or flower only to form the organic material for other plants and flowers to do the same. It was destined for much greater things. And as the days turned into weeks, and Mahvand's opening night for his debut conceptual art exhibition, *Notoriety*, drew ever closer, it let it be known, in no uncertain terms, that it yearned, above all else, to form the centrepiece to his exhibition. To be suspended at the epicentre of a Perspex cube, elevated on a plinth, and revealed to distinguished guests and a public, well versed in the vagaries of contemporary art, at a moment of maximum impact.

At first, Mahvand was wary. Was a seed, however much it beckoned and glistened, grandiose enough to form the centrepiece to *Notoriety*? Would it, as Jean-Baptiste put it, have the power to corrupt the onlooker on the spot? But the seed reminded him it was no ordinary seed, no blueprint for a piece of art floating in the worlds of ideas, but having actually materialised, as a result of powerful sex magick, it was a piece of art in its own right. Mahvand gradually came around to the seed's way of thinking. The seed was small and simple. And perfect because of it. Its power did not titillate. It was not in-yer-face, or conventionally avant-garde. Instead, it emanated a mysterious, captivating beauty which held Mahvand firmly in its grasp. To him, it was more than art. It was alive. And each time he opened the matchbox, he too came alive and was reminded; he, Mahvand Amirzadeh, was its chosen person. It made complete sense that it should befall him to choose its name. So, one night, gently closing the matchbox, and kissing the seed goodnight, he whispered the only name befitting of such a piece: *Untitled*.

He'd viewed a number of potential venues when considering where to showcase his work. He'd clambered to the bottom of a disused swimming pool in Haggerston and toyed with the idea of *Notoriety* sailing down Old Father Thames on a boat. He'd been given the grand tour of a dilapidated building in Hoxton by a waiflike indie chic, who either had an eating disorder or was a serious smackhead. In Dalston he'd traipsed through a World War II underground bunker. But the latter was dank and damp, littered with vintage pornographic magazines, and smelled of piss. That, in his humble opinion, was taking 'grunge aesthetic' a step too far. He'd even dared to venture south of the river to a gallery space in Brixton that was renowned for exhibiting work of a transgressive nature, including that of French artist Pierre Molinier, who'd gained notoriety for fucking himself in the arse with one of his own creations: the high heel of a shoe fashioned into a dildo. But none of these venues could compete with the kudos of the White Cube in Mayfair.

Even though Jean-Baptiste was a friend of the White Cube, he had reservations due to its size. But for Mahvand, it was the holy grail of exhibition spaces. Surrounded by boutiques, exclusive art galleries selling old masters, and specialist art bookshops, the White Cube had been instrumental in forging the careers of Young British Artists who were now virtual celebrities in their own right: Hirst, Emin, Gavin Turk and the Chapman Brothers. It had also exhibited the work of international artists including Hiroshi Sugimoto and Nobuyoshi Araki. But more than this, Mahvand considered it of great conceptual significance that his black seed, suspended inside a Perspex cube, would be unveiled to a jaded audience, eager for the next best thing, inside the confines of the White Cube.

At first, Jay Jopling, founder and director of the White Cube, was reluctant to agree to hold an exhibition for *Notoriety* at such late notice. White Cube decide which artists will showcase their work at least a year in advance and Andreas Slominski's exhibition of home-made traps, including cages, nooses, tripwires and nets, was booked for late November through to early January. It was out of the question. But not only was Jean-Baptiste a good friend of the gallery, he was also a high-profile client. So, after Jay had privately viewed Mahvand's collection, and referred to the *Holy Trinity* as 'a major piece of work with international appeal', a deal was struck in Jay's office on the second floor of the White Cube. (The details of which Jean-Baptiste would not elaborate to Mahvand.) The exhibition schedule was altered, and *Notoriety* was given the green light. Glossy invitations, in the trademark White Cube square shape, with a black-and-white portrait of the artist on the back, were sent to everyone on White Cube's mailing list: art gallery directors, art critics, clients, curators, all the Young British Artists as well as celebrities who'd attended previous opening nights. And, by virtue of Jean-Baptiste's membership, Mahvand started to hang out at an after-hours private members club in the heart of Soho.

At the Groucho Club one night in mid-November, his head buzzing with one too many glasses of Bollinger, Mahvand spotted a Damon Albarn lookalike sitting under a collage of eyes cut out from magazines and stuck to the surface of a shattered mirror. Then it sunk in. The pretty boy with the messy blonde hair and the Adidas tracksuit top really was Damon Albarn. *The* Damon Albarn from Blur. Mahvand wasn't really a Britpop type of guy – all that indie, straight boy, faux working-class posturing – but right then he felt like their number one fan. Damon sat in a secluded corner, reclining on a sumptuous leather sofa, engrossed in conversation with a skinny blonde. Mahvand had always had a soft spot for him, for that laddish charm, indie credentials and slightly affected Thames Estuary accent.

Piano cocktail music tinkled in the background, but in Mahvand's head all he could hear were the lyrics to *End of a Century*. While Jean-Baptiste was at the bar crunching on twiglets and talking to Damien Hirst about death, God and Margaret Thatcher's miraculous makeover courtesy of Saatchi and Saatchi, Mahvand saw his chance. Bolstered by his third super-strength line of cocaine in the toilets, he sauntered over to where Damon was sitting. With each bold step, a plan began to take shape.

'Hi. I'm Mahvand.'

Damon stopped talking to the blonde and looked up. He was even prettier close up: messy blonde hair, beautiful, long eyelashes and the nose of a pixie. Mahvand didn't usually go for pretty boys. He preferred his men rough, rugged, and preferably pushing forty. But he could see why Damon had been voted 'Most Fanciable Man' in *Just Seventeen* magazine.

'Just wanted to congratulate you on the Brit awards a few years back.' Mahvand held out his hand as if he was some music industry bigwig.

Damon smiled. 'Hey, man. Thanks.'

'And just to say, *Song 2* and *Beetlebum*. Two of my favourite songs on the new album, dude.' The truth of the matter was that Mahvand appreciated the alternative rock vibe on *Song 2* but still considered *Beetlebum* a bit too Beetles for his taste.

Damon laughed in a laddish way. 'What can I say? Trying to move away from the whole Britpop thing, I guess.'

Mahvand laughed, but more from the thrill of engaging in a bit of banter with a pop star, and reached a hand into his jacket pocket. 'Thought you might like to come to this. If you're free, that is.' He handed Damon the invitation. On the front, in the small print underneath, it read:

Feeling blasphemingly brazen?
Come as God in fancy dress
And you'll be entitled to a private audience
With Mahvand Amirzadeh
At a private members club in the heart of Soho.

'*Notoriety?*' said Damon with a quizzical smile.

'I'm showcasing my work. At the White Cube.' That moment for Mahvand was a game-changer. He was a celebrity in his own right. He'd laid to rest for good that self-conscious comics geek who'd gone grovelling to Adam Hudson at Forked Tongue. He was the one calling the shots now. And even though Damon didn't make it to the opening night of *Notoriety*, (he was on vacation in Reykjavik) he did attend a private viewing the day before and bought the papier mâché sculpture of Batman strangling Robin for a four-figure sum.

The next day, Mahvand was interviewed for *Frieze* magazine, hung-over and crashing from a cocaine comedown. DI White was waiting quietly in the wings. When the interview was over, Mahvand was taken to the local police station for further questioning. He was just about to have his fingerprints taken by a female police officer, who had something of Cherie Blair about her, when Candy showed up in fake fur with the bent copper from Charing Cross station and a mealy-mouthed solicitor in tow. Mahvand couldn't have been more grateful. The following week, when the new edition of *Frieze* hit the newsagents, bookshops and galleries, next to a washed-out black-and-white mugshot of Mahvand drinking a double espresso, the article headline ran: *The New Face of Brit Art?* It was the question mark that bugged him.

With less than a week to go, Jean-Baptiste recommended a little retail therapy. Arm in arm, they strolled down New Bond Street in Mayfair, like two Victorian aesthetes, searching for that perfect opening-night outfit. Mahvand remembered the first time Jean-Baptiste had given him the grand tour of Golden Dawn, arm in arm. How in awe he was with this handsome man who flattered and charmed and seemed to show such an interest in him. Mahvand tried to quell the voice of dissent. *But it wasn't me he was interested in, was it? Not the real me, anyway.*

At Prada, a security guard with an earpiece, and dressed, no doubt, from head to toe in Prada himself, opened the door to the store and a whole new shopping experience.

Prior to meeting Jean-Baptiste, Mahvand would have been far too self-conscious to even set foot in a store like

Prada. His old self, more familiar with the hustle and bustle of Top Man or C&A during the January sales, even found the mannequins in the shop window a little intimidating, with their chiselled fibreglass features, dressed in the finest of Italian fabric. But his new self felt more than at home in this top-of-the-range fashion emporium in the heart of Mayfair. This was where the beautiful people came to buy beautiful clothes, and now he was one of those beautiful people, well, he too could enjoy the spoils of the beautifully privileged. He deserved nothing less.

The sales assistants were the final link in the chain of the multimillion-pound Italian fashion house, and Mahvand sensed they were more than willing to bend over backwards when they sniffed out the potential for a little extra commission. He was right. Under the bright lights and gleaming surfaces of chrome, glass and Perspex, with one classically handsome and rather sycophantic sales assistant at his beck and call, Mahvand chose the outfit for his opening night (or, as he would later tell it, the outfit chose him): a tailor-fitted, two button, black wool suit with a price tag that would have previously induced ridicule and revulsion. Stepping out of the changing room, Mahvand gave himself the once-over in a full-length mirror.

'And Cinderella shall go to the ball,' said Jean-Baptiste, standing next to a rainbow-coloured array of shopping bags that bore some of the highest profile names in fashion: Dolce & Gabbana, Gucci, Cartier, Alexander McQueen, Vivienne Westwood.

The Italian sales assistant, who must have been hired, at least in part, because of his Latino good looks, stood behind him, chin cupped between thumb and forefinger, giving an admiring glance. 'And may I say, sir, Cinder's arse looks absolutely FABULOUS in that.'

Mahvand instantly rose to the bait. 'I'll take it.' A gaunt face with a haunted expression, sporting a new, closely cropped haircut, stared back at him in the mirror. *The New Face of Brit Art? Jean-Baptiste's fuck puppet? A disciple of the Brotherhood of the Skull and Crossbones? Just who in God's name am I?*

On Sunday, all the pieces for the previous exhibition, Christian Schumann's exhibition, *New Paintings*, were deinstalled. Like every exhibition held at White Cube, *Notoriety* was due to open on Thursday at 6 p.m. In between that time, the pieces for Mahvand's exhibition were installed in the gallery. Being more like a small family business, there was no curator, and everyone from the artistic liaison officer through to Sophie, responsible for archives, press and marketing, lent a hand installing the smaller pieces. Technicians, hired by the gallery, had to tip *Gay Man's Unmade Bed* on its side against one of the walls, and glue the sex paraphernalia to the mattress with industrial strength glue. Not one to miss an opportunity, Mahvand changed the title from *Gay Man's Unmade Bed,* to *Gay Man's Unmade Bed Tipped on its Side.*

The night before *Notoriety* opened its doors to the art world, no matter which way Mahvand positioned himself in bed, he just couldn't fall sleep. Somehow, details of the *Holy Trinity* exhibit had been leaked to the press and key figures in the Church of England and the Catholic Church had been wheeled on in their respective frocks to express their outrage and revulsion on current affairs programmes and late-night chat shows. Given the storm that was brewing in the Holy Chalice, Mahvand began to doubt the wisdom of asking distinguished guests in the art world to come dressed as God lookalikes. And as for the question mark in the *Frieze* magazine interview? It continued to eat away at his artistic self-confidence. As did the pieces of conceptual art that were Daimon Mount-Stuart's seeds of inspiration: the *Holy Trinity* exhibit, *No More Heroes* and *Gay Man's Unmade Bed*. He was a fraud. An imposter. He'd forged his career on the back of someone who lay six feet under, and as for the pieces of art themselves – they'd been crafted by the hands of young aspiring artists, fresh out of college, desperate for their own fifteen minutes of fame.

At 2:58 a.m., Mahvand lifted the dead weight of Jean-Baptiste's arm, snuck out of bed, and crept along the passageway to the end of the western wing and one of the many spare bedrooms. Gently lifting the lid of the sandalwood storage trunk, he carefully removed the layers of sheets and blankets and reached down for his magical masterpiece: the black seed suspended at the epicentre of a large Perspex cube. It was a modern-day ship in a bottle, a sex magick souvenir forever captured behind acrylic glass, a conundrum. He ceremoniously placed the cube on top of the chest of drawers under Daimon's light installation, 'PURPLE', and, like a good Catholic kneeling before the Blessed Virgin, got down on his knees.

The only other person who knew about *Untitled* was his cut-throat lawyer at the Farringdon office and, of course, the Mancunian assistant from Goldsmith's he'd commissioned to actually make the piece. (With pound signs in her eyes,

Ali had been paid a handsome sum and been made to sign a contract with a strongly worded confidentiality clause.) Mahvand had even managed to keep the seed (both its conception and gestation) a complete secret from its father – or was it its mother? – now sound asleep in the master bedroom. And, of course, there was the inevitable diverting and fending off of numerous questions concerning the empty plinth in the centre of the gallery from nearly everyone who worked at White Cube. But Mahvand sensed that the seed preferred it that way.

He gazed lovingly at his magical child. Tomorrow it would be unleashed onto an unsuspecting gathering of conceptual art aficionados. The black seed would have its day. He would have his day. And that question mark from the interview with *Frieze* magazine would be transformed into a resounding exclamation mark in every art magazine, tabloid and broadsheet that covered the private viewing.

Mahvand rose and lifted the cube to his lips. He kissed each of its Perspex faces in turn, placed it back in the trunk and went back to bed. When he finally managed to drift off, he found himself completely naked and all alone in the upstairs gallery of the White Cube, huddled in the far corner like a frightened animal. As the four walls began to close in on him, he came face to face with a hologram in green-and-yellow light: a magnified image of Daimon Mount-Stuart's corpse.

WHITE CUBE

They were wearing identical Prada suits, classic Berluti Italian shoes, and large-lensed shades courtesy of Giorgio Armani. 'We're the late nineties version of Gilbert and George,' joked Jean-Baptiste as the limousine careered into Piccadilly and got stuck behind the rear end of a double-decker bus.

Mahvand had wanted to get a black cab down to the White Cube. Stepping out of a chauffeur-driven limo was so not your typical Young British Artist behaviour. But Jean-Baptiste was adamant. It was all about creating an image, forging one's own brand. And yes, if it came down to it, turning oneself into a work of art.

Mahvand looked out of the window, at once twice removed, the tint of his shades and the limousine window casting all of London life in shadow. *Notoriety* opened its doors at six. Jean-Baptiste had persuaded him it was de rigueur to be late for one's own debut exhibition. Mahvand checked his new Cartier watch: a gift from Jean-Baptiste to celebrate his success. It was already five past. His stomach lurched as they cruised past the Palladian facade of Burlington House and the Royal Academy of Arts. Leonardo Da Vinci, with a paintbrush in one hand, palette in the other, along with Raphael and Sir Christopher Wren, looked down from the lofty heights of the upper storey, immortalised in granite. Underneath, glossy posters, showing the enlarged tip of a tongue touching the tip of an iron, promoted Charles Saatchi's private collection: *SENSATION*. Mahvand had already been inside. He'd seen Emin's ode to everyone she'd ever slept with – the blue tent – and Damien's tiger shark immersed in formaldehyde solution behind the glass panel of a vitrine. He was even there when a member of the public had splashed a tin of paint over the portrait of Myra Hindley. Catching himself staring up at Leonardo on the plinth, he wondered if his *Holy Trinity* exhibit would suffer a similar fate. Would an act of vandalism be the defining moment of his opening night? He looked across at Jean-Baptiste chewing a piece of gum: his jaw clenching, unclenching, tongue and saliva churning it round in his mouth like a washing machine stuck on the slow cycle. What was it he'd said? There's no such thing as bad publicity. Mahvand wasn't so sure. He reached for the remote. The cold gust of air and drizzle on his face was a welcome relief from Jean-Baptiste's incessant chewing and caustic remarks.

As they turned into Duke Street St James, Mahvand immediately spotted what he took to be paparazzi and members of the official press, who'd set up camp just up from the White Cube on the corner, outside Rare Books. Then he spotted Gran and Candy outside The Chequers Tavern, braving the rain and late autumnal chill. Candy was rooting round in her handbag, dressed in a luminous pink wig and fake fur that was usually only ever given an airing at weddings and funerals. Gran sat slumped in a wheelchair, wrapped up in her old winter coat, her lower half covered in a tartan blanket. It was the first time Mahvand had seen her wheelchair-bound. Candy had told him to come prepared, but nothing prepared him for that vacant expression on her face lit by the yellow glow of an Edwardian street lamp. It was as if she wasn't really all there. And he was struck by a crushing sense of guilt. *I should have been there. For her. Like she has been for me. All these years. Dear God, what have I done? What have I become?*

The limousine came to a stop and Jean-Baptiste squeezed Mahvand's hand. Nikolai came to the side door and opened it.

'Good luck, sir.'

This was it. His moment of glory. Only now he wasn't sure he wanted it. As he stepped out of the limousine and onto the wet tarmac, he caught a glimpse of the moon tinged with a reddish hue, then was momentarily blinded by a flurry of flash photography. When his eyes adjusted, he spotted a spectacled Jarvis Cocker in a crush-velvet suit making his way into the White Cube.

SPLAT!

Before he could fully register what had happened, something hit him hard on the left side of his face. He looked down. His shoes were covered in an amniotic-like fluid, yolk and egg shell. So too was the right shoulder of his Prada suit. Mahvand turned to see where the laughter was coming from.

'Forgive the sinner. But not the sin!' yelled an obese woman in sensible shoes from under her *Nationwide* umbrella.

'Thou shalt not take the Lord's name in vein! Go to hell!' shouted her friend clutching a black leather-bound Bible.

A small group of irate Christians had gathered outside the Whitford Fine Art gallery and were waving garish home-made placards, with their out-of-townie offspring in tow. They were marshalled on either side by two bored-looking policemen. An elderly man at the front in a duffel coat, all skin and bone, seemed weighed down by the doom-laden message of his sandwich board. *Repent, for the End of the World is Nigh!*

'Faggot!' screamed a rosy-cheeked, middle-aged woman in a blue anorak and bobble hat.

Mahvand saw red. He pulled his hand from Jean-Baptiste's and charged at the demonstrators. 'You fucking Jesus freaks! God is gay! Fuck the lot of you!' He spun around like a rabid dog as the press and paparazzi went into overdrive. Mahvand felt disorientated by a sudden frenzy of flash photography, and turned on the press. It was as if all the rage that had been simmering inside for months just came pouring out. 'Your mothers suck cocks in hell! D'yer hear me?'

Mahvand felt a firm grip on his elbow. It was Jean-Baptiste. *Is he smiling?* 'Best get the artist inside.'

SPLAT!

Another brown speckled missile. This time it hit the green panelled front door of the White Cube. Above the door, a sculpture of a bearded man's face, like some Greek god, looked on impassively as the egg white slid down the letter box.

The next thing Mahvand registered was Jean-Baptiste ushering him through the open door of the White Cube.

Inside, the glitterati of London's conceptual art scene were rammed up against the walls and the stairs that led to the first-floor gallery. The air was thick with cigarette smoke. *Why did I listen to Jean-Baptiste about being fashionably late? I should have been here to meet and greet each guest.* Mahvand reached for his inhaler, took several puffs and looked up at the surveillance camera. He felt his legs want to give way. For a split second, he thought he saw the grainy black-and-white image of himself on the screen flicker into a likeness of Daimon. When he peered closer, he realised it was himself staring up at the screen. Or, at least, a version of himself looking very much the part of a distinguished businessman. He squeezed past a gaunt-looking young man in wide-framed spectacles and a black polo neck jumper. *Get a grip. It's just opening-night nerves.*

The inside entrance was abuzz with laughter, gossip and art talk. 'Like totally,' said the woman in front with the New York accent. 'Who was it said Schumann's work was a bumpy road that seemed to lead towards a Technicolour adolescent apocalypse?' She was wearing a black beanie hat and paint-splattered overalls.

'Glad you decided to put in an appearance.' At the top of the stairs, squeezed next to Alex James, the bass player from Blur, was Jay Jopling. He stood tall above the crowd in his wide-rimmed glasses and grey suit. 'Thought you'd switched sides and joined the Christian crusaders outside.'

Mahvand saw his chance, gave JB the slip and pushed passed the Yank with the paint-splattered overalls

Mahvand could already feel himself retreat further inside behind the VIP mask, as the celebrity-artist took over and stepped into the limelight. He took some delight in blanking the woman from *Frieze* magazine who'd sown the seed of doubt with her question-mark-loaded article, and air-kissed the arts editor for *Time Out*. He made sure he was photographed shaking hands with Gilbert and George, who were already on their way down. In their trademark tweed suits, they reminded him of Tweedledum and Tweedledee.

'What did you think of the work?' asked Mahvand.

'Thought provoking,' said George in an upper-class English accent, the lighting reflecting off his bald patch. He gave Mahvand the once-over. 'Wonderful suit, by the way. I can't abide how everyone wears jeans these days. Such a uniform, don't you think?'

'Do you sell the pieces in the *Holy Trinity* separately?' asked Gilbert in an Italian accent.

Taking a leaf out of Jean-Baptiste's book, who was a master in the art of artificially inflating demand, Mahvand said, 'It's a set piece, I'm afraid.' And like some royal dignitary, he thanked them both for coming and continued up the stairs.

In the reception area, next to the sold sculpture of Batman strangling Robin, Jay was engrossed in conversation with Janet Street-Porter and Neil Tenant from the Pet Shop Boys. Mahvand ducked to avoid the low hanging papier mâché model Earth. It was strange. In the studio, the pieces had felt like an extension of himself. But here in the gallery, it was as if someone else had made them. *Context is everything.*

'Janet, Neil, this,' said Jay, 'is the artist.'

'Well, this is a first. About time we had an openly gay Young British Artist,' said Janet, guffawing and kissing Mahvand on both cheeks.

'Interesting name for an exhibition, by the way,' said Neil in a Geordie accent quite unlike Candy's.

'Oh, thanks,' said Mahvand.

'*Notoriety*. Makes one think of people who found fame for the wrong reasons. Serial killers, mass murderers and such like.'

'Take no notice,' said Janet. 'Personally, I think it beats *Sensation* hands down.'

'By the way. Can you put us all out of our misery? It's killing us. What exactly have you got hiding under the white sheet on the plinth next door?' said Neil with a deadpan expression. 'Or is it a piece of conceptual art in its own right?'

Everyone laughed; everyone, that is, except Mahvand, who was already beginning to feel the strain.

'All will be revealed,' said Jay. 'Hope to see you both at the Groucho Club for the after-party?'

He handed Mahvand a bottle of Corona beer from a crate on the floor and escorted him away. Jean-Baptiste had insisted on everyone having champagne. But Mahvand was adamant. The laying on of beer was one Young British Artist tradition he would not break with.

'By the way,' said Jay. 'Saatchi is offering five hundred thousand for *Gay Man's Unmade Bed*. And Meryl Lynch want to talk. They're after an Amirzadeh for the lobby in their London office.'

'*It's Gay Men's Bed – Tipped on its Side*.' said Mahvand caustically. 'And it's worth twice that. As well you know.' He knew he should be thrilled at the news. But it just felt like another piece of him had died inside.

At the entrance to the actual White Cube itself, he caught a glimpse of Tracy Emin in a black macintosh and knee-high black boots. She was standing in front of the fibreglass sculpture of Christ with the raging hard-on.

'Fucking brilliant!' she said to her friend, who was dressed in a tartan minidress and pigtails.

Mahvand didn't find out whether it was his sculpture she found fucking brilliant or something else, as he was distracted by a Jesus lookalike with an overgrown beard and shoulder-length black hair. Standing alone at the far end of the gallery, in front of the white blinds that emitted a glow from the street lights outside, he was looking straight at Mahvand. Mahvand couldn't help but notice the slogan on his T-shirt: *Fuck, Suck, Spank, Wank*. The exact same T-shirt Daimon Mount-Stuart was wearing when he'd first met him at Kaos. That had nothing to do with opening-night nerves. It was a sign. A sign that Daimon was there in spirit, if not in body.

While Jay was talking to Matthew Collins, artist, TV presenter and documentary film-maker, Mahvand saw his chance, slipped away, and headed for Jay's office on the second floor. And there, to the accompaniment of a conversation about video and large-scale light installations just outside the door, he tipped a greedy-guts amount of white powder onto the desk and racked up a huge line. A line of beauty, he said to himself, as he hoovered up every white crumb from the mahogany wood with a tightly rolled twenty-pound note.

Stepping over the threshold and into the actual gallery minutes later, his social anxiety was mercifully replaced by a rush of dopamine in the brain. The White Cube hummed with an other-worldly pristine white light. This was the future. And he was part of it. Correction. He was it! Cocaine dripped down his nasal passages to the back of his throat and numbed his front teeth. Everywhere he looked, an avatar, or a god from classical antiquity, seemed to be observing a piece of artwork with bemusement or curiosity. One of Mahvand's assistants from Goldsmiths, dragged-up as Krishna, with garlands of flowers and smeared in cobalt-blue body paint, was in deep conversation with Janet Street-Porter over by the *No More Heroes* exhibit. Aphrodite, sporting a revealing white toga, Roman sandals and Pre-Raphaelite hair extensions, was necking back the beer while seeming to ponder the philosophical ramifications of the Good Lord being anally penetrated by a shepherd's crook. Each exhibit was shrouded in a halo of white light, and the anger and Christian rhyme of the protesters outside seemed like a throwback to some earlier, more primitive civilisation. Mahvand felt in his trouser pocket for the key that would unlock his masterpiece. He pressed the sharp, jagged edges against the soft underbelly of his hand. It did little to open the channels of communication between himself and the seed. But he did find himself suddenly on the receiving end of a well-honed, seduction routine. A male model, who introduced himself as Giovanni, was just back from doing a photo shoot for Gucci in Rome.

'Prada, if I'm not mistaken,' he said, toying with one of the buttons on Mahvand's jacket. 'This year's winter collection.'

Mahvand looked around nervously in case Jean-Baptiste was in earshot.

Giovanni, who, for the second time, raked his fingers through his jet-black shoulder-length hair, made Mahvand feel as if he was the only one in the room. He asked all the right questions, and, with the ease of someone who'd done it a thousand times before, slipped him his business card. He also introduced Mahvand to his friend Marianna Sorrentino, whose windswept look and pouting mouth made Mahvand think she was no stranger to the surgeon's knife. She worked for the British Council and represented a range of cutting-edge British artists at the Venice Biennale art fair, which she assured him was the Cannes film festival of the art world.

'Daahling! You simply must exhibit next spring' she said. 'And in Venice, with the religious dimensions to your work, you're certain to cause a sensation!'

'And if you're ever in the south of France,' said Giovanni. 'Come and look me up. I have a charming little chateau just outside Marseille.' He paused. 'But lose the older guy in the matching Prada suit. He gives me the creeps.'

After inviting Giovanni and Marianna to partake in the ritual sniffing of snow in the upstairs office, Mahvand decided it was time to unveil the centrepiece to his exhibition. He alerted Jay, who began to usher people into an already overcrowded White Cube.

Mahvand felt light-headed. His heart was racing, and the palms of his hands felt clammy. He was seriously regretting having done that second line. Out on the street, a rousing rendition of *Onward Christian Soldiers* had just started up. There was a hush inside the gallery. Jay stood beside Mahvand, who stood beside his beloved *Untitled*, and cleared his throat. 'Where do I start? I think it will come as no surprise to friends of the gallery and those that work at the White Cube, that this particular exhibition is a rather unexpected addition to our programme.'

Mahvand felt Jean-Baptiste's fingers reach for his.

'But I think you'll agree,' said Jay. 'It is a welcome addition.'

A round of applause.

'This is an artist who references popular culture, religion and environmental concerns in one body of work. An artist who, like Marcel Duchamp in 1917, takes a ready-made object with no obvious aesthetic merit—'

Jay was suddenly interrupted by a commotion out on the stairwell. Everyone turned their heads.

'Let us through. Wheyaye, man. I'm fam'ly, like!'

Mahvand would recognise that Geordie accent anywhere.

And there, at the entrance of the White Cube, out of breath, and clutching her flask of gin, stood Candy. 'Ahm 'is Ma!' She adjusted her bra strap, hiccupped, and delivered her next line to Jay. 'Weors the bloody wheelchair access in this place, man?' She paused. 'Or is art the sole privilege o' the young an' able-bodied these days?'

Mahvand looked away in shame. There was a deathly silence.

'What's she doing?' hissed Jean-Baptiste with a look of contempt on his face. 'Disgracing you before your moment of triumph.'

Mahvand looked at the great and the not so good: celebrities, models, artists – all gathered together in his name. Apart from the odd smirk or rolling of the eyeballs, they seemed transfixed by Candy's performance, frozen in time like the waxworks in Madam Tussauds. He looked at Candy: bra strap showing, pink wig slightly skew-whiff, bosoms heaving. Jean-Baptiste was right. She was an embarrassment. To him. To herself. And to every decent, mild-mannered transsexual in the land.

Wagging a finger at him, she said, 'Just so as ye knaa, me and yer gran are s-s-still ootside The Chequers, leik.' She'd begun to slur her words. 'Remember yer gran? Remember yer ma?' Hiccup. 'She's the one in the wheelchair, asking herself what she's done wrong fre hor only grandson not even te gis her the time of day. And Ah is the one freezin' us tits off in fake fukin Versace, man.'

Mahvand couldn't believe she was outing him like this. Was it his fault he hadn't welcomed them, when he was already running ten minutes late and being pelted with eggs by Christian fundamentalists?

'Fre those of yee tha' are interested, me and his gran'll be signing autographs outside The Chequers.' And with that, she turned, nearly walked straight into the brick wall, turned ninety degrees, stumbled, and headed out of the White Cube.

Mahvand looked at the floor, wondering whether she'd make it down the stairs in one piece.

Jay exchanged a look with Mahvand, loosened his collar, and raised his bottle of Corona in the air. 'A toast. To Mahvand Amirzadeh.'

Mahvand looked up and out onto a sea of lime-topped beer bottles. 'To Mahvand.'

There was a ripple of polite laughter and head nodding in the crowd.

I don't see the point in it.

Why go to the bother of padlocking an exhibit?

Is it some kind of stunt?

It's all a bit cloak and dagger, darling.

'Get on with it,' hissed Jean-Baptiste.

Outside, the protest song continued. '*Onward Christian soldiers, marching as to war. With the cross of Jesus, going on before.*'

Mahvand fumbled in his trouser suit pocket for the key, and fished it out. As he fiddled with the key in the lock, he was filled with self-doubt. *Why did I let a little black seed dictate the proceedings for my opening night? What if no one gets the concept behind it?* His hands were trembling as he unwound the heavy-duty chain that was coiled around the plinth and cube. He handed the chain to Jean-Baptiste, and even though he was about to reveal his innermost being, he felt a burden unexpectedly lift from his shoulders. With one tug from his right hand, like Great-grandfather Harbuckle just about to reveal a woman supposedly severed in half, the cloth fell to the floor.

'*Christ, the royal Master, leads against the foe; forward into battle, see his banners go.*'

Inside the gallery, the white walls seemed to encroach and bristle with virgin malevolence. Silence gave way to whispering, nudging and coughing. Someone pushed through the crowd towards the exit. A flashback of the wolf, snarling in slow motion inside Jean-Baptiste's ribcage, forced Mahvand to reach out to the plinth to steady himself. Laughter erupted, cruel and mocking, accompanied by a bubbling of hostile and damning reviews.

'What is it?'

'Isn't that what they call virtual art?'

He overheard a monotonal voice say, 'Does this sound the death-knell to Britart?'

'What is it? I can't see.'

'A black dot inside some kind of transparent cube. Go figure.'

'Perhaps they should have named the exhibition *Vacuity*?'

More laughter.

The snippets of conversation told him all he needed to know: that the black seed was exerting its true power, poisoning the minds of everyone around him in a bid to discredit his artistic reputation. Mahvand looked around. He was greeted with looks of disdain, bafflement, and derision. And all he heard were the words Jean-Baptiste had spoken to him when he first saw his home engulfed with flames, *I'd go as far to say that it reminds one of the storming of the Bastille during the French Revolution.* And for a split second, he looked out onto a sea of highly decorated fans and white-powdered faces, smirking, averting their gaze or else gazing appreciatively into handheld mirrors at their own reflection.

'This better be part of some wow-factor performance art piece,' hissed Jean-Baptiste.

'Please tell me this isn't some form of twisted revenge for not being allowed to set fire to the *Mankind as a Cancer on the Face of the Earth* exhibit?' asked Jay

Someone over by the *No More Heroes* exhibit called out, 'The artist's got no clothes!'

Laughter reverberated around the gallery.

'What's the meaning of this?' asked Jean-Baptiste through gritted teeth.

Aphrodite, whose Pre-Raphaelite wig had slipped towards her eyebrows, said, 'It's twue. How sweet. Look! There's a little black seed.'

'I dig the concept,' said the Jesus lookalike over by the blinds in the *Fuck, Suck, Spank, Wank* T-shirt. 'Black. Perspex. Seed. Cube. Fucking genius, man!' He was laughing.

'It's no ordinary seed!' cried Mahvand. 'It's a magic seed.'

'Don't tell us. It's going to grow into a giant beanstalk,' shouted Mahvand's student assistant dragged-up as Krishna.

'Fee, Fi, Fo, Fum. I smell the blood of someone's—' said the Jesus lookalike.

'Cum,' called out a woman behind him. More laughter.

Giovanni squeezed passed him with a look of contempt, closely followed by Marianna, who would, no doubt, have registered the same disdainful look if her face hadn't been partially paralysed with a live bovine virus.

Jean-Baptiste grabbed him by the elbow. 'Get a grip. You're scaring people.'

Mahvand broke free. 'It's all your fault! If you hadn't summoned Belial. If you hadn't pushed me into the abyss.' He gripped Jean-Baptiste by both shoulders and began to push.

Jean-Baptiste pushed back. 'Free will, Mahvand. Free—'

Mahvand heard squeals of protest as those nearest to him spilled beer and were elbowed out of the way. His smooth-soled Berluti shoes were unable to establish a grip on the polished parquet wood flooring and he kept slipping back. Like a ram locking horns, he pressed the crown of his head hard against Jean-Baptiste's. The next thing he knew, the right side of his face was smarting with pain, and a great force had come to bear on the centre of his chest. As he hurtled backwards at great speed towards the far end of the gallery, he caught sight of people's shocked expressions and his Giorgio Armani sunglasses somersaulting in mid-air. He ended up in a crumpled heap on his back, bathed in the warm glow of a street lamp outside, gazing up at *The Erection of Christ*. It was as if Mahvand was seeing his own creation for the very first time. The crown of thorns. The uncircumcised hard-on. The ripples of sculpted fibreglass flesh. The trickle of blood from his nostril. *Wait. That wasn't part of the brief.* Mahvand's annoyance turned to horror as it dawned on him that it was actual blood trickling from Christ's nasal passages. He tried to stand but some dark force had immobilised him, and he was forced to witness the trajectory of each drop of blood as it dripped down Christ's fibreglass lip and chin, and splashed onto his T-shirt and the expensive Italian fabric of his suit. Somewhere between finding himself immobilised and the nosebleed, Christ's face had morphed into Daimon's.

Suddenly, a crack appeared in the right shoulder. The crack became a jagged tear. The tear grew, and before Mahvand could register exactly what was happening, the right arm had ripped clean away from the shoulder and crashed to the floor. Mahvand stared at the dismembered limb and then at the gaping hole. *It's the black seed. The dark forces that summoned it into being.* His vision blurred and the hole metamorphosed into a stump, uncanny in its resemblance to Daimon's. Mahvand looked away. He struggled to his feet and staggered forward. Everywhere he looked a white surface reflected back at him – more interrogation room than cutting-edge art gallery. He squinted under the glare of white light and searched the crowd for Jean-Baptiste. There was no sign of him. He removed his jacket and flung it over the offending dismembered limb. Emblazoned across the front of Mahvand's white T-shirt were the words: *I Need Art Like I Need God.*

'Encore!' shouted a woman at the front. Everyone started clapping.

Beside himself, Mahvand addressed the remaining guests. 'You don't understand. I'm not who you think I am.' He spotted the woman with paint-splattered dungarees at the back. She was hysterical. He was on the verge of tears. 'I'm an imposter. A fraud. A charlatan.'

He overheard a woman at the front laughing and talking to her friend. 'Sweetie-dahls, I've seen some way-out performance art in my time. But this is in another league entirely.'

'Hey, David Copperfield. How did you make Christ's arm fall off?' shouted a dreadlocked white guy in a donkey jacket filming the whole thing with a camcorder.

'And the nosebleed. Pure genius!' said another.

A slow clapping started up.

Mahvand dropped to his knees. 'I stole the ideas. I stole them ...' Tears were running down his cheeks. 'From a dead man.'

A few guests had started to chant his name. Others joined in until Mahvand got the feeling he was at some Black Sabbath Mass for arty fashionistas and A-listers.

'MAH-VAND! MAH-VAND!'

'If you want to congratulate anyone, congratulate Daimon Mount-Stuart.'

'MAH-VAND! MAH-VAND!'

'The black seed. Don't you see?! It controlled my mind. And now ... now it's controlling you!'

He could bear it no longer and stormed through the gallery, the guests parting on either side. There was no way he could face the media and paparazzi out on the street, so he took the stairs, two at a time, past the flat on the third floor and on up to the fourth. Pushing the emergency exit doors at the top of the building, he gulped mouthfuls of cold air and stepped out onto the roof. He gazed up at the rust-red moon and the scattering of stars haphazardly flung against the bulging black eye of God and walked across the puddles to the ledge. He peered over. The demonstrators had disbanded. All, that is, except the old man proclaiming the end of the world, who Mahvand now saw as a much misunderstood modern-day prophet. Gran and Candy were still outside The Chequers Tavern, and Mahvand experienced himself as if in a fable, the moment deeply imbued with symbolic meaning.

He glanced down at his T-shirt, *I Need Art Like I Need God,* now spattered with blood, and sat himself down on the ledge of the building. Under normal circumstances, he'd be suffering the effects of vertigo: racing heartbeat, clammy hands and dizziness. All he felt was icy cold water seeping through his suit trousers and Calvin Klein underpants. So, it had come to this. Sitting in a puddle on the roof of the White Cube on the night of his debut exhibition. Caught between the devil and the deep blue sea, his recurring nightmare of falling from tall buildings now made complete sense. As did his daytime predilection for gazing up at them. Looking up at an office block or 1970s' high-rise, he'd often wondered what happened if you jump. Does your life really flash before you? Do a few seconds feel like an eternity?

'Mahvand!'

Mahvand gripped the guttering and turned around.

Jean-Baptiste was on the roof, arms stretched out, walking towards him.

'Stop! Don't come any closer.'

Jean-Baptiste kept walking. '*La lumiére de le lune!*'

'I mean it. I'll jump.' Mahvand lifted both arms in the air as if about to launch himself off the building. 'See. I have wings. I can fly. I conjure objects from thin air. And I can fly.'

Jean-Baptiste stopped and crouched down. 'Come away from the edge.'

'I always knew that one day my flesh would turn to feathers.'

Mahvand heard the tremor in Jean-Baptiste's voice. 'Just move away. From the ledge. Slowly. I swear, by the light of the moon, everything I've done, I've done for you. You must know that. If I've done anything wrong, I apologise. If I've hurt you, please, forgive me.'

Mahvand laughed. It was a laugh that brought him back to himself. 'I'm not falling for it. Not this time. It's over. All of it. You. Me. Art. Magic. Fame. Fortune. OVER!' When Mahvand looked down onto the street, Candy was pointing up at the roof. She staggered into the middle of the road, craned her neck and hollered.

'What in heaven's nyame are yee deein up there, man?

Guests were beginning to spill out of the gallery onto the street.

'What happened inside. It means nothing,' said Jean-Baptiste. 'It was a blip. A blip in a career that will see you exhibit in every major gallery of every capital city in the Western world.' He held out his hand with a crazed look in his eye. 'Today – the White Cube. Tomorrow – the Royal Academy. The Guggenheim.'

'Keep away from me.'

'The Pompidou.'

'If you take a step closer.'

'The Serpentine.'

'I'll do it.

'The Millennium Dome.'

'I'll jump.'

Mahvand was saved from carrying out his threat by Candy hollering on the other side of the street. 'Will yee stop making a fool of yorsel dowtah, an' come down, man.'

Several people were now standing in the middle of the street, pointing up. Mahvand spotted an open-mouthed Janet Street-Porter, and the woman who'd interviewed him for *Frieze* magazine. Vivienne Westwood, looking like an aged Elizabeth I with her white-powdered face and a shag of marmalade hair, stood gawping up at him, arm in arm with a bespectacled Nicholas Serota. The man with the sandwich board was still in the same spot, gazing into space. Members of the press had positioned themselves at particular vantage points along the street, as if they were vultures ready to swoop and feed off the carrion of his corpse, should he but choose to jump.

'*Cariño!*'

Mahvand recognised the voice immediately. And there he was, a Catalonian avatar smeared in blue body paint, sporting a bushy black wig, grass skirt, and what appeared to be a necklace of skulls: Octavi dressed as the Hindu goddess, Kali. In place of the pink feather boa, a moustachioed severed plastic head hung from his neck. Mahvand gripped the roof guttering with both hands as he suffered a sudden flashback of Jean-Baptiste's face mid-coitus morphing into that of John the Baptist.

Octavi was walking backwards from the entrance, waving something in his hand. 'It's finished,' he shouted. 'The last *Kattalin Kemen* zine. Ever.'

'We can turn this around,' said Jean-Baptiste.

'*La Prohibida*. The transexual Basque terrorist. She finally lays down her arms!'

'Use it—' Jean-Baptiste suddenly stopped.

'*Cariño*!'

'Mahvand,' cried Jean-Baptiste.

'Wanna trade?' shouted Octavi.

Mahvand looked at his grandmother bent double, still gripping on to the Edwardian street lamp. *She's more of a magician than Jean-Baptiste ever was. I'm more of a magician.* He thought of her love for him, and there she was, despite suffering the daily indignities of Sunny Pastures, still standing. *It's a deeper kind of magic.* He shuffled back, swung his legs, and hoisted himself up. As he did so, his left foot slipped on a wet lead slate. The last thing he saw was Jean-Baptiste, grinning like the Joker from Batman, offering him his jacket. Then, pinpricks of light in a black canvas of sky, as his legs went from under him, and he toppled sideways over the edge. His ears were filled with screams below and Jean-Baptiste's shouts above. *This is it. The end.* But somehow he managed to reach out just in time. A sudden, sharp pain in his fingers shot down his arm and into his left shoulder. He was clinging to the plastic guttering which he could already feel was about to give way.

'Divvent let gan, dowtah!' he heard Candy shout. 'Ahm coming up te help yee. Just hold on!'

The guttering was cutting into the joints in his fingers. When he looked up, a pair of bloodshot eyes were staring down into his. Jean-Baptiste. *Oh, God. Please. Not like this.* Jean-Baptiste reached out, his watch dangling from his wrist like an exquisite bracelet. Mahvand was certain Jean-Baptiste was just about to peel his fingers from the guttering. *Please. His face can't be the last thing I see.*

Jean-Baptiste suddenly retracted his hand and stood up '*Il est impossible*! If I try and pull you up you'll send us both to an early death.' His skin was beginning to glisten and pulsate with particles of dark light. Mahvand yearned, more than anything, for the rung of ladder under his feet. His vision blurred as Jean-Baptiste's eyeballs, cheekbones and Adam's apple were slowly sucked, one by one, into an egg-shaped vortex of dark light. Jean-Baptiste's Prada jacket fell from his shoulders. The trousers dropped from his waist. That watch, an exquisite piece of Swiss *horlogerie*, clipped Mahvand on the left ear before smashing onto the pavement below. The Giorgio Armani sunglasses followed suit. Only when the metamorphosis was complete did the creature kneel down and ceremoniously offer Mahvand his hand.

Mahvand felt an overwhelming sensation to let go.

'Oh my God!'

'He's going to fall!'

'Hold on!'

'MAH-VAND!'

The last shout was his grandmother's. He managed to glance back to the other side of the street. She was still clinging to the lamp post, her wisps of white hair uprooted by the wind. But she'd positioned her bow. Taken her aim. And released her arsenal of riddles. Up they soared to the parapet and battlement of the White Cube. 'There is a veil that covers your heart. A blind spot you choose not to see. I've seen it in the cards. I've seen it in the tea.'

Gran's arsenal unleashed in Mahvand a power beyond will, a force greater than gravity – a super power. There was no way he was letting go.

'Put on the full armour of God,' she cried. 'For our struggle is not against flesh and blood.'

Belial fought back. He lowered his featureless, egg-shaped head until it was inches away from Mahvand's. Inside the swirling dark light, a montage of images vied for Mahvand's attention. An older, more distinguished version of himself, sporting a powdered wig at the Palace of Versailles, applied a delicate shade of pink to an emerging portrait on canvas of Marie Antoinette; an even hotter imposter, posing as a bisexual porn star/aspiring actor, drooled from a distance over a drug-fucked Jim Morrison spouting poetry at The Factory; himself as himself, only infinitely more handsome, more charming, more desirable, MORE EVERYTHING, arm in arm with Jean-Baptiste – this time blinded by flash photography outside the Royal Academy. Blinded by his own megalomania.

He received Belial's words telepathically. 'All this is but a taste of what I will give you, if you will only bow down and worship me.'

Despite the excruciating pain, Mahvand clung ever more tightly to the guttering. He craned his neck and looked below to the other side of the street. Gran was still clinging to the lamp post as if it was the mast of a ship. Once again, her words soared up to the battlement. 'But against the rulers, the principalities and the powers of this dark world. And against the spiritual force of evil in the heavenly realms.'

A sudden gust of wind above Mahvand's head whipped up sodden autumnal leaves, empty crisp packets and a Fortnum and Mason carrier bag. Belial appeared in fits and starts, flickering back and forth between that lower-ranking fallen angel and Jean-Baptiste. Mahvand registered a re-emergence of square jawline, the tip of a nose, the outline of that macabre tattoo, before Belial ruffled his feathers and spread his wings. They rose majestically to form a pinnacle, so it seemed that the blood moon balanced precariously on their very tip. Two black, horizontal slits on a bed of aqueous yellow stared down from above.

Belial spoke. 'Then the Lord said, "*You are to entice him and also prevail. Go and do so.*"'

There was a flapping of wings. One hoof followed the other, as the creature launched itself off the roof of the White Cube.

'Alreet. Yor Mutha is heor noo.'

Mahvand glanced up. Jean-Baptiste had been replaced by Candy, who was leaning over the edge, gravity pulling the flesh from her bone. She released an almighty burp and Mahvand got a face-full of alcoholic fumes and fag-ash-breath.

'Gissies yer hand,' said Candy.

'And give me the other,' said another voice.

Mahvand looked up. A sudden flashing blue light lent him an other-worldly appearance, but there was something about his eyes that made Mahvand trust him implicitly. Then he realised. He was looking into the face of the Jesus lookalike. Only, in that moment, there was nothing 'lookalike' about him. Mahvand felt a strong hand grip his right forearm. He was Peter being pulled from a turbulent Galilean sea back on board the fishing boat. Candy's red lacquered fingernails reached down to clasp his other arm, and the entire length of guttering fell away. His arms felt like they were coming away from the shoulder joint as he was lifted above the ledge and pulled to safety.

Mahvand finally staggered to his feet and Candy embraced him, squeezing so hard he felt her nails dig into his back. When she finally drew back, he noticed she was missing her pink wig. Tears, blackened from mascara, were running down her cheeks. He glanced down at his wet T-shirt. Christ's nosebleed now resembled an open wound.

His teeth were beginning to chatter and he turned to Jesus. 'Go downstairs. Take *Untitled*. To a landfill site. Bury it. Just get rid of it.'

All three were momentarily distracted by a giant bat-like shape flying over the treetops of St James's Park. They stood dumbfounded and followed its trajectory over rooftops and office blocks until it was nothing more than a black dot against the blood moon.

'What in heaven's name is tha'?' asked Candy, wriggling out of her fake fur and draping it over Mahvand's shoulders.

Mahvand was about to embark upon a rather convoluted explanation when he stopped himself. Candy would never believe him. And anyway, not even he could answer her question definitively. Who, or rather what, was that creature that had taken flight? Was it Jean-Baptiste, Belial, or Baphomet the Sabbatic Goat? Or perhaps all three?

Jesus walked towards the exit doors.

'Thanks fre yer help, like,' called out Candy. 'Divvent think Ah could hev managed it on me aan, pet.'

'I'm sorry, Candy,' said Mahvand

'There's nought te be sorry fre. Yee just lost yer way, that's aal, pet.'

He felt like that six-year-old child again, with only the adventures of Wonder Woman and The New Mutants to keep him company, holed-up in a musty-smelling bedroom on the fourteenth floor of an East End tower block with mould on the wall. An old woman he hardly knew was furiously knitting in the room next door. He yelped like a wounded animal.

Candy staggered forward. 'There, noo. Mutha's heor. The worst is ower, dowtah.' She stroked his hair. His body shook uncontrollably in her arms.

Mahvand felt Candy's nails dig sharply into his back. He lifted his head and looked over to the emergency exit double doors. They were wide open. A man in a suit with a port-wine birthmark was walking towards them. He was flanked on either side by two policemen.

Detective Inspector White dug his hands into the pockets of his trench coat. 'Mahvand Amirzadeh. I am arresting you on suspicion of murder. You do not have to say anything, but it may harm your defence if you do not mention when questioned something you later rely on in court.'

WHITE ROOM

Mahvand lies in a private room on a single bed in the nether regions of the psychiatric hospital. The rotating blades of a giant fan on the ceiling whir like the continual flickering of those disturbing images captured forever somewhere in the region between retina, optic nerve and cerebral cortex.

The sergeant with pinpricks for eyes and a double chin had ordered a strip search with the perfunctory manner of some pen-pushing bureaucrat on the verge of retirement. Detective Inspector White, stretching his stubby fingers into those pale blue surgical gloves with an evil glint in his eye, had said, 'we hate this as much as you do, son. But you were in possession of an illegal class A substance.'

In the hospital, Mahvand curls up into the embryo position: knees to chest, chin tucked in, eyes shut tight. But it's no good. It's been nearly two months, but the movie in his head that switches from black and white to colour, and back again, still plays him: 'Belgravia Police Station.' The humiliation of standing, bent over, legs apart, still high, stark bollock naked, White's sheathed trotters spreading his clenched cheeks apart, attempting to probe his back passage.

That police cell. Nothing to mark time. No clock. His Cartier watch, along with his wallet, keys and Prada belt, had been confiscated by that pen-pushing porker slumped behind the desk. Intermittently having to piss a few yards away in something vaguely resembling a toilet. Lying on that wooden block. Those grooves and crevices where names like 'Mozart Bloods', 'Maida Vale Mob' and 'Fuck Da Police' had been carved deep into the wood. The stench of human excrement. The interview. Still high on cocaine. Without a solicitor. Quicker that way, White had suggested, dangling the carrot of police bail before him like an unscrupulous hypnotist. Mahvand remembers every word. As if it was yesterday.

'Was that before or after Christ's nosebleed?' White's sidekick asked, snorting with laughter before he racked up a white line from Mahvand's coke and proceeded to snort it right there on the desk in front of him.

'Did you find the guy with the camcorder?' asked Mahvand. 'White. Dreadlocked. Donkey jacket. It's all on tape.'

'Is that so?' said White with a sardonic smile. 'Don't think a jury is quite ready to see a fibreglass sculpture of the Nazarene bleeding from his nasal passages.' He turned to his partner. 'Do you?'

Mahvand leant forward and stared into White's grey eyes. 'What have you done with it?'

The other pig just made a snorting sound at the back of his throat.

'And as for that limb dropping off—' said White.

'Not to mention the miraculous disappearing act of your homosexual lover on that rooftop,' said the double act.

White undid his top button and loosened his tie. At first, Mahvand thought he was seeing things.

'No. Upstanding members of the Great British Public …'

said White. In the hollow between his two collarbones was a tattoo not dissimilar to the sigil of Belial. 'Not quite ready for all that,' said White, leaning forward.

What diabolical deity was White enthralled to?

'The tape's destroyed, son.'

Mahvand's vision blurred. *How far do the tentacles of the Brotherhood of the Skull and Crossbones reach?* His mouth was bone dry.

'And so are you.'

Mahvand stretches out, turns, and lies on his back. He stares at the rotating blades of the fan that cut the air and he relives every minute of it: the look of concern on the trainee police officer's pockmarked face – the one who came bearing a Charles and Diana royal wedding souvenir mug full to the brim with tea as weak as gnat's pee. The female PC with the greasy ponytail and no soul, who led him back to the cell, snout in the air, handcuffs swinging from her backside, like she owned the joint. Filth. That's what Gran would have called them. If only she knew.

Mahvand's head is propped up by a single waterproof, wipe-down pillow. His fingertips rest on the too-tightly-tucked, starched-cotton sheets. Bare white. White floor. White ceiling. White walls. White on white. Inside he wants to explode.

Sanctuary.

That's the word Dr Hoffman, his psychiatrist, uses. It makes him think of the science fiction movie *Logan's Run*.

'When did you experience your first hallucination?'

'How old were you when your mother died?'

'We should perhaps think about upping your dose of Clozaril.'

His psychiatrist's words whir in his mind like the constant hum of the fan. In his mind he is Michael York as Logan 5 escaping Carousel for the wilds of the outdoors.

Two months spent in the purgatory of police custody, and then the jury at the Old Bailey had taken less than an hour to arrive at the verdict. Candy had squeezed his hand so hard his knuckles turned white as the final verdict was read out. The judge's voice had sounded muffled. It was as if the courtroom was submerged in water.

On the count of murder: not guilty. Manslaughter: not guilty. Perverting the course of justice: guilty. Possession with intent to supply class A drugs: guilty. Theft of intellectual property: guilty. The hammer rose and fell in slow motion. *Ten-month suspended prison sentence. Psychiatric assessment – late-onset paranoid schizophrenia. Mandatory six-month stay in a secure psychiatric unit.*

Mahvand smoothes the creases on the white cotton sheets. *Just because you're paranoid doesn't mean they're not out to get you.* A chill comes in through the open window. Outside it's starting to snow. He stares up at the never-ending rotation of the fan on the ceiling. Whenever Candy came to visit, she always refused to tell him what had happened to the pieces from his exhibition. So, right there and then, he decides their fate. He imagines each exhibit from *Notoriety* rising like the soul or spirit or essence or whatever the fuck it is that's rumoured to leave the body at the moment of death. *The Erection of Christ.* Up he rises, feet first, up, up, up before the giant blades slice his fibreglass flesh to pieces. *The Good Shepherd* follows a similar fate, but seems to levitate midway, before he too is spliced, and gobbets of dismembered limbs and splintered fragments of shepherd's crook are spewed and flung to the four corners of the room. The papier mâché model of Batman is decapitated in one swift swipe of blade. No blood. No gore. Simple. His head bounces from wall to wall like a ping-pong ball before hitting the floor and rolling towards the door. *Mankind as a Cancer on the Face of the Earth* is a total mash-up. A snowstorm of newspaper. Mahvand is struck by a sudden insight and sits up in bed. *If discarnate beings can assist in creating diabolical pieces of art, there must be opposing communities of discarnate beings that can help create art that lets the light through.* He hears the concerned voice of his psychiatrist again. The barrage of questions. As predictable as the rotation of each steel blade.

Do you believe in Heaven?

Have you ever tried to harm yourself?

Do you believe demons and angels are here on Earth with us?

Perhaps we should try you on a new aantiiipsyyychotiiic.

Mahvand would not be drawn on those topics. Nor would he mention Detective Inspector White, Belial or the Brotherhood of the Skull and Crossbones to anyone ever again. Especially anyone who saw life through a psycho-analytical lens. He was beginning to accept that he sensed and saw things most people didn't; It was both a blessing and a curse.

Mahvand walks out into the corridor. There is the distinct and overpowering smell of disinfectant. A patient in a floral nightie and oversized cardigan shuffles towards him. He's seen her before. Marjorie Braithwaite. She shuffles. Then stops. Shuffles. Then stops. Stares at him. Right through him. Her burgundy slippers remind him of Gran. She's drooling. The spit from her bottom lip slithers down her chin, hangs in mid-air and swings pendulum-like before dropping to the linoleum flooring. He sees past all this and imagines her as a young girl then in the first bloom of love. Even though she doesn't respond, he engages in small talk in the hope that there's a part of her that can hear him, and then continues down the corridor. He passes the art therapy room, Dr Hoffman's office, the group therapy room, down another labyrinthine passage and out into the communal living space.

On the telly, an elderly game show host with a dyed hairpiece, flanked on either side by two scantily clad assistants, comes out with catchphrase after catchphrase. Mahvand walks over to the patio doors. He looks out onto the twisted vine clinging to the granite slabs of a nearby cottage. Inside his head he hears the voice of Dr Hoffman: *It's wisteria, you know. Come the summer, you should see the flowers, Mahvand. A shower of purple rain. A shower of purple*. At the time, Mahvand could think of nothing else but the photo of his mum outside their home in Tehran. The one that used to hang in Gran's front room. The one his father had taken. It was if he'd known all along what he needed to do. *And I'll do it*, he says to himself again. *As soon as I'm out of here. I'm going. Back to Tehran. I'll risk national service. I don't care. I want to see my dad*. He feels hot tears spill down his cheeks.

When he turns around, an elderly lady smartly dressed in a pleated navy skirt, white blouse and pearl necklace is walking towards him. She reminds him of someone – a younger, slimmer version of Gran. She's smiling. As she moves closer, unaided by walking stick or wheelchair, he realises. It is Gran. *What's she doing here?* It feels as if he's dreaming. It feels like he's more awake than he's been for months. She takes him by the hand and guides him towards two armchairs facing the patio doors. They both have wooden armrests, like the ones at Sunny Pastures. Doilies, crocheted with pink roses, cover the backrests. For Mahvand there's a cushion to support his lower back. He lowers himself into the chair. Gran sits next to him. He stares at her upper back. Her dowager's hump – it's miraculously disappeared.

'I've come to say goodbye,' she says, and rests a hand on his.

'But you've only just got here.' He looks around. 'Where's Arthur? Did he drive you down from Sunny Pastures?'

She pauses. 'I don't live there no more.'

He looks at her hands. The liver spots have disappeared. 'I'm sorry, Gran.' His eyes well with tears.

She smiles. A smile that reminds him of his mother. 'I'm sorry too. I had my own blind spot. My faith, on more than one occasion, eclipsed my love for you.'

'I let you down.'

She looks away. 'That's all water under the bridge.'

'No. It's not. I abandoned you.' He pauses. 'Your own flesh and blood.' In place of the powdered rouge, he detects a youthful flush. Something about her, meeting her like this, makes him confess. 'I've seen things.'

'I know, sweetheart.'

'Things I never should have seen.'

She squeezes his hand.

'Done things. Things I never should have done.'

'Ain't we all. Let he who is without sin cast the first stone. John 8:7.'

'I crossed to the other side.'

'And you crossed back again.'

'I lost my way.'

She smiles. 'You silly old sausage. You took a detour. That's all.'

The world outside is magically transformed by a dusting of white. 'Dark night of the soul. So they say. Happens to everyone, sweetheart. Eventually.' She pauses. 'Remember, Mahvand. Why you came. Remember. Who you are. You're a Harbuckle through and through.'

Her hand loosens its grip. He feels her fingers slip from his. 'Be tempted. By the light.' Her eyes are flecked with gold. She is luminous. 'You are a son. A son of the light.'

Where have I heard that before? A hand rests on his shoulder. He turns round. Dark brown eyes peer down through black-rimmed spectacles. Dr Hoffman says, 'Who are you talking to, Mahvand?'

When Mahvand looks back, there is only the empty armchair. The pink roses.

'And what's that smell?' Dr Hoffman asks, resting his other hand on Mahvand's other shoulder.

A familiar scent of Lily of the Valley lingers in the air. Mahvand follows the trajectory of a single snowflake.

And remembers.

ACKNOWLEDGEMENTS

I would like to thank Sally O-J for her insightful comments on an earlier draft of *Pharmakeia*. Thanks also to Julia Bell, Clayton Littlewood, Jeremy Sheldon, Leah Larwood, Veena Sharma, Victoria Grigg, Thaddeus Hickman, Fiona Melrose, Terry Eeles, Karin Salvalaggio, Tanya Datta, Farhana Gani, Emma Lever and everyone at Birkbeck for their constructive feedback and support.

For their support and encouragement, thanks to: James Kapalo, Emma Flint, Alex Dalton, Oliver Berman and Elspeth Elliot. Thanks to Mike Harth and everyone at Paradise Press, to Richard Sheehan for copy-editing and Kristen Harrison and everyone at The Curved House publishing company for the great work on typesetting and the design for the cover. Thanks also to Sophie Greig, Head of Archives at White Cube gallery.

Last but not least, a special thank you to Sina Shamsavari for his love, inspiration, and insight into the world of conceptual art and comics.

ABOUT THE AUTHOR

Timothy Graves is 46 and lives in London. His debut novel, *Homo Jihad*, was short-listed for the Polari First Book Prize in 2010. He has a Master's Degree in Creative Writing from Birkbeck, The University of London, and his short story, *Bright Fire of Morning*, is published in The Mechanics Institute Review 8. He enjoys acting, a good red wine and Buddhist meditation.

www.paradisepress.org.uk
www.timothygravesauthor.com